GL♥SS
SUMMER SCANDAL

She looked at the clock again. It was quarter to seven. And she'd finished her Coke. 'I should go.'

'I guess you've got something else to do,' Jack said.

She nodded.

'Could we go out again sometime?' he ed. 'Like, on a real date? For a whole ening?'

Why did his eyes have to be so brown, so deep, so soft? Why did he have to look so sincere?

End it now, she told herself. Stop this, fore you get in any deeper. Tell him you're busy, tell him you've got a boyfriend, tell him anything.

But what she said was, 'Yes. I'd like that.'

Books by Marilyn Kaye

Gloss
Gloss: Summer Scandal

Marilyn Kaye

GL♥SS

SUMMER SCANDAL

MACMILLAN

First published 2014 by Macmillan Children's Books
a division of Macmillan Publishers Limited
20 New Wharf Road, London N1 9RR
Basingstoke and Oxford
Associated companies throughout the world
www.panmacmillan.com

ISBN 978-1-4472-2399-3

1 3 5 7 9 8 6 4 2

A CIP catalogue record for this book is available from
the British Library.

Printed and bound by CPI Group (UK) Ltd, Croydon CR0 4YY

With deep affection, this book is dedicated to Luce-Claude and Jean-Pierre Duquesne, who appreciate the English language (even when it's spoken by an American!)

Author's note

Dear Readers,

This book is set in the year 1964, and I have used many words and expressions which were popular at that time, though they are not common today.

The words 'Black' and 'African-American' were not in use in 1964. In the United States, the most respectable and appropriate term was 'Negro'. I realize that this is not an acceptable word today, and I apologize to those who might take offence from my use of it. But in order to make the story sound authentic in the context of the time period, I needed to use this word.

I hope you'll understand.

Chapter One

Sitting behind her desk, Sherry Forrester looked down at the photo of the four grinning young men with shaggy hairstyles. John, Paul, George and Ringo. The Beatles.

There hadn't been a music phenomenon like this since Elvis Presley. It seemed as if the whole world had gone positively crazy over the four boys from Liverpool, England. In the US, their recording of 'I Want to Hold Your Hand' had sold a million and half copies in less than three weeks. And when the band arrived in New York, thousands of hysterical fans had waited hours at the airport, hoping to get even just a glimpse of them.

More than seventy million Americans were glued to their TV sets the first time the band appeared on a popular variety series. Sherry herself had watched the show, barely able to hear the music over the screams of the audience. And at their live concerts, teenage girls had fainted.

It was now only four months since that first appearance on TV, and a word had already been coined to describe the group's popularity: Beatlemania.

GL♥SS

'Try to come up with a new angle for an article,' her boss, managing editor Caroline Davison, had pleaded. The so-called 'Fab Four' had already appeared on the covers of practically every magazine, teen *and* adult. *Gloss* had always prided itself on being up to date when it came to anything that affected girls between the ages of thirteen and eighteen, whether it was fashion or beauty or popular culture. Somehow, they'd missed the boat this time. They had to catch up and hit the readers with something different.

Sherry opened a yellow legal pad, took up a pen and waited for inspiration to hit. English . . . British . . . the American Revolution! On the pad she scrawled the words 'The British are coming!' No, that wouldn't work. These guys were already here. She drew a line through the words.

Then she quickly wrote, 'Why do we love the Beatles?' Just as quickly she scratched that out too. Not catchy enough.

Her mind was a blank. A figure appeared at her doorway, and she raised her head, glad for a distraction.

'Hi, Doreen. What's up?'

'I haven't seen Caroline all day,' the beauty editor said. 'Is she out?'

'She's with the new interns,' Sherry told her.

'Oh, right, it's that time again.' Doreen closed her eyes and sighed. 'I hope I get a better one than I had last year.'

Sherry gave a non-committal shrug. Of course, Doreen wouldn't know that the intern assigned to beauty last summer had been one of Sherry's closest friends. She probably didn't even remember that Sherry herself had been an intern just one year ago. But even Sherry sometimes had a hard time remembering this. She felt as if she'd been working at *Gloss* forever.

Doreen strode away, and Sherry got back to work. She looked at the photo again, and considered what she already knew about them. Paul was the cute one, John was the smart one, Ringo was the funny one, and George – actually she couldn't remember reading anything at all about George. But thinking about them as individuals gave her an idea.

'Who's your favourite Beatle?' she scribbled on the pad. She looked at the words, and realized they sounded familiar. From a stack of magazines on her desk, she pulled out the latest issue of their new rival, *Modern Girl*. Sure enough, over a picture of the group on their cover ran the words 'Who's Your Favourite Beatle?' With a sigh, she scratched out that idea too.

She leaned back in her chair and stared up at the ceiling. Caroline had offered her this office, a converted supply room, three months ago. Sherry had been promoted from general editorial assistant to special assistant to the managing editor, and this had taken her out of the bullpen. But there were no windows, and the four walls seemed to be closing in on her.

Restless, she shoved her feet back into the princess-heeled white shoes she'd taken off that morning as soon as her feet were hidden behind the desk. The toes pinched, but she had to get used to them – everyone was wearing pointed toes this summer. She thought longingly of the penny loafers she'd had on the first day she came to *Gloss*. They'd been so comfortable.

Of course, footwear wasn't the only major change in her life. A little over a year ago she'd been a small-town girl from North Georgia, just out of high school, with plans to attend an elite women's college in Atlanta, after which she would marry her high-school sweetheart. Now she was living the life of one of the heroines in those paperback novels that she along with millions of others were reading these days – a young, single woman in Manhattan, with an apartment and a roommate and a job at a glamorous magazine. Of course, those novels always involved a romance as well, something that was completely absent in her life. Maybe it was just as well, given her history with guys . . .

She stood up, stretched, made a futile attempt to smooth out the wrinkles in her cotton shift dress with the large blue-and-yellow flower print and went out into the bullpen. Although she was happy to have her own office now, sometimes she missed the huge space where over a dozen employees had desks. Frequently she left her office door open, just so she didn't feel so isolated. The soft clicking of electric typewriters and the hum of conversation made for pleasant background noise. Plus, one whole wall was lined with windows. The sun was shining, the sky was azure and the magnificent New York City skyline was in plain view . . .

At the closest desk, Caroline's secretary, Gloria Patterson, was gazing dreamily in the same direction. Sherry could understand why. 'Seventy-two degrees and not a cloud in sight,' she commented.

Gloria nodded. 'Just our luck, right? It rains all weekend and now it's gorgeous out there.'

'I can't believe it's the end of June and I don't have a tan yet,' Sherry remarked. 'It's too warm to wear stockings, and my legs are so white . . .' she stopped suddenly, and flushed. Was that an appropriate comment to make in front of someone whose skin was always dark?

But she didn't have to worry. Gloria smiled. 'At least that's something *I* don't have to think about.'

Sherry was relieved. Being from the South, she tried to be so careful in everything she said. She was always afraid people might assume she was a racist.

Gloria turned off her typewriter. 'I'm going on my coffee break,' she announced. 'Do you want me to bring anything back for you?'

'No, thanks. I'll take a break when Caroline returns.'

Sherry lingered in the bullpen for another few

minutes, trying to absorb some natural light before going back into her office. She'd just turned to leave when the main doors to the area opened and Caroline entered, followed by eight girls. They ranged in size and shape and hairstyle, but they were all seventeen or eighteen years old, and they were all wide-eyed, gazing in awe at everything and everyone, especially Caroline, with her sleek, polished Grace Kelly elegance. Sherry could totally identify with what they must be feeling. Nervous, excited, with no idea what the summer would hold for them . . . For a moment she was almost envious. It was all ahead for them, the newness, the adventures.

'Girls, this is the bullpen,' Caroline was saying as she led them across the room. 'Most of you will have desks in this area. Later I'll be assigning you to work with specific editors in different departments. George!'

A balding man with wire-rimmed glasses stopped. 'Yes?'

'Girls, this is George Simpson, our features editor. George, these are the new interns.'

There were murmurs of 'hello' and 'pleased to meet you' from the interns, but George Simpson didn't bother with pleasantries.

'Who's the fastest typist?' he asked Caroline.

'I don't know, George. The interns don't take a typing test.'

'Well, they should.' That was all he said before moving on.

Watching this exchange, Sherry had to work at keeping an impassive expression. Mr Simpson had been her boss when she was an intern, and he was the worst, never wanting her to do anything beyond clerical work. That was all he thought interns were good for. Or maybe not just interns, but working women in general. After a year at *Gloss*, Sherry still couldn't understand why he wanted to work for a magazine devoted to teenage girls when he had no respect for the female sex.

Caroline was used to George, and she'd managed to maintain her professional smile. 'Girls, I also want you to meet Sherry Forrester, my personal assistant. Sherry first came to *Gloss* as an intern, just like you.'

The girls looked at her with interest.

'I'll bet you've got some good stories,' one of them said, and another added, 'Anything you want to warn us about?' This was followed by a few nervous giggles.

Sherry suddenly felt terribly old and mature, and she tried to imitate Caroline's smile. 'You'll have a better experience learning it all on your own,' she said, and Caroline nodded with approval.

'And now,' she said, 'I'm going to show you something very special. The famous *Gloss* samples closet.'

The eager interns followed closely in her footsteps. Except for one.

The girl who lingered was about Sherry's height, with straight, shiny jet-black hair and dark eyes. Her name tag read 'Liz Madrigal'.

'How did that happen?' she asked Sherry.

'How did what happen?'

'You coming here as an intern and then getting an actual job on the staff. That's kind of unusual, isn't it? What did you do to make them want to hire you?'

Sherry was slightly taken aback by the girl's directness. 'Well . . . it's a long story.'

'I'd like to hear it.'

'Sherry!'

Relieved at the interruption, she turned to see her roommate, Donna Peake, hurrying towards her.

'Excuse me,' she said to the intern. 'We can talk another time. You should go catch up with the others. The samples closet is really amazing.'

Liz Madrigal left without another word, and Sherry turned to Donna. 'What's up?'

Donna waved what looked like a postcard. 'I've got something to show you.' They went into Sherry's office and Donna set the card down on the desk. 'It's addressed to both of us, but the mail boy came to my department first so I got it.'

Sherry picked it up. The picture was an aerial view of a city, identified as Pittsburgh, Pennsylvania. Turning it over, she immediately recognized the round, almost childish handwriting; she knew only one person who actually dotted every small letter i with a little heart.

Hey, girls! Here's my news. Pittsburgh is boring and so is my job, and I haven't met one decent guy. So I'm coming to New York!

There was a line of x's and o's, and a signature: *Pamela*.

'Is she saying she's going to visit or move back here?' Sherry wondered.

'No idea,' Donna said. 'But my guess is that she wants to take another shot at living in the Big Apple.'

Sherry smiled. 'Wow. It would be great to have her here.'

Donna nodded in agreement. 'She was a lot of fun.'

'As long as she stays away from married men,' Sherry noted. She shuddered as she recalled Pamela's disastrous relationship last summer with the *Gloss* advertising manager.

'I'm so glad Alex Parker left the magazine,' Donna said with feeling. 'I couldn't bear seeing him around here after the way he treated her.' She looked at the clock. 'I have to pick up some stuff in the samples closet. I hope those interns are finished in there. You gonna be home for dinner?'

'Where else?' Sherry asked, shaking her head ruefully. 'It's not like I have a date.'

After Donna left, Sherry went back to her desk.

With no new bright ideas, she pushed aside the Beatles for the time being and attacked a different job. It was something she was supposed to do on a regular basis – scan the daily newspapers for items and topics that might lend themselves to *Gloss* articles.

The front page of that day's *Herald Tribune* wasn't exactly uplifting or inspiring. The feature article was accompanied by a grainy photograph of a lunch counter in Alabama, where a civil-rights demonstration had turned violent. In the picture, a sheriff was holding his baton over the head of a Negro man sitting at the counter. A woman next to him had her hands over her face, as if she was protecting herself. In the background, a group of white people held signs demanding 'Segregation Forever'.

Sherry shivered. The scene had taken place in a town she didn't know, but the counter looked exactly like one she used to frequent with her friends after school, for Cokes and burgers and ice-cream sundaes. She wondered if this kind of activity was going on back in her hometown. Mama hadn't mentioned anything in her weekly letters, but that didn't mean nothing was happening. Mama didn't like to dwell on unpleasant topics.

Nor did Sherry usually. But she couldn't stop staring at the photo. It really did look just like the Hillside Luncheonette back home. Of course, you never saw people who weren't white there. Except for the lady who mopped the floor.

She forced herself to look elsewhere on the page. An earthquake in Japan, a serial killer in Boston . . . a war in Vietnam that was escalating. Nothing for *Gloss*.

She flipped through the pages until she came to the society section, which included the gossip column, and scanned this for anything about celebrities popular with teens. A name jumped off the page.

Pop singer Bobby Dale hasn't had a major hit for some time, and maybe that's why he's heading to the silver screen. The teen idol will be taking a featured role in Tangled Hearts, *a romantic drama starring Lance Hunter and Monica Caine. Shooting begins on location in New York this month.*

Now, *that* was interesting – for *Gloss*, and for herself too. Bobby Dale was going to be in New York. Would Allison Sanderson be with him?

Sherry wasn't even sure if the two were still together. The former *Gloss* intern, another good friend from last summer, wasn't a good correspondent – but then, neither was Sherry, and they had lost touch over the last year. Sherry's thoughts went back to the last time she saw Allison – in August, at the Copacabana nightclub, where Bobby was performing and had treated the four friends to an evening. Sherry, Donna, Pamela and Allison – that was the last time they'd all been together. It had been so exciting for all of them, having a friend who was dating a real pop star.

She turned a few more pages and stopped at the fashion-and-style section. Men's fashions were being featured that day, so there wasn't much of interest. She did note a photo of a man in an odd-looking hip-length coat with a mandarin collar. The caption read:

The Nehru jacket, named for the Prime Minister of India and worn by Sean Connery as James Bond in Dr. No. *Is this the next big thing in menswear, or just another fad?*

Definitely a fad, Sherry thought. And then, out of nowhere, it hit her. She pushed the newspaper aside and grabbed the yellow legal pad.

The Beatles – Fab or Fad?

A new angle, she thought happily. And feeling very pleased with herself, she picked up her handbag and left the office. Her job entitled her to two coffee breaks a day, but she always felt better when she thought she'd earned them.

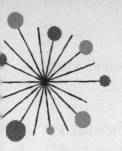

Chapter Two

'Hey! What are you doing back here?'

Allison glared right back at the muscular man with the fierce expression who was blocking her way in the corridor. She lifted the tag that hung from a string around her neck and held it up. The guard squinted at the all-access backstage pass and then lifted his eyes to her face. His grimace disappeared and he almost looked apologetic.

'Oh, yeah, I know you. You're his girl.'

Allison bristled. 'I'm nobody's girl. I'm Allison Sanderson. I'm a guest of Bobby Dale.'

The man looked confused. 'But you're the girlfriend, right? You're Bobby's girl.'

Allison gave up. Until someone came up with a better word to describe her role in Bobby's life, there was no point in arguing.

In the distance she could hear the audience chanting, 'Bobby! Bobby! Bobby!' As if in response, from a door at the other end of the corridor, Bobby emerged. The man mumbled something into his walkie-talkie gadget, and from the unseen stage came the sound of a drum roll. The chanting grew louder.

Bobby paused to plant a kiss on Allison's lips. 'Wish me luck.'

'Break a leg,' she said.

He rolled his eyes. 'That's for dancers, not singers.'

'Develop a severe case of laryngitis?' she suggested.

He grinned, and turned to run out on the stage. The chanting turned into shrieking as the band struck up the opening to Bobby's latest recording. Allison knew she could go and watch him from the wings, but she'd done that at the concert the evening before, and Bobby didn't expect her to do it again. He hadn't even expected her to do it yesterday.

'You've seen the show. Why would you want to see it again?' he'd asked.

That was such a Bobby thing to say. The adulation of a gazillion teenage girls had never turned him into an egomaniac.

So instead of hanging out in the wings, she made her way down the corridor to the staff lounge. It was just a little room with a sofa, some chairs, a coffee machine and a pay phone, but it was better than waiting out the concert in his dressing room.

Unfortunately the lounge was currently occupied by an usher and an usherette, engaged in some heavy necking on the sofa. So she snatched up a magazine from the top of a stack on the table and headed to the dressing room.

The reason she hadn't wanted to go there in the

first place was still in the room. Bobby's manager, Lou Mareno, was sitting at the make-up table, going through some papers and frowning. He glanced up when Allison entered and grunted something that was supposed to pass for a greeting.

She sat down on the small, hard, uncomfortable sofa. 'Bobby sounds good,' she murmured in an effort to make conversation.

'He always sounds good,' the harried-looking man muttered. 'Too bad he's not sounding good to a full house.'

'The concert didn't sell out?'

'Where have you been?' he barked. 'The last *five* concerts haven't sold out.'

Bobby hadn't mentioned that to her. Probably because it wasn't that important to him.

It was clearly important to Lou Mareno though. 'No one's interested in teen idols any more,' he grumbled. 'All they want are bands. And not even American ones.'

That was true, Allison thought. Walking down any hallway in her dorm, she invariably heard the Beatles or one of those other English bands. Back in February, a couple of girls she knew at school actually cut classes so they could go to New York for a Beatles concert.

Lou Mareno hadn't finished complaining. 'It doesn't help that Bobby insists on singing those folk songs in concert.' He glared at Allison, as if this was *her* fault. It wasn't, but she would have been happy to take the credit. She loved folk songs, and she'd been very happy when Bobby admitted his own passion for the music.

'It makes Bobby happy to sing those songs,' she murmured.

'Well, it's not winning him any fans.'

'Maybe in some other venue . . .' she began, but the look on the manager's face made it very clear that he wasn't open to suggestions.

'You don't go from concert halls and arenas to coffee houses and playing in parks,' he declared. 'That's like telling the world you're on your way out. It's for losers.'

Now she was getting annoyed. 'Bobby is not a loser. He's going to be in a movie, for crying out loud!'

'Yeah, well . . .' He looked at his watch. 'I gotta make some calls. You ever heard of this band, the Rolling Stones? A bunch of fellows who look like hoodlums? I want to find out if they need representation in the US.'

What a hypocrite, Allison thought. He complained about the British Invasion but given half a chance, he'd jump on the bandwagon.

'There's a phone in the lounge,' she told him, and he left. She knew it wouldn't bother him if a couple were making out on the sofa. He wouldn't even notice. And from the way that couple had been going at it, they probably wouldn't notice him either.

His words hadn't bothered her at all. *She* wasn't worried about Bobby. The fact that until recently he'd been *the* teen idol had never impressed her, and it hadn't been what drew her to him a year ago. In fact, if anything, it had made him totally uninteresting to her.

She'd never been a fan of this kind of music, or the guys who sang it – cute, wholesome, non-threatening clean-cut types, the object of a typical thirteen-year-old girl's fantasy. As an intern at *Gloss* magazine last summer, she'd been less than thrilled when she was given the assignment to interview him.

But Bobby wasn't at all what she'd expected. He didn't take himself or his success too seriously, and he wasn't interested in the glamorous life at all. Raised in New York, he preferred to stay with his grandmother in suburban Queens than at a fancy Manhattan hotel when he was back in town. He was sincere, he was real, he was kind and generous. And it hadn't been all that hard to fall in love with him.

And they'd been together for almost a year now! Well, not really together all the time. She'd been here, just across the river in Cambridge, in her freshman year at Radcliffe College. Bobby had been touring the country, or at home in California. But he'd come east to see her almost every other month.

It was probably no bad thing that he hadn't been around more. Radcliffe was demanding, and for the first time in her life Allison really had to apply herself academically. She rarely had time to read anything that wasn't required for a course, and she could count on one hand the movies she'd seen over the past ten months. She missed Bobby, of course, and she was glad he was wealthy enough to afford a long-distance phone call almost every night. But with all the work she had to do for school, she certainly didn't need the distraction of a full-time boyfriend.

And maybe this was why the relationship was still going strong. Maybe it was true that absence made the heart grow fonder. Would the romance endure if they were together more? Would familiarity breed contempt? She'd find out soon enough.

She took the chair Lou Mareno had vacated and checked to see what magazine she'd picked up in the lounge. Funnily enough, it was the latest issue of *Gloss*, the first issue she'd seen since she left the internship last August.

Flipping through the pages, she could see that the magazine hadn't changed at all. Pages and pages of clothes, and all the usual ads with more clothes, plus silverware and china patterns. Lots of beauty and fashion advice. Should you match your eyeshadow to the colour of your eyes, your handbag to your shoes, your lipstick to your nail polish? There was a review of the latest Elvis Presley movie, *Viva Las Vegas*, and an interview with Patty Duke, the teen star of her own TV comedy. And an article about Sean Connery, who played James Bond, and his upcoming movie in the 007 series, *Goldfinger*. She remembered going to see him in *Dr. No* last summer, with Pamela, her roommate from her time at *Gloss*.

Thinking about Pamela made her smile. She'd been quite a character, with her platinum-blonde hair, tight skirts and low-cut tops. They'd had a lot of fun together, and they'd been pretty close. But they'd lost touch completely since the internship ended, and she didn't even know where Pamela was living, or if she'd gone on to secretarial school as she'd planned.

It was like that with the other interns she'd been friends with too. None of them had been any good at corresponding. At least she knew where the other two were, still working at *Gloss*, and checking the magazine masthead she made sure they were still there. Yes, Sherry was still listed as Caroline Davison's assistant in editorial, and she found Donna's name under photography, as an assistant to David Barnes.

She heard voices in the hallway. Looking at her watch, she realized it was already intermission time. Sure enough, seconds later Bobby opened the door. He was accompanied by two of those muscular guards and some girl who was making efforts to wipe the beads of sweat from his brow.

'Can I get you anything, Bobby?' the girl asked. 'A beer, a Coke?'

'Just some water, please,' Bobby said. And then,

'Wait a minute,' as the girl started out. He turned to Allison. 'Do you want something?'

'No, thanks,' she said.

The girl gave Allison a hard look before going off to get Bobby his water. She knew the expression – she'd seen it whenever she and Bobby encountered fans. Jealousy, combined with bewilderment. What was that great-looking pop star doing with that ordinary-looking skinny redhead?

It didn't bother Allison at all, not even when they tried to flirt with him. Bobby only seemed to have eyes for her. It was really an amazing relationship. But still the doubts were with her. Was their romance so amazing because they spent so much time apart?

Bobby dismissed the guards and turned to Allison. 'I'd kiss you, but I'm all sweaty.'

'I'd kiss you but . . .'

She handed him a box of tissues. As he mopped his face she asked, 'How's the show going?'

Before he could answer, the girl reappeared with a pitcher of water and a glass. Just one, of course. She clearly didn't want to acknowledge Allison's existence.

'Thank you,' Bobby said. The girl lingered, and he managed a smile. 'Thank you,' he said again, then gently but firmly ushered her out of the dressing room. Closing the door, he sank into a chair.

'I am *not* going to miss this,' he declared.

Allison smiled. 'You think making a movie will be easier? Movie stars have groupies too.'

'I have no idea what it's going to be like,' Bobby admitted. 'I still can't believe this is even happening. I'm no actor, Allison. What am I doing?'

'The director must think you've got talent, or he wouldn't have offered you the part in the movie.'

Bobby shook his head. 'He gave me the part because he thinks my being in the movie will draw a teen audience.'

Allison wanted him to feel better about it. 'Hey, maybe you'll discover a talent you never knew you had.'

He shrugged. 'I'm nervous,' he confessed. 'I just hope I'll be able to get away every weekend to come up here and see you.'

It was the perfect opening for her news. 'You won't have to do that,' she told him.

'What do you mean?'

'I'm going to be in New York all summer.'

His eyes widened. 'You're kidding!'

'I found a summer job as a day nanny for some family. And friends of my parents are letting me sublet their apartment, on the Upper East Side.'

Bobby was momentarily speechless, but his actions spoke for him. He leaped up and embraced her. That led to a massive kiss, which quickly led to the both of them falling on to the little sofa, which had miraculously become less uncomfortable.

It was the worst moment for someone to start rapping at the door.

'Go away!' Bobby yelled. A split second later his good manners kicked in and he added, 'Please!'

'Five minutes, Mr Dale!' a voice called.

'Damn,' Bobby muttered, but he got up. 'I have to change my shirt.'

'I was thinking,' Allison said as he took a fresh shirt from a hanger, 'this apartment I'm subletting, it's supposed to be pretty big. You could stay there with me.'

There was clear regret in his eyes and he shook his head. 'No, how would that look, living together? For you, I mean. Your parents would have a fit if they found out. I'm better off staying at my gran's in Queens.' Then he cocked his head to one side and looked thoughtful. 'Of course, there will be times when we're in Manhattan, it's late at night, I can't find a taxi . . .'

Allison laughed. 'Yes, I can see that happening frequently.'

He finished buttoning his shirt, gave her one more kiss. 'I'm really, really happy,' he declared before running out the door.

And so was she. She just hoped that they'd both still feel that way at the end of the summer.

Chapter Three

D onna slipped the contact sheets into an inter-office envelope, and scrawled 'Belinda Collins – Fashion' in the address box. Picking up some other mail, she went out into the hall. Just as she was dropping the items in the out tray on the receptionist's desk, the elevator doors opposite opened and a tall, very slender girl ambled out.

The receptionist was off on her coffee break, so Donna turned to the girl with a slightly nervous smile. 'Oh, hello, Bonnie. Have a seat. I'll go get David.'

She hurried down the corridor to the darkroom. The red light was on over the closed door, so she couldn't enter. Rapping on the door, she called, 'David! Bonnie's here!'

'I'm developing!' the photographer yelled. 'Tell her to wait.'

Tell her to wait. Tell Bonnie Bailey, the number-one, most-sought-after teen model in the universe, to *wait.* Oh, David, Donna thought mournfully, why do you do this to me? Even after almost a year working here, she was still intimidated by the celebrities of the fashion world who occasionally crossed her path. Would she ever feel secure and confident? Would she ever stop seeing herself as a fraud, with no business whatsoever being in this glamorous world?

She hurried back to the reception area. Bonnie was sitting on the small sofa, her mile-long legs crossed as she flipped through a magazine.

'David's in the darkroom. He'll be right out,' Donna told her, and hoped fervently that was true. Seeing that the receptionist was still on break, she asked, 'Can I get you something? Coffee? A soda?'

'No thanks, Donna.'

She couldn't believe Bonnie Bailey actually knew her name! True, Donna had seen her maybe half a dozen times, but most of the models who came in here looked right through her, as if she wasn't even there. Although, if she was to believe what David told her, half of those models were such airheads they probably had a hard time remembering their own names.

Bonnie yawned, and then clapped a hand to her mouth. 'Wow, sorry, that was so rude! Late night – you know what it's like.'

Donna didn't, but she nodded understandingly.

'I'm sorry you have to wait.'

Bonnie shrugged. 'I'm used to it,' she said cheerfully. 'Ninety per cent of this job is standing around and waiting! People think modelling is glamorous. If they only knew how boring it really is.'

'You don't love it?' Donna asked curiously.

Bonnie grinned. 'Of course I love it. What other job would pay so much for just hanging around and waiting!'

Donna thought about all the other models who complained incessantly. Bonnie's frankness was a nice change.

The model yawned again. 'Maybe I *should* have some coffee after all. I don't want to fall asleep during the shoot.'

'Of course. Milk? Sugar?'

'Just black,' Bonnie said. 'And only if it's no trouble,' she added, flashing her dazzling smile.

Donna ducked into the little staff lounge and searched for a clean mug. Finding one, she held it under the coffee machine and held her breath as she turned the spigot. Thank heavens there was some coffee left. And there were the cookies she'd brought in the day before. She placed a few on a plate.

Bonnie accepted the cup gratefully but eyed the cookies with mock horror. 'Oh, get those away from me!'

'You don't like chocolate chip?' Donna asked.

'Are you kidding? I *love* chocolate chip! And those look home-made. Are they?'

Donna nodded. 'I made them.'

Bonnie's eyes widened, and she looked at Donna as if she'd just claimed to have painted the *Mona Lisa*. 'Wow.'

'Have one,' Donna urged.

Bonnie's face took on an expression of extreme despair. 'I'm a model, Donna. I eat a cookie and I'm out of a job.'

'I won't tell,' Donna promised.

Bonnie turned her head from one side to the other, as if to make sure no one else was watching. Then she grabbed a cookie. Biting into it, she rolled her eyes in ecstasy.

Donna couldn't help laughing. Bonnie had a reputation for being terribly theatrical, but she did it with a sense of humour. This was probably one of the reasons she was so successful as a model – she was able to communicate strong feelings and reactions.

'I have a fantasy,' Bonnie confided. 'Someday, when I'm too old for this gig and I can quit modelling, I'm going to walk into a pastry shop and buy one of everything.' She paused. 'Maybe two.'

They were laughing as David finally emerged from the darkroom. The handsome photographer, who bore a marked resemblance to the actor Rock Hudson, headed towards them.

'So good-looking,' Bonnie said as she watched him approach. 'And so unavailable – or so I've heard. He's gay, right?'

'Um . . . I think so.' Donna knew this, as did just about everyone at *Gloss*, but no one ever came right out and *said* it. Once again, she was impressed by Bonnie's forthright attitude.

'Let's get to work,' David declared. He sent Bonnie down to see the hairdressers and make-up people, and told Donna what equipment he would need.

Twenty minutes later, they were ready to start shooting. Donna had followed David's instructions and set up the appropriate tripods and umbrellas. Bonnie had changed into the first outfit she'd be modelling – a long-sleeved forest-green flannel dress with a flared skirt and narrow leather belt. Totally inappropriate for a hot June morning, but this was for the September issue.

Personally, Donna thought the model had looked better before she went into hair and make-up. Her hair was still in her trademark style, a chin-length straight bob with bangs that came to her eyebrows, but it was shinier now, due to a heavy application of lacquer. A thick layer of pancake foundation made her skin look artificial, almost like porcelain, and the rouge on her cheeks had been applied so heavily it looked almost clownish. But Donna knew from experience that under the heavy lights required for this kind of photography, the model needed this make-up. When the pictures appeared on the pages of the magazine, Bonnie would look completely natural. In a perfect sort of way.

Belinda Collins from fashion arrived to supervize the shoot, and Donna was surprised to see that she was accompanied by Caroline Davison. She couldn't remember ever having seen her at one of these sessions before. Nor had she ever seen the elegant managing editor pay so much attention to a model. She greeted Bonnie warmly, and chatted for a bit while Belinda hung a handbag on the model's arm. Then the fashion editor stepped back, frowned, shook her head and tried another bag.

At this point, Donna stepped into her role as 'gofer'. If necessary, she'd run down to the samples closet for more handbags, or fetch the make-up artist to do touch-ups, or gather different cameras. There was always something, and she never knew what it would be. That was part of what made the job so interesting.

'Oh no,' Bonnie moaned.

'What's wrong?' Caroline asked in alarm.

'I think I feel a drop of sweat on my forehead.'

'Could someone turn the air conditioning up?' Caroline asked, and Donna took off to do this. Then she returned with the make-up artist to touch up the spot on Bonnie's forehead.

'Thank you, Donna, you're the best!' Bonnie cried out. To Belinda she said, 'I always like working here, because of Donna.'

'Mm,' Belinda murmured, not really listening as she pinned a brooch on the flannel dress. But Caroline was looking interested.

David heard what she said too. 'Thanks a lot,' he called out, pretending to be hurt.

Bonnie laughed. 'Oh, David, darling, you know I adore you too. But Donna keeps me company.'

Finally everyone was ready, and the shoot began.

'Bonnie, look to the left,' David ordered. 'No, not that much! Now tilt your head to the right. A little more.'

'Extend your arm so he can see the bag,' Belinda called out.

'Not so far out!' David yelled. 'Now relax your left shoulder. Look this way. Smile. Stop smiling.'

'Wait!' Belinda shrieked. 'Her nose is shining. Make-up!'

It went on and on like this, with both David and Belinda shouting directions at the poor girl. Despite the air conditioning, Donna thought she looked awfully hot. She ran back to the lounge to get a glass of cold water for the model. When she returned, David was letting her have a break. Donna hurried over to her with the water.

'You read my mind,' Bonnie cried out. 'Thank you, Donna.'

The receptionist appeared at the door. 'Miss Bailey, there's a message for you. A Susie Phillips called and said she can't meet you for lunch.'

'Oh fudge,' Bonnie moaned. 'We were going to the Russian Tea Room and I am so craving a little caviar. Donna! Want to have lunch with me there when we're finished?'

Donna had never been to the famous restaurant, but she'd certainly heard of it. And she knew it was very expensive. Bonnie probably didn't realize that a photography assistant's salary wasn't in the same league as a top model's.

Before she could respond, Belinda was ushering the model to the changing room to get into her next outfit. And Caroline approached Donna.

'I want you to have lunch with Bonnie,' she declared. 'And don't worry, *Gloss* will pay.'

Donna's mouth fell open. 'Why?'

Even though the model was out of the room, Caroline lowered her voice and pulled Donna aside. 'Did you know that every time Bonnie's on our cover, our newsstand sales double? We're trying to get her to sign an exclusive contract with *Gloss*, so she won't work for any of our competitors. Clearly you've got a rapport with her.'

'You want *me* to ask her to sign a contract?' Donna asked nervously.

'No, no, nothing like that. Just be her buddy – it will make her want to be here more. Get a real friendship going. Believe me, Donna, this will help when I approach her about the contract. Will you do it?'

'Well . . . OK. Sure.' It wasn't as if she'd be doing anything under false pretences, Donna thought. She *did* enjoy being with Bonnie.

Caroline beamed. 'I'll call the restaurant now and

tell them to charge the lunch to *Gloss*.'

'I only get an hour off,' Donna warned her.

'Don't worry about that. I'll tell David you can take all the time you want when you lunch with Bonnie. After all, you won't just be eating, you'll be working!'

So one hour later, Donna found herself entering the Russian Tea Room on West 57th Street with Bonnie Bailey. The doorman recognized the model and ushered them both in with a tip of his hat and words of welcome. Then a man hurried forward and practically bowed.

'So pleased to see you again, Miss Bailey! And Miss – Miss. . .'

It took a few seconds before Donna realized he was asking for her name. 'Peake,' she squeaked out. 'Donna Peake.'

'Oh, of course!' the man exclaimed, as if he should have recognized her. 'Right this way.' He led them through the opulent room, all red and gold with floor-to-ceiling mirrors and sparkling lights, to a large red banquette. Then he snapped his fingers, and a uniformed waiter magically appeared with enormous menus. Donna accepted hers, but Bonnie didn't want one.

'I know exactly what I want,' she said.

The waiter smiled. 'Your usual, Miss Bailey?'

Bonnie nodded happily.

'And you, miss?'

Donna stared at the menu. It was in English, but she still didn't understand what half these items were. She looked up helplessly.

'The same?'

'You'll love it,' Bonnie assured her. 'Oh, there's someone from my agency. I have to go say hello. Do you mind, Donna?'

'Not at all,' Donna assured her. She was happy to have a moment alone to absorb what was happening to her.

She'd been in New York for a year now, and she'd had a multitude of new and exciting experiences. But she didn't think she'd ever get used to them. Now, as she gazed around this luxurious and terribly chic place, she couldn't help remembering who she was and where she came from.

Poor Donna. From a dreary, Midwest working-class town where the word 'restaurant' meant a diner or the Dairy Queen. Where she'd grown up in a trailer in the worst part of town. Struggling at school because she had a condition that made it hard for her to read. Struggling at home because her mother was an alcoholic and there was no father in residence. Two young siblings to take care of. Kathy and Billy . . .

It used to be that she couldn't let herself dwell on them, since tears would come to her eyes. But now that the little ones had gone to stay with their father and his new wife, they had a better life. And Donna could actually play a part in this life too. This past Christmas, Martin Peake had flown her out to their home in Michigan to spend the holiday.

Only Sherry and the other two friends from last summer, Allison and Pamela, knew the truth about Donna's background. They even knew about her wretched ex-husband, Ron. They knew about the baby she'd lost, the fighting, how scared she'd been. That she'd stolen someone's application to become an intern at *Gloss* and had run away to New York.

Watching Bonnie table-hop now, she wondered if they could ever be real friends. What would the model think of Donna's past? Not that Donna had any plans to reveal her story to Bonnie. Or anyone else, for that matter. Somehow she'd managed to avoid getting too close to anyone over the past year. She'd never been plied with questions, and she'd never had the temptation to tell.

But now Caroline wanted her to get close to Bonnie. Well, Donna would be happy to have the occasional lunch, chat about fashion, listen to Bonnie's tales of her dates and parties and whatever else she did in her free time. Bonnie must have lots of friends, so she probably wouldn't start confiding in Donna, telling her secrets and expecting her to do the same.

Meanwhile, she should sit back and enjoy herself. Think about where she had been just over a year ago, and where she was now. No longer an abused housewife in a broken-down trailer. No longer 'Poor Donna'. She was Donna Peake, a New York career girl, having lunch with a celebrity model in a glamorous restaurant.

And as Bonnie returned to the table, Donna found it pretty easy to smile happily and wonder what caviar tasted like. She wasn't even sure she knew what it *looked* like.

Chapter Four

Pamela had snagged a window seat on the bus, but it didn't provide any real entertainment. Billboards were not all that interesting, and that was pretty much all there was to see on the highway.

She'd been on the Greyhound bus for four hours, and she was only about halfway through her journey. Thank heavens she'd stayed out really late the night before, so she'd been able to sleep for the first two hours of the ride.

But now she was awake, and bored. She'd already eaten the sandwich she'd brought along. There were magazines she'd picked up at the station stacked on the empty seat next to her, but she didn't feel like looking at them. And there was a candy bar in her handbag, but she wasn't hungry.

No one had sat next to her, which was just as well. It wasn't like any interesting people would ride a Greyhound bus from Pittsburgh to New York. With some exceptions of course. Like herself.

In any case, she didn't really feel like talking. She was nursing a headache, the result of too much beer the night before. She didn't even *like* beer. But that joint she'd been in wasn't the kind of place that offered cocktails. People from the office had taken her there for a little going-away party. Pamela hadn't expected anything really fabulous – after all, she'd only been working at the insurance company for three and a half months. It wasn't as if they were going to dig deep into the petty-cash fund to splurge on a real celebration. Even so, she thought they could have come up with something better than that dingy dive around the corner from their building.

The so-called party consisted of two other secretaries, the receptionist from the downstairs lobby, the pimply guy from group claims whose name she could never remember and that creepy lecher Mr Quimby, who was their division manager and always looking for an excuse to touch her.

She'd been out with most of them at one time or another after work, but she wouldn't call them friends. In a way, the evening was very good for her. It was so dreary she became more and more excited about leaving and was certainly willing to put up with an eight-hour bus trip.

Pittsburgh in general had been a disappointment to her. Growing up in a town less than an hour away, she thought it was a glamorous big city, a place you visited maybe once a year, if that. She could remember going there a couple of years ago with her mother and one of her older sisters on a shopping trip for her sister's bridal gown. It was noisy and crowded and exciting, everything her hometown was not. At secretarial school, girls talked about moving to Pittsburgh and finding jobs there, as if it was paradise for the single girl.

Pamela knew better. She'd *been* to paradise, otherwise known as New York City. Just out of high school and before secretarial school, she'd spent a summer there as a magazine intern. The job hadn't meant much to her, but *New York*! It was the thrill of a lifetime, being in the city she'd seen in movies and on TV. And it was every bit as glamorous as she'd imagined.

But intimidating too. A little scary. And more than a little heartbreaking. And when she finished her secretarial training in December, she'd decided to give Pittsburgh a shot.

It was a misfire. First off, the rents for apartments were more expensive than she'd thought they would be, so she had to answer an ad for a share. Her roommate turned out to be a real nerd who sat watching TV every night and went home every weekend to her parents so she could watch her shows on a colour TV. The job was deadly. She'd accepted it because it was in a big company where she thought there would be plenty of eligible men – and there probably *were*, only she never got to meet them. Her position kept her in a tiny department where she sat with the same dull people all day. Even at lunch in the company cafeteria, they all sat together.

On her own, she'd tried hitting a cocktail lounge once in a while, but realized that Pittsburgh was a lot less sophisticated than New York. Single women in cocktail bars were considered to be 'working girls', and not the working-in-an-office type. She found herself thinking about New York more and more, remembering the good times, wondering what Sherry and Donna were up to in the city that never sleeps.

And even when the memory of Alex Parker crept into her mind, she couldn't think badly of New York. It had been her own fault, she decided. She was just too naive a year ago. Now she knew that despite what Helen Gurley Brown had written in *Sex and the Single Girl*, an affair with a married man wasn't all fun and games. A gullible girl could end up falling in love. And getting very, very hurt.

But she was a different girl now. And she knew what she wanted. Closing her eyes, she conjured up the man of her dreams.

In her imagination he didn't always look the same. A couple of years ago she'd have envisioned someone who looked like a cute teen idol – Fabian, or Frankie Avalon, or Bobby Rydell. Now her fantasies took the form of men, not boys. But not just any men.

First and foremost was Sean Connery. Tall, dark and beyond handsome. And the sex appeal! As James

GL♥SS

Bond, he was the ultimate in sophistication. So elegant in his tuxedo as he ordered his martinis shaken, not stirred. (Of course she knew this was a role and not the real man, but she couldn't help feeling that the real Sean Connery *had* to have a James Bond personality. No one could act *that* well.)

But just a month ago she had seen a movie starring Steve McQueen. A completely different type – blond, and not elegant at all, more rough and cocky. But still so sexy. She could fantasize about him too, and not feel like she was cheating on Sean/James. In fact, she was pleased to realize that she was so open-minded when it came to taste in men. All he had to be was incredibly good-looking with lots of sex appeal. That wasn't much to ask.

And it would help – a *lot* – if he had money too. Not only because she liked going out to nice places. She wasn't just out for a good time any more; she was thinking about her future. She did *not* want to spend the rest of her life typing. Maybe if she was the brainy type, like Allison, she might entertain thoughts of having her own career that could bring in a good salary. Not that she herself was dumb, but academic stuff just wasn't her thing. If she didn't want to be a secretary forever, marriage was the only answer.

But marriage to whom? With her eyes still closed she saw herself walking up the aisle, on her father's arm. And waiting for her at the altar was . . .

When she next opened her eyes, she looked through the window and saw a city. Her heart leaped. New York! But then she heard the bus driver call out, 'Philadelphia. Philadelphia. Pennsylvania next stop.'

Well, that meant only two more hours. She took up a magazine from the stack on the seat next to hers. Around her, people were gathering their things and lining up in the aisle to leave. The bus stopped, they left, and new people got on.

'Is this seat taken?'

Reluctantly she glanced up. A young man stood there. He was short, and a little chubby, but he looked clean, he was wearing a business suit, and he had a pleasant smile. For a second she thought he seemed a little familiar, but that was probably because he looked so ordinary.

'No,' she said, and removed her magazines from the seat. He sat down, and as he took off his suit jacket he eyed her with interest. Uh-oh, Pamela thought. He wants to flirt. She bowed her head and stared resolutely at the magazine in her lap.

Then he spoke. 'Don't I know you?'

Pamela silently groaned. What a corny line. Without taking her eyes off the magazine, she shook her head.

'Yes, I do! You're Bud Mackle's sister!'

Startled, she turned to him. He took her reaction as an affirmation.

'Paula, right?'

'Pamela.'

He snapped his fingers. 'Of course, Pamela. Sorry. But it's been a while! Bud and I were pals in high school. We used to hang out at your house a lot.'

'I did think you looked a little familiar,' Pamela admitted. 'But I don't remember your name.'

'Larry. Larry Taylor. You know, I haven't seen Bud since we graduated.'

Pamela calculated. 'That would make it seven years.'

He smiled. 'I'll bet he's changed. *You've* certainly changed.'

'Well, I should hope so,' Pamela retorted. 'I would have been twelve years old last time you saw me.'

'You had pigtails,' he said.

Pamela nodded. 'My mother wouldn't let me cut my hair. Not until I cried and told her the boys were always pulling on them.'

'I'm sure they were just trying to get your attention,' Larry said. 'That's what we used to do when we liked a girl. When we were little kids, I mean,' he added hastily.

'Oh, they got my attention all right. Especially when I slapped them for doing it.'

Larry grinned. 'Yeah, as I recall, you were a pretty gutsy kid. In fact, I remember one night . . .' He started laughing.

'What?'

'A bunch of us guys were at your place, playing

cards. We must have been about fifteen, sixteen. Your folks were out, and somebody had brought beer. I guess you were about ten or eleven. Anyway, you came downstairs and told us to shut up, we were making too much noise. Then you saw the beer.'

'And asked you for some?'

'No. You demanded five dollars from each of us or you'd tell your parents.'

Pamela lit up. 'I remember that! I made twenty bucks that night!'

'You still into blackmail?' Larry asked.

Pamela laughed. 'No. I guess I missed that career opportunity.'

'So what's Bud been up to these past seven years?'

'He's married, he's got two kids. They bought a house in the old neighbourhood, just down the street from my folks.'

It turned out that Larry remembered all of Pamela's siblings, as well as her parents, and he was interested in all their stories. He laughed when she told him about the disaster at sister Laura's wedding when the groom cut into the wedding cake and the top three tiers fell over. He was dismayed to hear of her father's surgery and relieved to know it was successful. He was sympathetic when she reported her sister Janet's divorce, and intrigued that her brother Ralph was now a grandfather.

'That means you're a great-aunt,' he noted.

'Ralph's twenty-two years older than me,' she quickly pointed out. She looked out the window. The bus was crossing the George Washington Bridge, which meant they were entering New York. She couldn't believe how quickly two hours had passed.

'And what about you?' he asked. 'What have you been up to?'

'I've been working in Pittsburgh,' she said. 'Now I'm moving to New York.'

He seemed pleased to hear that. 'I live in New York. Upper West Side. Where are you?'

'Well, nowhere at the moment,' she admitted. 'I have to find a place.'

> 'Now I'm moving to New York.'

'Where are you working?'

'I don't know that yet either.'

She could see the concern in his eyes. 'I'm staying with some friends till I find a job,' she explained.

He still looked concerned. 'Do you know the city at all?'

She nodded. 'I spent last summer here working at *Gloss* magazine.'

'I don't think I know it.'

'You wouldn't, it's for girls. I was in the Hartnell Building on Madison Avenue.'

'*That* I know,' he said. 'It's on the same block as the

Eastside Coffee Shop. I eat lunch there almost every day. Best grilled cheese sandwich in town. Good BLT too.'

The bus pulled into the Port Authority Terminal. Pamela shoved her magazines into her tote bag and stood up. Larry stepped out into the aisle and paused so Pamela could precede him. Once outside, they waited together while the driver opened the baggage compartment.

'Which one's yours?' Larry asked.

She pointed, and he pulled it out for her.

'Thanks,' she said. 'Well . . . it was nice talking to you.'

'Maybe we can get together in the city sometime,' he said.

'Sure, maybe,' she said, and started walking towards the exit.

'Wait, I don't know how to reach you?' he called after her, but she pretended not to hear and kept on walking. He was a nice guy, that Larry Taylor. Nice but ordinary. But she hadn't come to New York to meet ordinary guys. She could have done that back in Pittsburgh.

Chapter Five

Donna had something on her mind. After living with her for a year, Sherry could always tell when something was bothering her. She could read the expressions. As they sat across from each other in the Hartnell cafeteria, Donna's brow furrowed. She opened her mouth, as if on the verge of saying something. Then she bit her lower lip, as if she was trying to decide whether or not to speak. But no words would leave her lips and she raised her coffee cup for a sip.

Sherry not only knew something was bothering her roommate, she had a pretty good idea what it was, and strongly suspected that it was the same problem that was on *her* mind. So she said it first.

'How long do you think Pamela's going to stay with us?'

Donna exhaled a sigh of relief, clearly glad that the topic was now out in the open. 'I guess till she finds a job.'

'But how long is that going to take?' Sherry wondered, knowing full well Donna couldn't answer that. 'I mean, I see all these ads in the newspaper for secretarial positions. And she's been hunting for three full days now. At least, we *think* she's been hunting,' she added darkly. Each morning, as she and Donna were leaving for their jobs, Pamela was still asleep. When they returned from work, she would regale them with her unsuccessful efforts. But Sherry was beginning to wonder how much real effort Pamela was putting into her job search.

'She wouldn't be making up those stories,' Donna declared.

'No, I guess not. She doesn't have that much imagination.' Sherry clapped her hand over her own mouth. 'I can't believe I said that! I sound terrible! You know I adore Pamela.'

'So do I,' Donna said quickly. 'It's just that, well . . .'

Sherry nodded. 'Yeah, I know.'

Both Sherry and Donna were pretty tidy people. Sherry, because she'd been raised that way, and Donna, because she'd lived a chaotic life in a trailer with an alcoholic mother and two young siblings, and she'd spent a lot of time picking up after all of them.

Pamela, on the other hand, was *messy*. Her enormous suitcase remained open in the middle of their living room, and items of clothing were strewn all over the place. She left dirty dishes piled up in the kitchen sink, and the bathroom surfaces were covered with face powder, blobs of toothpaste and crumpled tissues. And she seemed to take up so much space! The apartment really wasn't big enough for three residents.

'She must want her own place,' Donna remarked. 'That sofa is so lumpy she can't be comfortable sleeping there.'

'I don't understand why she hasn't had a successful interview,' Sherry said. 'Do you think it's the way she dresses?' Pamela had a penchant for tight skirts and tops that showed her cleavage. Not exactly appropriate business attire. And with her platinum-blonde hair and her heavily applied make-up, people could get the wrong idea about her.

'I guess it depends who's doing the interview,' Donna noted. 'If the personnel manager is male, her look might be very appealing. But for all the wrong reasons.' She sighed. 'Remember how pleased we were when she came?'

It had been an unexpected arrival. True, Pamela had sent them a postcard telling them she was coming to New York, but she hadn't said when. Nor had she declared her intention to stay with them until she could find a job and a place of her own.

But at the time, neither of them cared – they were so happy to see her. It had been like old times, three of the four friends who had bonded during the *Gloss* internship. They'd ordered a pizza and stayed up half the night talking and laughing, reminiscing and catching up.

As if reading her mind and remembering how they felt the next morning, Donna yawned. Then Sherry remembered Donna had been out late the night before too.

'Going out with Bonnie again tonight?' she asked.

'Thank goodness, no. She's got an early booking tomorrow.' Donna shook her head wearily. 'I wish she'd remember that I have early bookings every morning.'

Sherry grinned. 'Must be rough being a jet-setter.'

'It's been fun,' Donna admitted. 'Bonnie's really nice, and we've been going to neat places. Pamela was so jealous when I told her we went to the Peppermint Lounge!'

'I heard her asking if she could come along next time.'

Donna nodded. 'I had to tell her this is a job. And if Caroline wasn't giving me money, there's no way I could afford to go out so much with Bonnie.' She laughed. 'It's funny though. Bonnie rarely has to pay for anything herself. Guys are always buying her drinks and stuff.'

'Have *you* met any interesting guys?' Sherry asked curiously.

Donna's smile faded. 'I don't know. Not really. But maybe I'm not looking to meet anyone. I'm just not ready for . . . you know.'

Sherry knew. Donna had a history that none of her friends shared. She'd actually been married, to a wretched guy who treated her terribly. She'd run away from him, and for the entire summer she'd interned at *Gloss* she'd lived in fear of him finding her. It was only after his death in an accident that she began to feel safe. Sherry could totally understand her reluctance to jump into the sea of dating.

Donna looked up at the clock on the cafeteria wall. 'I've gotta go. David has a shoot downtown and I have to get the cameras ready. See you tonight.'

Sherry still had another five minutes of coffee-break time left, and after Donna took off she looked around to see if anyone else she knew was on break. At a table in the back she spotted Gloria, Caroline's secretary, with several other women, all Hartnell Publications secretaries. At another table, not far from them, sat another group of secretaries. But all the women at Gloria's table were Negroes, while the women at the other table were white.

It was strange, Sherry thought. Being from Georgia, she knew all about segregation. But here in New York there weren't those laws that separated the races. The two races ate in the same restaurants, used the same restrooms, drank out of the same water fountains. Why then did these women *choose* to separate themselves?

She got up and strolled towards Gloria's table. As she approached, she picked up on their excited conversation.

'It's terrible,' one woman was saying. 'They were

having a peaceful demonstration. Nobody was making any trouble. And the police turned hoses on them! People were knocked down, and some of them were really hurt.'

'I heard a little boy broke his leg,' another woman declared. 'And a dozen people were arrested.'

At that moment, Gloria saw Sherry standing there. The other women followed her eyes. And they all went silent.

'Sorry, I couldn't help overhearing,' Sherry said. 'Where did this happen?'

Gloria answered. 'Alabama.'

'Oh.' And then, for no reason she herself could understand, she said, 'I'm from Georgia.' Even as the words left her mouth, she knew how stupid she sounded. Was she trying to excuse herself from any blame, by pointing out that she was from a different Southern state?

Gloria raised her eyebrows. 'Did you want something, Sherry?'

'No . . .' Clearly there would be no invitation to join them. 'I'll see you upstairs.'

It was strange, she thought, as she rode the elevator up to her floor. Gloria was usually so friendly. Surely she must know that Sherry wasn't racist, even though she came from a segregated state. She'd been raised to respect all people, whatever their colour, and her parents had never espoused any racist attitudes. Of course, they didn't know any Negroes socially, but that's just how things were. There was no reason for Gloria to act so cold.

But all thoughts of Gloria and racism left her mind when she entered her office and saw one of the new interns by her desk. And not simply standing there – she was actually reading something.

'Excuse me!' Sherry said sharply. 'What are you doing?'

The girl, Liz, – Sherry remembered her name – looked up.

'Hi. I was waiting for you, and then I saw this list. Are these ideas for stories?'

Sherry took the paper from her and glanced at it. 'Yes,' she said, and put it back on her desk, face down. 'But you really shouldn't go into people's offices without permission. And you definitely shouldn't be looking at things on their desks.'

Liz had the courtesy to look a little embarrassed. 'Oh, I'm sorry. I'm so curious about everything.'

Sherry managed a small smile. Maybe she was a little jumpy after that encounter with Gloria. 'Well, don't do it again, OK? What did you want to see me about?'

'I wanted to talk,' Liz said. 'I think it's so amazing, how you went from being an intern to a real editorial assistant. How did that happen? What did you do to make them want to hire you? Was it what you wanted all along? I mean, when you came to *Gloss* as an intern, did you already know you wanted to work here?'

She certainly *was* curious – this was the second time she'd approached Sherry with these questions. Sherry addressed the last one first. 'No, I just came to be an intern. I was planning to go to a college back home when the summer was over.'

'So what happened?'

Sherry hesitated. She didn't want to be rude, but she had a lot of work to do. Fortunately, at that moment, Caroline appeared at the door.

'Liz, I was looking for you! The interns have a talk from the circulation manager up on the twenty-third floor.'

'Oops, I lost track of the time!' Liz exclaimed. She turned to Sherry. 'Can we talk another time?'

'Of course,' Sherry said. Liz left, and Caroline smiled.

'I'm glad you're taking an interest in the girls,' she said. 'They need to feel welcome here.'

Sherry smiled back and nodded. 'Sure, I'm happy to help. That one seems like a real eager beaver.'

'She does, doesn't she?' Caroline said thoughtfully. 'I've got my eye on her.'

Sherry smiled and nodded again. She didn't mention that she'd caught the girl in her office and reading something from her desk. But she made a mental note to keep an eye on her too.

Chapter Six

It was late on a Saturday afternoon when Allison emerged from the taxi to see her summer residence for the first time. The location alone told her it was a pretty snazzy place – Fifth Avenue, facing Central Park. The lobby of the building confirmed this. Several chandeliers hung from the ceiling with its engraved mouldings, ornate red and gold paper lined the walls, the carpet was oriental and there were heavily brocaded loveseats that looked as if no one had ever sat on them.

There were two doormen, not one. Both wore dark perfectly starched uniforms and equally starchy expressions. After checking Allison's identification, one of them took her suitcase.

'I can carry it,' Allison offered, but he ignored her. He escorted her into the elevator and rode with her up to the twelfth floor. Unlocking the door, he led her into a foyer. He spoke.

'The maid arrives at ten a.m. every weekday morning,' he told her.

'Oh, I don't need a maid,' Allison assured him, but again he ignored her remark. He went on to point out light switches, the air-conditioning controls, and the central-heating unit – as if anyone would be turning on heat in a New York summer. Finally he handed her the keys and left.

Allison had assumed any friends of her parents would be upper-class types, so she wasn't surprised to find the apartment so elegant and spacious. There were two bedrooms, two bathrooms, a huge living room and dining room, and a kitchen with a breakfast nook. The people who owned it had a house in Connecticut, and only used this apartment for occasional weekends in the city. They were currently away in Europe, so they wouldn't need it at all this summer. It was all hers, and hers alone. Unless she could convince Bobby to stay here with her. It was funny, how he was so much more concerned about her reputation than she was! But Allison had always been the rebellious type.

She picked up the phone and dialled the number of his grandmother in Queens. Bobby picked it up on the first ring, and his 'Hello' sounded breathless. She figured he'd probably been anxiously awaiting her call to let him know she'd arrived.

'Hi, it's me! I'm here in New York. Oh, Bobby, just wait till you see this place—'

He broke in. 'That's great, babe, but listen, I can't talk now. We've got a meeting for a read-through.'

'A what?'

'We're going to read through the script, the whole cast, with the director, out at his place in the Hamptons, on Long Island. It's a marathon session; I won't be back till tomorrow night.'

'You're going to be away the whole weekend?'

'That's showbiz,' he said. 'Call you from there later, OK?'

Hanging up, she realized he'd been in such a rush he hadn't even asked for the phone number where she was staying. And she sank down on the plush sofa with a frown on her face. Was she really going to be alone on her first Saturday night back in New York? Rattling around in this big silent apartment? Suddenly she wasn't so happy about having so much space to herself. She didn't want to stay on her own tonight.

She picked up the phone, dialled 411 for information and got a number. Then she dialled it.

She thought she recognized the voice that answered. 'Sherry?'

And the girl at the other end identified her too.

'Allison?'

'Yes, it's me! I'm here, in New York.'

'Oh, Allison, so great to hear from you!' She must have turned away because her voice became fainter. 'Y'all, it's Allison!'

Allison started laughing. 'I can't believe you still say "y'all". You've been in New York for a year, Sherry!'

'Well, you know what they say: you can take the girl out of the South but you can't take the South out of the girl.' There was the sound of a voice in the background, and Sherry spoke away from the phone again.

'She's here! In New York!'

'Who are you talking to?' Allison asked.

'Donna and Pamela. So you get yourself over here right this minute so we can have a reunion! You have our address?'

Hanging up, it occurred to Allison that there would be no answer here when Bobby called her back later. But then she remembered that he didn't even have the number here. So far she certainly didn't have to worry about them spending so much time together they would lose interest in each other. She supposed that should be a relief – but it wasn't. In the back of her mind she'd assumed they'd be spending this evening together, celebrating her arrival.

Well, at least she wouldn't be spending Saturday night alone.

Sherry lived downtown, and when Allison consulted the New York subway-system map, she saw she could get a direct train from the West Side. To get there, she could walk through Central Park.

The sun was shining, and early on a Saturday evening the park was lively. Kids were still riding their bikes on the paved walks or gliding along on roller skates. A game of softball was happening on an open field, and couples old and young were strolling hand in hand. She passed a typical New York hot-dog cart, and a rush of memories came back. Sam . . .

Maybe that guy behind the cart was the same one who'd sold her and Sam hot dogs just a year ago. Sam had offered to pay for his dog with a song. The man naturally preferred cash.

At the time, Allison had been so impressed with Sam. She'd admired the way he didn't seem to care about money or success. She saw him as a true poet and beatnik, with a pure heart and soul. But she'd been so naive. In the end Sam turned out to be a total fraud. She could only be grateful that she'd realized this before she gave herself completely to him. And that she'd learned the old cliché was true – you can't judge a book by its cover. If she hadn't realized this, she might never have been open to Bobby.

When she arrived at the address Sherry had given her, she could see immediately that it wasn't anything like the building she'd left. There was no canopy over the door, and the lobby was a dingy, vacant space. There was a doorman, but he was nothing like the polite uniformed men on Fifth Avenue. Here, slumped behind a rickety desk, there was a skinny, scowling guy who needed a shave.

He glanced up when Allison entered. 'Yeah?'

'I'm here to see Sherry Forrester,' she said.

He let out a weary sigh, as if some huge favour had been demanded of him. Then he checked a list and picked up the phone. He mumbled something.

'What?' Allison asked.

'Name!' he growled.

'Sherry Forrester.'

This elicited a sigh that was more like a groan.

'*Your* name!'

'Oh. Allison.'

He punched in some numbers. Someone must have responded, because he muttered, 'Allison's here,' into the phone. Then he hung up.

'Third floor.' He cocked his head, and Allison moved through the scruffy lobby in that direction. There was no elevator, so she climbed the stairs and found herself on a hallway with doors down both sides. The jerk downstairs hadn't bothered to tell her the apartment number.

Fortunately, at that moment, one of the doors was flung open and Sherry stuck her head out. 'Allison!'

She opened her arms and enveloped Allison in a hug. 'Come on in! Excuse the mess.'

The place *did* look a little cluttered, with items of clothing draped over a chair, some magazines on the floor, and a tipped-over handbag spilling out its contents on a coffee table. From another room, Donna came out and they threw their arms around each other.

'So great to see you!' Allison exclaimed. Released from the embraces, she got a good look at both girls, and she was impressed.

Sherry had lost that small-town prim and proper

GL♥SS

look – in her slim capri pants and blouse, she seemed much more sophisticated. And Donna was transformed. The girl Allison remembered as shy and shabby, with a generally downtrodden air, now looked like a sleek and glamorous New York career socialite, in a black sheath with a single strand of pearls around her neck.

'You both look fantastic!' she exclaimed.

'You too!' Donna and Sherry cried out in unison.

'And what about me?' That question came from Pamela, who emerged from what Allison assumed was a kitchen with a glass in her hand. She set the glass down on the coffee table and they had their hug.

Sherry snatched the glass off the table. 'Pamela, use a coaster!'

'Sorry,' Pamela sang out.

'Are you all living here together?' Allison asked.

She didn't miss the look that Sherry and Donna exchanged.

'Actually, it's just Donna and me,' Sherry explained. 'Pamela's only staying here while she looks for a job.'

'Which is not easy,' Pamela declared. She tossed some clothes off a chair on to the floor and sat down.

Allison grinned. 'Finding a job or staying here?'

'Both,' Pamela replied. 'There's not enough closet space in this apartment.'

Allison caught another look from Sherry and Donna. The situation was becoming clear.

'And I can't find a job,' Pamela continued. 'I don't

get it. My typing is OK, I can do shorthand now and I can even transcribe from a dictation machine.'

Allison could only guess that it might have something to do with her appearance. At that moment Pamela was wearing shorts and a halter top. Personally, she loved the fact that Pamela had her own unique style, but she could only hope that she wore more suitable clothes when she went on interviews. Knowing Pamela, she couldn't be sure.

Donna changed the subject. 'What are you doing in New York?' she asked Allison.

'I've got a summer job as a day nanny. This way I can be in New York while Bobby is shooting the film.'

'I'm so glad you two are still together,' Sherry said warmly. 'After that awful Sam, you deserve someone special.'

'As do we all,' Allison declared. 'So tell! How's your love life?'

'*What* love life?' Sherry shook her head ruefully. 'All I do is work.'

Allison turned to Donna. 'What about you?'

Donna shrugged. 'I'm not even looking.'

Knowing Donna's past, Allison could understand why she wasn't ready to even think about a relationship yet.

But Pamela certainly was. '*I'm* looking. Don't worry,' she added hastily. 'Not like I was looking last summer.'

'That's a relief,' Allison said with feeling. She could

remember too well the sobs of her former roommate when she realized Alex Parker wasn't going to leave his wife for her.

'Only unmarried men,' Pamela assured her. 'I want a husband.'

'Right now?' Allison asked. 'Don't you want to enjoy being a single girl in New York for a while? Go out on dates, have some fun?'

'Not if it means I have to go on being a secretary,' Pamela declared. 'It's boring.'

Sherry was looking anxious, and Allison thought she could read her mind. She was worried Pamela would go on living with them until she found that husband.

'No one says you have to be a secretary. That's not the only job in the world,' she murmured. 'You could go back to school, study to be something else.'

'Like what? I don't want to be a nurse or a teacher. I talked to someone at an airline about becoming a stewardess, but it turns out there's a height requirement, and I'm not tall enough.'

'Maybe you could be a nanny, like Allison,' Donna suggested.

'Take care of kids?' Pamela shuddered. 'No, I'm stuck with this. I signed up with a secretarial temp agency yesterday, so at least I can start making some money while I look for a real job.'

'Oh, that's great!' Sherry exclaimed, with a lot more

enthusiasm than Pamela was demonstrating.

Allison nodded. 'Then you'll be able to get your own apartment.'

Pamela shrugged. 'Not right away. Do you know what it costs to rent an apartment here? Before you can even move in, you have to give the landlord the first and last month's rent plus a deposit! It'll take me ages to save all that up. Plus, if I'm only doing temp work, I won't have a real salary. I don't know how much work I'll get, so I don't even know what I can afford to pay in rent.'

Allison looked at Donna and Sherry. Their smiles were getting thinner and thinner.

Donna got up. 'Sorry, girls, I have to leave.'

'Are you meeting Bonnie tonight?' Sherry asked.

Donna nodded. 'She wants me to come with her to a cocktail party.' She indicated her dress. 'Does this look OK? It's from the samples closet.'

'Perfect,' Sherry declared.

'Who's Bonnie?' Allison asked.

Donna explained how Caroline wanted her to help convince the model to sign an exclusive contract with *Gloss*.

'Can I come this time?' Pamela asked eagerly.

The look on Donna's face told Allison they'd had this conversation before. 'It's a work thing, Pamela. I can't invite friends to come along. I'm sorry.'

Pamela pouted, and Donna looked extremely

uncomfortable. Allison could practically *feel* the tension in the room.

Suddenly she had an idea. 'Pamela, why don't you come stay with me this summer?'

Pamela's eyes widened. 'Stay with you?'

'I've got this big apartment with two bedrooms for the whole summer.' She grinned. 'I wanted Bobby to stay there with me, but he thinks living together would give me a bad reputation. Anyway, he's going to be busy filming, and I hate rattling around alone in that big apartment. What do you think?'

Pamela clapped her hands. 'Roomies again!'

And Allison didn't miss the look of relief on the faces of the other two.

It was the perfect solution. She'd be doing Sherry and Donna a favour, and she knew from the summer before that Pamela could actually be a lot of fun to have around. And if Bobby would be working a lot of evenings and weekends, she wouldn't be lonely.

But looking around this place and all of Pamela's chaos, she decided to tell the doorman she'd definitely want that daily maid service after all.

Chapter Seven

The cocktail party was being held in a huge, cavernous Soho loft. It was the home of Rafe Bryant, an up-and-coming young designer who had made a big splash at the spring fashion shows. The place was teeming with beautiful people and jet-setters. Uniformed catering staff moved through the crowd with trays laden with canapés.

As a member of the *Gloss* staff, Donna had attended events like this several times, and still found them intimidating. But she'd figured out a way to deal with them. She had her own special routine. It varied from place to place, but it usually only took her a minute or two to work out a plan that would get her through the evening.

Bonnie was immediately swept up by a group of guests, and she tried to pull Donna along with her. But Donna immediately went into her routine – first she'd pleaded the need to find a toilet, assuring Bonnie she would catch up with her in a few minutes. Once Bonnie was out of sight, she stepped back to a corner of the room and surveyed the place.

In an alcove, behind an antique desk, there were

bookcases against the wall. She walked purposefully towards them and began studying the titles as if searching for something in particular. One of the catering staff passed by, and she took a little sausage wrapped in pastry from the tray. She ate it slowly, all the while staring at the books and hoping she looked busy.

After about ten minutes of doing that, she moved on to another wall, which was covered with framed black-and-white fashion photographs of Bryant's designs. This was easier and more interesting to observe, and she recognized a couple of photographs that her boss, David, had taken.

Then it was over to another corner, where a drinks bar had been set up.

'Vodka gimlet?' the bartender asked. It was the fashionable cocktail of the moment.

She nodded and accepted one. Personally she didn't like the bitter lime taste, but it gave her something to carry and helped her blend in with the crowd. She circled the room, gazing around as if searching for someone. When she came to a big potted plant, she took a quick look around to make sure no one was watching and emptied the cocktail into the dirt.

After that, she located a bathroom, where she drew a comb through her hair and reapplied lipstick that didn't need reapplying. Then she went back into the main room and started the routine all over again.

Oh, *Gloss*, what I do for you, she thought mournfully as she stood in front of the bookcase, staring blankly at the spines. Desperately she hoped Bonnie would sign that exclusive contract with the magazine very soon, so she wouldn't have to keep on going to these functions. She *liked* Bonnie – the model was sweet and warm and easy to be with. She just didn't like the places she had to go to with her.

'See anything good?'

The voice startled her, and she turned to the figure that had suddenly appeared by her side.

'What?'

The young man smiled, revealing perfectly straight white teeth. 'Anything good to read here?'

'Oh! Gosh, I don't know . . . I mean, I wasn't really looking.' She knew she sounded stupid. Here she was staring at thick book spines with titles on them, and now she claimed she wasn't even looking at them.

But he didn't comment on that. He moved closer to the bookcase, and she was suddenly aware of how tall he was. Handsome too, in a clean-cut preppy way, with a square jaw and neat wavy brown hair. Then he took a pair of wire-rimmed glasses from his suit jacket pocket and put them on. She could still make out how deep brown his eyes were.

'Can't read a word without these,' he murmured. 'Let's see what we have here. *Birds of America.*

Masters of the Italian Renaissance. A History of the Peloponnesian War . . .'

'The *what* war?'

'Ancient battle between Athens and Sparta, around 400 B.C.'

'Oh.' She flushed. Should she have known that? Had she just revealed how uneducated she was?

He grinned. 'Don't worry. Only people who went to ridiculously pretentious boarding schools would know about the Peloponnesian War.' He looked at the shelves again. 'You know what I think?'

'What?'

'Somebody bought these books by the yard. You know, for decoration. Notice how they're all about the same height? I'll bet you anything half of them have uncut pages.'

'But why would somebody do that?' she asked.

'To show off – to look intellectual or something. My parents have a library in their apartment, and they hired a decorator to buy books for the walls.'

A library in an apartment? She'd never heard of such a thing.

He extended his right hand. 'I'm Jack.'

'Donna,' she said, and shook his hand.

'What's your connection here?' he asked. 'Are you a model?'

'Me? A model?' She made it sound as if he'd called her a Martian.

'Is that an insult?' he asked.

'No! It's just that models, well, they're all tall and beautiful.'

He shrugged. 'You're not exactly short and ugly.'

She felt her face redden.

'Sorry,' he said quickly. 'Am I being too pushy?'

'No.' Should she thank him for the compliment? She felt so flustered by his attention she didn't know how to react. So she went back to his earlier question, about her connection to this event.

'I work for a magazine, *Gloss*. You've probably never heard of it.'

'Are you kidding? I have a teenage sister. It's been my Christmas gift to her the past three years – a subscription to *Gloss*. What do you do for the magazine?'

'I'm the photographer's assistant. What about you? Are you involved in fashion?'

He shook his head. 'I've got a summer internship at a bank. This really isn't my scene at all.'

'Mine either,' Donna admitted. 'I'm not much of a cocktail-party person.'

'How about the new dancing places, the discotheques?'

Donna shuddered. 'They're even worse than cocktail parties.'

'My feelings precisely,' Jack said. 'So why are we both here?'

GL♥SS

'I came for work,' Donna told him. 'Kind of a requirement for my job. You?'

'I'm only here because a buddy of mine from Yale dragged me along. He's always trying to meet models.'

Yale. One of the most elite universities in the country. Jack was either very, very smart or very, very aristocratic. Or maybe both.

And then he reddened. 'I can't believe I said that.'

'What? About your friend wanting to meet models?'

'No, about going to Yale. You know, dropping the name like that. I guess I wanted to impress you.'

She stared at him. 'Why would you want to impress *me*?'

'Are you kidding? Because – because I wanted you to be interested in me. Because I'm interested in you.'

He smiled again. And this time she had the oddest sensation. It was as if someone had turned on more lights in the room. Everything seemed brighter.

'Well, since neither of us really wants to be here, maybe we could go someplace else,' he said. 'Someplace more quiet, where we could talk.'

'I can't,' she said, and realized she was actually sorry to have to say this. 'I'm with someone.'

'Oh.'

Was that disappointment she saw in his face?

'A girlfriend,' she added quickly. 'Bonnie Bailey, the model.'

There was no mistaking the expression on his face this time. He was relieved.

'So . . . you're single, right?' he asked.

She hesitated. Fortunately, at that very moment, some other man, maybe his Yale friend, joined them.

'Jack, you gotta talk to this guy I just met. He's thinking about switching his investments to your bank.'

Jack looked pointedly at Donna.

'Oh, sorry,' the man said.

'Brad, this is Donna. Donna, this is my incredibly rude buddy Brad.'

Brad grinned. 'Nice to meet you, Donna, and I'm sorry to interrupt you guys. But this fellow, he's talking about a major deal. You really need to meet him, Jack.'

'You go ahead,' Donna urged. 'I'll be around.'

'I'll find you,' Jack promised, and left with his friend.

Donna stared after him, and suddenly realized that her heart was pounding rapidly. She'd met attractive men over the past year, and some had even flirted with her, but she'd never felt so . . . so interested. That last question though – 'you're single, right?'

Was she? Technically, she supposed she was a widow. She'd been married to Ron, and Ron was dead. But she didn't feel like a widow. Maybe because she'd run away from him while he was still alive, and hadn't shed a tear when she found out he'd died.

GL♥SS

Bonnie suddenly emerged from the crowd and clutched her arm. 'How are you doing?'

'Fine,' she replied.

'No kidding!' she exclaimed. 'I saw who you were talking to!'

'You know him?'

Bonnie shook her head. 'One of the other girls knows him. He's a Vanderwill, Donna!'

Donna looked at her blankly.

'The Vanderwills are one of the wealthiest families in New York,' Bonnie told her. 'Old money, high society, very la-di-da.'

Donna managed a thin smile. 'He seemed nice.'

'Listen, a bunch of us are going to the Electric Pig, that new disco uptown,' Bonnie went on. 'You'll come with us, won't you?'

'Oh, gee, Bonnie, I'm kind of tired . . .' she began, but she was interrupted by the appearance of Caroline Davison.

The editor gave Donna an approving nod and beamed at Bonnie. 'Hello, girls. Having fun?'

'I'm trying to talk Donna into going to the Electric Pig,' Bonnie told Caroline.

'Oh, how fantastic,' Caroline gushed. 'I'm sure Donna won't need much convincing.'

Inwardly Donna sighed, but she forced yet another thin smile. 'No, not at all.'

Bonnie put her arm through Donna's. 'Let's go say

goodnight to the host and take off.'

They were on their way to the door when Jack caught up with them.

'Are you leaving?' he asked Donna.

Bonnie answered for her. 'We're going to the Electric Pig. Want to come?'

'That's a discotheque, right?' Jack asked. He looked at Donna and winked. Then he turned back to Bonnie.

'Sure. Why not?'

Chapter Eight

On Monday morning the weather was gorgeous, not too humid, so Sherry and Donna got off the bus early so they could walk the rest of the way to work.

Sherry picked up the conversation they'd been having the day before.

'I'm still surprised he didn't call you yesterday.'

'Who?' Donna asked innocently.

'Jack, of course! That was his name, right?'

Donna nodded. 'Jack. Jack Vanderwill.'

'And he was all over you Saturday night, right?'

'I wouldn't say *that*,' Donna said. 'But yeah, we talked a lot. Until we got to the Electric Pig. We were with all those other people, and it was way too loud to talk.'

'Were you with him all the time there?'

'Yeah.'

Sherry gave her a sideways look. 'You're smiling. It was nice, huh?'

'Well, it's funny in a way. We'd been talking before, at the cocktail party, about how neither of us liked these new discotheques. Because they're so noisy and crowded. And there we were, in the most popular one of the moment. Kind of weird.'

'You told him you had to go because of Bonnie, right? So he went because he wanted to stay with you. Even if it meant going to a discotheque.'

Donna shrugged. 'Maybe.'

Sherry wasn't going to let her get away with *that*.

'Come on, it's obvious! The guy's interested in you. Did you dance?'

'Not really. It was so crowded we just sort of stood there, facing each other, and kind of swayed to the beat.'

'I call that dancing,' Sherry declared. 'And he offered to see you home, right?'

'Well, yeah, he's got nice manners. But there was another girl who was going downtown, so it made more sense for us to share a taxi.'

'And he kissed you.'

'A peck on the check. It wasn't a big deal.'

Sherry frowned. 'Even so, I don't understand why he hasn't called.'

'I didn't give him my number,' Donna told her.

'So what? He could have looked you up in the phone book. Or called information.'

Donna bit her lip. 'I didn't give him my last name,' she finally admitted.

'Donna! Are you crazy? Is he good-looking too?'

'Very.'

'And he has a job?'

'He's at Yale. He's working in a bank this summer.'

Sherry ticked off his attributes on her fingers. 'Nice, good-looking, attentive, employed, Yale . . . He sounds perfect.'

'I guess he is.'

'Then why aren't you more excited? What else do you want in a guy?'

'I don't know that I want a guy at all,' Donna said. 'Not now. Not yet.'

Sherry sighed. 'Oh, Donna. Look, I understand how awful your love life was. But the past is the past. You have to move on.'

'It's not just that,' Donna confessed. 'What would happen when he found out about me? Bonnie says his family is very important, high society and all that. You think he's going to be interested in a girl from a trailer park, a girl who got pregnant and married a bum?'

Sherry wanted to argue, but she couldn't, not honestly. Because she knew there were people who would care. Her own parents, for example. If she started seeing a guy who wasn't their kind . . . well, they wouldn't be pleased. And she really loved her parents. She wouldn't want them to be unhappy.

Talking had slowed their walking, and they had to pick up the pace to get to work on time. They were almost out of breath when they arrived at the Hartnell Building, but they stopped short when a taxi pulled up and Pamela got out.

GL♥SS

'What are you doing here?' Donna asked.

Pamela grinned broadly. 'Can you believe it? My first assignment from the temp agency! Right here at *Gloss*!' She reached through the window of the taxi to pay the driver.

Sherry was puzzled. 'You're staying with Allison over on Fifth Avenue. Why did you take a taxi?'

'Now that I'm making some money, I thought I'd splurge. I'm supposed to report to a Mr Anderson. Do you know who he is?'

'Merchandizing, eighteenth floor,' Sherry told her. 'And we'd all better get a move on. We're late.'

'Isn't this great!' Pamela enthused as they got into the elevator. 'It's almost like old times. We can have lunch together.'

'I can't,' Donna said. 'I've got an all-day shoot across town with David.'

'And it's Monday, which means I'll be swamped,' Sherry added. 'Don't count on me for lunch; I'll be having a sandwich at my desk.'

Pamela looked at them both in surprise and disappointment. 'Really?'

The elevator doors opened. 'Maybe we can take a coffee break together,' Sherry said as she walked out. 'Call my extension.'

She practically ran the rest of the way to the office. From her desk Gloria mouthed, 'She's waiting.' Sherry ran into her own office, snatched up a notepad and

76

a pen and hurried back out. She rapped lightly on Caroline's door.

'Come in!'

Sherry was glad to see that Caroline didn't appear annoyed at her tardiness. But she was surprised to see someone else in the office.

'Sherry, you know Liz, one of our interns. Liz asked me if she could join in on some of our meetings, to observe the editorial process.'

'Great,' Sherry said, hoping she sounded more enthusiastic than she felt. She sat down next to the girl and whipped open her notebook. Liz promptly took a notebook out of her bag and did the same.

'I've been getting some disturbing news,' Caroline began. 'We all know that *Gloss* isn't alone in its field, that there are other magazines oriented towards teenage girls. We've always been ahead of the pack, and we've never seen them as a threat to our popularity. But this new magazine, *Modern Girl*, seems to be really taking off. Last month their newsstand sales exceeded ours, and their subscriptions are rising at an incredible rate.'

Liz leaned forward. 'Well, it's new and people are curious. Maybe that's the only reason.'

Sherry thought it was a little pushy for an intern to jump in like that, and she wished she'd said it first.

'Possibly,' Caroline admitted. 'But I'm beginning to realize we've got some serious competition here and we need to step up our game. We can't sit back and assume that *Gloss* will always be in the lead. It's time we started thinking about moving in new directions, extending our scope.'

Sherry spoke up before Liz could. 'Take some risks maybe? Solicit articles on less traditional topics?'

'Precisely,' Caroline said, and Sherry was pleased. 'Precisely' was a lot better than the 'possibly' she'd offered Liz.

'We could even assign writers to some controversial subjects,' Caroline went on. 'Any ideas?'

This time, Liz got in first. 'Ear piercing!'

Caroline's brow furrowed. 'Ear piercing?' she repeated.

'Yes! It used to be something only gypsies did. Now ordinary girls want to get their ears pierced. And a lot of parents are against it.'

'That could be an interesting piece for our beauty or fashion people to address,' Caroline said. 'But it's not really what I had in mind when I said "controversial."'

Liz was clearly crestfallen by the response, and Sherry couldn't help feeling a little pleased. She had a pretty good idea what Caroline wanted.

'Articles about newsworthy topics, not connected to fashion or beauty, but still of interest to our readers,' she suggested.

Caroline nodded. 'For example, the new birth-control pill. Should doctors offer prescriptions to teenage girls? It would decrease unwed pregnancies, but some people think it would encourage promiscuity.'

'What about this war in Vietnam?' Sherry asked. 'I was reading in the newspaper about some demonstrations against the war on a college campus. Some boys burned their draft cards.'

'Girls read *Gloss*,' Liz piped up. 'This doesn't have anything to do with them; they don't get drafted into the army.'

'But their boyfriends do,' Sherry countered. 'So they should be interested.'

Caroline was nodding again. 'You're right.'

Encouraged, Sherry continued. 'And I've got another idea. You know the book *The Feminine Mystique*, by Betty Friedan?'

'Never heard of it,' Liz declared. 'What is it – something about how women need to act mysterious to get a man?'

Caroline smiled. 'No, Liz, not at all. The author suggests that women in America are generally unhappy, that they've been forced into roles as wives and mothers and that this is not enough for them.'

'I haven't read it yet,' Sherry admitted, 'but I've been hearing about it. Do you think there's something in there that would be interesting for our readers?'

'*Gloss*'s readers aren't housewives and mothers,' Liz pointed out.

'No,' Sherry agreed, 'but for a lot of them, that's their ambition.'

Now Caroline looked really intrigued. 'I think you've got something there, Sherry. From what Friedan writes, women's roles in America are on the verge of changing. And this is going to have an effect on our readers.' She cocked her head thoughtfully. 'What if we arranged an interview with a psychologist who specializes in teenagers? The writer could ask her about how teenage girls are going to deal with the changing roles.'

'Yes!' Sherry exclaimed. 'Are girls ready to become the women of tomorrow?'

Caroline snapped her fingers. 'And that's our title!'

Sherry couldn't help noticing that Liz was writing rapidly. Surely the intern didn't think Caroline was going to assign an important article like this to *her*. Even Sherry wouldn't get a crack at this.

'Sherry, go up to the library and look in some of those local medical directories,' Caroline said. 'See if you can find a therapist who specializes in treating teenage girls. And Liz, you need to get over to the conference room for the film screening. OK, girls, that's all for now. Oh, Sherry, I've got something for you.'

From her desk drawer Caroline took out a brochure. 'It's about the Columbia University School of Journalism. You might want to start thinking about this. You can only get so far in publishing without a degree.'

'I'll read it,' Sherry promised, folding the booklet

carefully and putting it in her handbag.

Once outside the office, Sherry pointed in the direction of the conference room. 'It's just down that corridor.'

But Liz didn't take off. 'Maybe, instead of seeing that film, I could help you with your research.'

'You need to do what the other interns are doing,' Sherry told her. And to make the assignment more appealing, she added, 'You know, that was my first break at *Gloss*. Writing a review of a new movie we were shown. Caroline was very impressed.'

'OK.' But she looked at Sherry curiously. 'Are you going to do it?'

'Write the article? No, interviews like this are always conducted by professionals.'

'No, I mean, go to the university.'

'I don't know. Maybe, some time. Why?'

'Just wondering,' Liz said, and walked away.

That was when it hit her. *She wants my job.* That's why she keeps hanging around. Well, Sherry couldn't think about that now, she had too much to do. The library, then her daily search of the newspapers . . .

She was distracted from her thoughts by Caroline's secretary.

'There's a call for you, Sherry.'

'Thanks, Gloria.' She took the receiver Gloria held in her direction. 'Hello?'

'Hi, it's me! Want to take a coffee break?'

'Oh, Pamela, I can't. I'm so swamped right now.'

'And no lunch either, right?' She sounded more than disappointed, almost hurt.

'Look, we can take a coffee break together this afternoon, I promise. I'll meet you in the cafeteria at three.'

Hanging up, she left the offices and went upstairs to the company library. There, she searched through a variety of directories and eventually found the name of a woman doctor, a psychologist who specialized in the problems of teenage girls. Back at her office, Gloria was on her way to lunch and offered to bring back a sandwich from the cafeteria. Sherry gratefully accepted.

She began going through the daily ritual of perusing the newspapers for articles of interest to *Gloss* readers.

'Disappearance of civil-rights workers' was one of the lead stories. And even though this wasn't something that screamed '*Gloss*', she read it anyway.

It seemed that three young men – Michael Schwerner, Andrew Goodman, and James Chaney – had vanished in central Mississippi while investigating the burning of a Negro church by the Ku Klux Klan.

It was a very upsetting story, and there was a detail which intrigued her. Goodman and Schwerner were white.

So, white people were getting involved in the

civil-rights movement, she mused. That was interesting . . .

She continued reading. It turned out that Goodman was a twenty-year-old college student. Chaney was twenty-one, Schwerner twenty-four. Young men, just starting out in the world.

There was a Ku Klux Klan chapter back in her own hometown. She didn't know any of the members, but she knew the reputation of the organization. And the thought of what might have happened to those three young men made her shudder.

Suddenly she realized it was after three, and she'd promised to meet Pamela. She took the newspaper with her, and hoped that Pamela might be late so she could finish reading the article.

But Pamela was already there, and she looked annoyed. 'I've been waiting for ages,' she complained. 'I'm so bored!'

'With waiting?'

'With this job! It's deadly, Sherry. This Mr Anderson, he's got me filing stacks and stacks of old invoices. And guess who else is on that floor? Remember Felix Duncan, the creepy accountant? He keeps hanging around my desk. And putting his arm around my shoulders.'

'Well, at least it's just temporary,' Sherry said. 'I'm sorry I'm late, but I was reading this article. Look.'

Pamela scanned the article and wrinkled her

nose. 'That's terrible. I don't understand these racist types. Personally I only have one prejudice: against married men who flirt with single girls.'

Sherry grinned. 'Like Felix Duncan?'

'And others I won't mention.'

Sherry considered this. 'You know, that could be an article for *Gloss*. "How to avoid married men on the job".'

'Isn't that a little too serious for *Gloss*?' Pamela asked.

'We're going to get into a lot of heavier stuff. It's really exciting. Like, how women are demanding new roles, and how teens feel about this. I found the name of a woman psychologist Dr Cutler, and I'm going to try and arrange an interview for *Gloss*. And this article in the newspaper, about the missing civil-rights workers, there might be something there for *Gloss* too.'

'That's nice,' Pamela said vaguely, but she didn't look terribly interested. 'Hey, do you think I should come down to your department and say hello to Doreen and Darleen? They might give me some make-up samples.'

When the coffee break was over, Sherry hurried back to the department and went to Caroline.

'Have you seen this?' she asked, and handed her the newspaper.

'Yes. Terrible, isn't it?'

'I was thinking . . . young white and Negro people working together, for civil rights. Do you think there might be an article for *Gloss* here?'

Caroline frowned, but it was the kind of frown that went with her furrowed brow. It meant she was seriously considering something.

'This would be a major leap for us,' she murmured, 'getting into something so . . . so . . .'

'Controversial? But isn't that what you want?'

Caroline's brow cleared. 'Yes. You're absolutely right. Sherry, write up the idea, like a proposal for a piece.'

Sherry nodded happily. 'And we'll have to find a really modern, up-to-date writer.'

Caroline looked at her thoughtfully. 'You know, Sherry . . . maybe *you* could write this article.'

Sherry drew in her breath. She'd written bits and pieces for *Gloss* – some movie reviews, a little article on modern etiquette – but nothing big, nothing major like this.

'I'm not promising anything,' Caroline added quickly. 'But see what kind of angle you can come up with, and we'll talk about it.'

Sherry immediately headed back up to the library. This time she solicited the help of the librarian in searching for articles about the involvement of young people of all races in working for civil rights. She became so engrossed in her reading that she completely lost track of the time. Even though it was after five, she was reluctant to leave.

Back downstairs, the *Gloss* offices were practically empty, but Gloria was still at her desk.

'Working late?' Sherry asked.

'Just waiting for my brother,' the secretary told her. 'We're going uptown to my mother's for dinner.'

Uptown. Did that mean Harlem? Sherry wondered. She knew absolutely nothing about Gloria's private life.

The phone on Gloria's desk rang, and she picked it up. '*Gloss* editorial,' she said. 'Yes, he's my brother. Please send him up.'

Sherry went into her office, covered her typewriter and gathered her things to leave. When she emerged, a young man was standing by Gloria's desk.

'Hello,' she said.

The man turned. It was clear to Sherry that this had to be Gloria's brother. He had the same café au lait skin, deep-set eyes, high cheekbones – but not feminine at all. In fact, extremely masculine.

'William, this is Sherry. Sherry, this is my brother William.'

Sherry extended her right hand for shaking. But William didn't take her up on the offer. He nodded abruptly, coldly, and turned back to Gloria.

'C'mon, sis, let's get moving, Mom will have a fit if we're late.' Together they headed towards the exit.

'Have a nice evening, y'all,' Sherry called after them.

Gloria looked back. 'You too, Sherry.'

But the young man didn't turn, and he said nothing at all.

Chapter Nine

Allison did something completely out of character on Monday morning. On the first day of her summer job, she changed clothes four times.

She'd never been a fashion hound. Even while working at *Gloss*, she wasn't terribly interested in the samples closet. When she was told that pants weren't acceptable office attire, she wore the same black pencil skirt almost every day. At Radcliffe, fashion was not an issue – it was even considered anti-intellectual to care too much about clothes. In the winter, everyone wore bulky cable-knit sweaters, with stretch pants or wool skirts. Warmer weather meant cotton pants with blouses or shirtdresses.

What was a nanny supposed to wear? In the back of her mind, she conjured up a vision of a lady in a prim tailored suit with a hat. But that was ridiculous – they weren't expecting Mary Poppins.

She could only come up with one other image of a nanny. Five years ago, when she was fourteen, she'd come to New York with her parents, and her mother had taken her to a matinee on Broadway to see *The Sound of Music*. But she couldn't see herself prancing around in a dirndl skirt singing, 'Doe, a deer, a female deer.'

Why was she making such a fuss? After all, a nanny was just a babysitter. But even babysitting wasn't a concept she was familiar with. She'd known other girls who made spending money that way when they were teenagers, but she'd always received a decent allowance for doing nothing at all. Allison had no experience with little kids, and that was why she was so nervous. She'd never been around them and she never wanted to be. Kids were noisy and dirty and you couldn't have a decent conversation with them.

Standing in front of the mirror, she assessed her current look: navy-blue capri pants and a sleeveless white shirt, the tails tied in a knot an inch above the waistband. No, maybe she shouldn't reveal any skin. She untied the tails and tucked the shirt in.

Pamela had left the apartment earlier, but her presence could be felt. Allison almost tripped over the suitcase that still lay open on the floor of the living room. And in the kitchen the remains of her new roommate's breakfast were all over the place – unwashed dishes, a coffee mug bearing traces of pink lipstick, crumpled napkins. Still, she was glad to have Pamela living here with her. It wasn't as if Bobby was around to keep her company.

It was ironic, in a way. She'd only organized this stupid nanny job so she could be in New York with him, and she hadn't even seen him since she'd arrived. She'd be seeing him tonight though. The producer of the film was having a cocktail party for the cast and crew, and they could bring dates. She had no idea what she'd be wearing for *that* either.

She'd be seeing him tonight . . .

The family she was going to work for lived just three blocks north and two blocks over, on Lexington Avenue. As she walked, she considered what she knew about them. From the letters she'd exchanged with Mr Markham, she knew that he was a widower with two children, a seven-year-old girl and a five-year-old boy. Unfortunately she couldn't remember their names.

She *did* remember Mr Markham writing that he was a university professor. He'd said he wouldn't be teaching this summer, but would be spending a lot of time at the university library doing research. He'd also be writing at home, but he needed someone to keep the kids occupied so he could work. She imagined him in heavy glasses, grey-haired, smoking a pipe and wearing a cardigan with leather patches on the elbows. A quiet man, serious – maybe even dour, considering that he'd lost his wife just two years earlier.

So she was pleasantly surprised when the door to

his apartment was opened by a trim, youthful-looking man with sandy hair and a warm smile.

'Hi, you must be Allison. I'm Tom Markham. Come on in.'

The living room she entered was large and comfortable, with overstuffed furniture, thick carpeting and lots of bookshelves. There were pretty paintings on the walls, mostly landscapes. On the mantel over the fireplace there was a large framed photograph. She recognized Tom Markham right away. In the picture he stood behind a chair that held a beautiful woman, with long brown hair. On her lap was a toddler, and a girl who looked to be about five stood next to her. They looked like such a lovely, happy family.

An upright piano stood against one wall.

'Do you play the piano, Mr Markham?'

'Call me Tom. No, my wife did. And Karen's taking lessons.' He turned in the direction of a corridor. 'Kids! Come meet Allison!'

An adorable little boy with a freckled face and his father's sandy hair came tearing into the room. He stopped short at the sight of Allison.

'You have red hair,' he declared, making it sound like an accusation.

Allison nodded. 'Is that OK?'

'You look like my Howdy,' he replied. 'I love my Howdy.'

'Howdy's a puppet,' Tom explained.

The child raced out of the room and returned with his doll. Allison recognized it immediately. She wasn't sure if she should be pleased with a comparison to an ugly puppet on an old children's TV show, but at least the little boy seemed to approve of her.

'This is Tom, Junior,' Tom Markham said. 'More commonly known as Tommy. Tommy, what do you do when you meet people for the first time?'

The boy came closer and stuck out his right hand. Allison shook it.

'Pleased to meet you,' Tommy said.

'Pleased to meet you too,' Allison replied.

The girl who followed him entered the room more slowly, mainly because she had an open book in her hands and her eyes were glued to it.

'And this is Karen,' the man said.

'Hi, Karen,' Allison said.

The girl mumbled something that could have been a greeting.

'Karen,' her father said pointedly.

She sighed and looked up. 'Hello, pleased to meet you.' Her tone, however, made it clear that she was far from pleased.

This child had no freckles and no warm smile either. Her solemn face was framed by two long brown braids.

'Hi,' Allison said. 'What are you reading?'

'*The Little House on the Prairie*,' Karen replied.

'I remember that book!' Allison exclaimed. 'I read it when I was nine.'

'I'm only seven,' Karen declared. 'I'm very advanced for my age.'

'And very modest too,' her father added with a smile. 'So, Allison, I guess I should explain your duties. If the weather's nice, you can take them out somewhere in the mornings. Then bring them home and give them some lunch around one.'

Allison flinched. She'd thought her only responsibility was to keep them alive and out of his hair. She hadn't considered feeding them.

'I'm not much of a cook,' she admitted.

'They don't require much of a chef,' he said. 'Can you open a can of Campbell's Chicken Noodle Soup and heat it up?'

'Yes.'

'How about making a peanut-butter-and-jelly sandwich?'

'I can do that too.' Another culinary talent occurred to her. 'And I know how to make a grilled cheese sandwich with an iron. That's how we do it in the dorm. I could probably figure out how to do it in a pan.'

'Grilled cheese with an iron,' he repeated. 'I remember those days. You're at Radcliffe, right? I went to Harvard.' He smiled in reminiscence. 'The Brattle Theater. Are they still showing *Casablanca* on Valentine's Day every year?'

'Absolutely.'

He went on with her schedule. 'Karen's piano teacher comes at two o'clock today, and you can play something with Tommy while she's doing that.'

'Checkers,' Tommy interjected. 'You do know how to play Checkers?'

'Yes, I do. But I'm not very good at it. You'll probably beat me.'

Tommy grinned happily.

Mr Markham – Tom – went on to talk about more regular events on other days during the week. There was Karen's ballet class, Tommy's swimming, the story hour at the local branch of the public library . . . It dawned on Allison that she should be writing all this down.

Tom must have read her mind. 'Don't worry about memorizing the schedule. Karen will remind you.'

Karen bestowed on Allison a condescending smirk.

Tom took out his wallet and extracted some bills, which he handed to Allison. 'In case anything you do requires an admission charge.' Then he turned to the kids.

'I am now retiring to my study,' he declared. 'And I will not be disturbed, right?' Clearly this was a regular request, and Tommy recited what seemed to be the traditional response.

'Except in case of emergency.'

'Precisely. And emergency doesn't mean we're out of Cheerios.'

With that, he left the room, leaving Allison alone with her two charges. They looked at her expectantly.

Allison hoped that her own expression didn't betray her lack of confidence. 'So . . . what do you want to do?'

'I want to see Whaley,' Tommy stated.

'Who's Whaley?' she asked.

He stared at her in disbelief. 'The whale! In Central Park!'

'There's a whale? In Central Park?'

Karen rolled her eyes in a distinctly unchildlike way. 'He's not a *real* whale.'

Whaley turned out to be a huge structure in the shape of a whale, through which kids passed to get into the Central Park Children's Zoo. Zoos had never been Allison's favourite places. She'd always hated seeing large animals trapped in small cages. But this zoo was different; it was more of a fantasy land for children. Everything was small, child-sized. There was a replica of Noah's Ark, a Gingerbread House and a home for the Three Little Pigs. The animals were mostly small – turtles, frogs, ducks, and there were rabbits that the children could pet.

Tommy was skipping happily in front of Allison but Karen proceeded at a more sedate pace, mainly because she had her book open and was reading as she walked.

'Karen, don't you want to look at the animals?' Allison asked.

Karen's eyes didn't leave the page as she replied, 'I've seen them before.'

'Well, you're going to bump into people if you don't look where you're going.'

This time Karen actually turned away from her book, but only to give Allison a steely look. A memory of herself at that age suddenly hit Allison. She too had preferred reading to all other activities.

Karen sat down on a bench. 'I'll just stay right here.'

'You can't,' Allison said. 'Tommy wants to run around and I have to keep my eyes on both of you.' At that moment she realized she couldn't see the little boy.

'Tommy!' she yelled. 'Tommy, where are you?'

Unfortunately, since her younger charge had one of the most common names in the world, half a dozen little boys turned to her. And their mothers, or nannies, or whatever adult was with them glared at her suspiciously.

'He's counting the turtles,' Karen said. 'He likes to count the turtles.'

'Come with me,' Allison demanded.

Karen gave her another one of her ice-cold looks. 'I don't want to count the turtles.'

Allison took a deep breath, and tried to calm her rising panic. What to do? Leave Karen here alone and go in search of Tommy? Grab Karen, who might start kicking and screaming, and drag her along with her?

Fortunately Tommy reappeared. 'Twenty-two turtles,' he announced.

Karen raised her head long enough to say, 'Who cares?'

Apparently Tommy was accustomed to her attitude, because he paid no attention. 'I wish there was a bug farm.'

The image made Allison smile. 'Do you like bugs?'

'Most of them. Especially spiders.'

'Spiders are disgusting,' Karen declared.

Tommy's expression darkened. Anxious to avoid a battle, Allison said, 'Come on, Karen. You don't think Charlotte is disgusting, do you?'

'Charlotte who?'

'You don't know *Charlotte's Web*? It's only the best book in the whole wide world! It's about the friendship between a spider and a pig.'

Karen didn't look impressed, but at least she didn't look away.

'I tell you what,' Allison continued. 'We'll walk around the zoo for a while. All of us, together. And then we'll stop at the library on the way home and look for *Charlotte's Web*. What do you say? Want to do that?'

Karen said nothing. But Allison thought she spotted a glimmer of interest in her eyes as she sighed, closed her book and got up.

'I think it's going to be OK,' she told Pamela that evening as she tried on her third possibility for the cocktail party. 'The boy's adorable. The girl's tough though. It was hard getting through to her.'

Sitting on Allison's bed, Pamela shrugged. 'Maybe she had a bad nanny before you. Wait – maybe she thinks you're after her father! He's a widower, right?' She cocked her head thoughtfully. 'Hey, what does he look like? I mean, if *you're* not interested . . .'

'Pamela, he's over thirty. And do you really want to be a stepmother? Zip me up.'

She did, and then Allison turned to face her. 'What do you think of this?' Personally she wasn't too crazy about the navy sheath with the yellow piping at the neck – a little too prim and proper, she thought. It was something her mother had given her. Since she never got dressed up, she didn't have any dress-up clothes.

Pamela wrinkled her nose. 'It's not very glamorous. There are going to be movie stars at this do, Allison. Real Hollywood types.'

'*I'm* not a Hollywood person,' Allison pointed out.

'But Bobby is,' Pamela countered. 'Don't you want him to be proud of you?'

Allison laughed. 'Bobby never notices what I'm wearing.'

Pamela gazed at her wistfully. 'You know, I have a dress that would be perfect for a cocktail party.'

Allison shook her head. Pamela was curvy – *she* was not. 'It wouldn't fit me.'

'Oh, I know that. I was just thinking . . . couldn't you guys bring me along? I mean, it's a cocktail party, not a sit-down dinner. No one will notice if there's one more person wandering around.'

Allison was torn. 'Gosh, Pamela, if it was something *I* was personally invited to, I'd say sure. But I'm Bobby's date. I don't think it would be appropriate.'

'I know,' Pamela sighed. 'It's a work thing. Like what Donna does with her model friend. Maybe if I had a real job, I'd get to go to work things too. Hey, guess where the temp agency is sending me tomorrow? *Modern Girl*.'

'What's *Modern Girl*?'

'It's *Gloss*'s competition.'

The house phone in the kitchen sent out its distinctive chirp, and Allison hurried across the apartment to answer.

'Yes?'

The doorman spoke solemnly. 'A Mr Dale to see you.'

'You can send him up,' Allison said.

She hadn't seen Bobby in almost a month. And the

last time she saw him he'd needed a haircut. Now his hair was falling into his eyes. She'd been prepared to rush into his arms the minute she opened the door, but instead she gaped at his shaggy locks.

'Yeah, I know,' he said with an abashed grin. 'They're making me let it grow for the role. It's the new style for guys – Beatles' influence and all that.'

A voice behind her exclaimed, 'Sexy!'

'Hi, Pamela,' Bobby said. So now, with Pamela in the room, all Allison got as a greeting was a little peck on the cheek instead of the real kissing activity she craved.

'Let me show you the apartment,' Allison said, thinking she could get him alone in her bedroom for a few minutes.

He checked his watch. 'We should get over there,' he said apologetically. 'I feel as if I have to be on my best behaviour with these folks.'

'You spent a whole weekend with them!' Allison pointed out.

'Just with the cast and the director,' Bobby said. 'The producers are going to be there tonight, and they're the really important guys. How about coming back here after? Then we can, you know . . . *relax*.' He glanced a little apprehensively in Pamela's direction.

'Don't worry,' Pamela said with another one of her dramatic sighs. 'We each have our own rooms. And

I'll make myself scarce if you want to get it on in the living room.'

Allison groaned, Bobby laughed, and they left the apartment. As usual, Bobby didn't comment on her appearance, but thinking about Pamela's comments, Allison couldn't help asking. 'Do I look OK for this thing?'

'Sure, fine,' he said distractedly, without really looking.

She was surprised to see a white stretch limo waiting in front of the building. So was Bobby.

'Damn, I told him not to wait. We're only going five blocks, for crying out loud.' He sounded irritable, and it dawned on Allison that he really was nervous.

The chauffeur jumped out and held the door open for them. Once inside, Allison took his hand, and he squeezed hers back. Clearly he was in need of some support.

'I'm sorry,' he said.

'For what?'

'I'm a little out of it. Everything's just so . . . different.'

'How do you mean?'

'The weekend was intense. Being around these people like Lance Hunter and Monica Caine, it was pretty intimidating. And Perry Coverdale. He's the director. Did you know he's been nominated for an Academy Award? Twice!'

'So he must be a pretty good director, huh?'

'Yeah. They're all good, and they've all had so much experience. I feel like I'm . . . I don't know . . . unworthy or something. Like I'm a fraud.'

'You're not a fraud,' Allison said, but he didn't seem to have heard her.

'Plus I'm the youngest,' he said. 'Well, except for Beverly. She's about my age. But even *she's* had experience.'

'Who's Beverly?'

'Beverly Gray. Remember that horror movie a couple of years ago, *I Married a Werewolf*? She was in that.'

All Allison remembered about that movie was covering her eyes every five minutes or so. It had been seriously scary.

'She was the kid sister, with the pigtails and the glasses.'

Allison vaguely remembered her. 'Is she nice?'

'Yeah, she's OK. She's been in a lot of TV shows. *Bonanza*, *Ben Casey* and an episode of *The Twilight Zone*. She's got a pretty big role in *Tangled Hearts*.'

The limousine set them out in front of a Park Avenue building, similar to the Fifth Avenue place where Allison was staying, with the same kind of awning that extended from the door to the street, and stony-faced uniformed doormen.

The apartment itself, though, was far grander. It took up an entire floor. As they entered a foyer that was bigger than the living room on Fifth Avenue, a silver-haired man in a suit strode up to Bobby and shook his hand.

'Hal DeSalvo, producer,' he announced. 'And you're Bobby Dale!'

'Uh, yes,' Bobby said. 'And this is Allison Sanderson.'

The man barely glanced at her. 'Yes, yes, delighted, so glad you could come. Have some champagne.'

As if by magic, a woman wearing a short black uniform with a frilly hat and apron and carrying a tray of champagne glasses appeared by their side. Bobby took two, handed one to Allison, and they strode into the main room.

This living room, or ballroom, or whatever it was called, was vast, but even so, it was crowded. At least a hundred people were milling about.

'Who *are* they all?' Allison asked Bobby in a whisper.

'You know how after a movie ends, when you're walking out, there are all these names rolling across the screen? They're all here. Cameramen, lighting people, hairdressers, make-up artists . . . And all the actors of course.'

Moving through the crowd, Allison recognized the handsome Lance Hunter, and she thought she spotted Monica Caine too. A couple of other faces looked vaguely familiar. At the other end of the room they saw sliding glass doors that led on to a terrace. By silent mutual agreement, they headed in that direction.

The terrace extended all around the building. A few others had sought refuge from the crowd there, but even so, there was a lot more breathing space. And it was quiet.

Plus the view was spectacular. Central Park lay far below, and beyond it the lights of Manhattan were coming on as the sun was setting.

'It's magical,' Allison breathed. 'And so romantic!'

Bobby agreed. 'I want to kiss you, right this minute.'

'Then why don't you?' Taking his hand, she moved down to a dark corner of the terrace. Bobby put his arms around her, and finally she got the kiss she'd been waiting for. Their bodies pressed against each other so tightly she couldn't breathe, and she didn't care. And she wanted more . . .

'Bobby!'

A high-pitched squeal came from just a few feet away. They both froze, and then separated. The owner of the squeal came into view.

'Oh, hi, Beverly,' Bobby said.

Allison turned, and hoped her face didn't betray her shock at the sight of Beverly Gray. No pigtails, no glasses, no sign at all of the 'kid sister' in the werewolf movie. Beverly Gray had become a stunning young woman, with pale blonde waves cascading to her shoulders, a real movie-star body (big boobs, tiny waist), full red lips, a tiny nose and porcelain skin. Her strapless ice-blue dress set all this off to perfection.

Fortunately Bobby had recovered from any annoyance at the interruption, and his natural good manners took over.

'Beverly, this is Allison Sanderson.'

The actress turned to her with a smile, but Allison got the feeling she was being looked over.

'Hi, Allison. What do *you* do?'

Allison looked at her blankly for a second. 'Me? I'm a student . . .'

Now Beverly looked puzzled, and Bobby stepped in. 'She's not with the film.'

'Oh!' Her eyes darted back and forth between Bobby and Allison, as if she was trying to assess the connection between them. For once Allison wished he'd said something about her being his girlfriend. But he knew she didn't like those identifying titles, those words that suggested possession. He was just respecting her feelings. Though he could have said, 'She's with me,' or something like that . . .

Beverly didn't seem particularly concerned with her status. She pretty much dismissed Allison and turned her huge blue eyes exclusively to Bobby.

'I can't believe we start real rehearsals tomorrow! Have you learned your lines?'

'Not completely,' Bobby replied.

'Me neither, but I'm working on it. I want to stop reading and start *acting*. If you know what I mean.' She winked.

Bobby reddened slightly, and Allison realized there had to be some sort of inside joke here that she wasn't getting.

'I just hope I don't disappoint you,' he said.

She gave him an odd little smile and a sidelong look. 'Oh, I don't think that's possible.'

It dawned on Allison that she was flirting. Bobby must have realized that too, because he spoke quickly.

'I mean, I hope I'm a decent actor.'

'Maybe you won't need to act,' she replied in a teasing voice.

An older woman arrived on the terrace. 'Beverly, there's someone from *Life* magazine here. You must meet him.'

Beverly produced an exaggerated pout. 'My manager. See you later, Bobby.'

How rude, Allison thought. It was like *she* wasn't even there. 'She was flirting with you!' she said to Bobby.

He shrugged. 'She flirts with everyone.'

'And what was all that stuff about not needing to act?'

'She plays my girlfriend in the movie. There are some scenes that are a little, you know, romantic.'

'Oh.' She moved closer to him, in the hope that they might resume what they were doing before Beverly interrupted them. But Bobby had other ideas.

'Let's get some food. I'm starving.'

Over the next couple of hours, they ate, drank, drifted through the crowd and met a lot of people with titles related to film-making. At least, Bobby met them. He would always introduce Allison, but once they realized she had nothing to do with the movie, they barely acknowledged her.

And the way they all spoke to each other! Everyone was 'darling' or 'sweetheart' or 'baby', everything was 'marvellous' or 'fabulous' – it all sounded so artificial, totally phony. It really wasn't her scene, and she didn't think it was Bobby's either. She understood that he had to be here, that it was part of his new job, but surely they'd been here long enough. She was about to suggest to Bobby that they leave, go back to her place and engage in more interesting activity, when a photographer latched on to him.

'We want to get a shot of you and Beverly together, something we can feed the newspapers,' the man declared.

Bobby released Allison's hand, gave her an apologetic look and allowed the man to position him beside Beverly, who was checking herself in a little pocket mirror. She dropped the mirror into her bag and beamed at Bobby.

'Just be casual,' the photographer said. 'We want this to look like a candid shot.'

Beverly's idea of casual clearly surprised Bobby. She moved in very close and put a hand on his arm.

Gazing up at him, she tossed her hair and started laughing, as if he'd said something funny.

'Fabulous, darling!' the photographer declared. 'Bobby, smile! Look at her, not me! Beautiful, love it!' There were about half a dozen flashes from the camera.

'Great, we've got it,' the photographer announced. But Beverly kept her hand on Bobby's arm and stayed close.

Allison moved in. 'Bobby,' she murmured urgently.

He got the message. 'I'll see you tomorrow, Beverly,' he said, and carefully pulled away. He took Allison's hand and they started towards the door. It took another fifteen minutes to get out – Bobby had to say the appropriate goodbyes to the host – but finally they escaped.

Allison was relieved not to see the limo out front. She needed to walk and feel normal again.

'Bobby, how do you stand it? What a bunch of phonies!'

'Yeah, I know. They're always performing. Even the ones who aren't actors.'

'And that Beverly! She's so – so –'

'Affectionate?' he suggested.

'Aggressive!'

'Yeah, I was warned about her. Whenever she's in a romantic role, she goes after the actor who's playing opposite her. She thinks it makes the performance more realistic.'

Allison looked at him in alarm, and he laughed. 'Don't worry, she's not my type.'

'I didn't know you had a type.'

'Well, I do. I can only fall in love with redheads named Allison.'

He came up to her apartment with her. Pamela wasn't there, or maybe she was in her room – the door was closed. Allison showed him around, saving her own bedroom for last.

'Nice,' he said, looking around. 'How's the bed?'

'Try it and see,' she replied.

He did, and she followed him. They fell into each other's arms.

It had been so long since they'd been this close, this physical. But there was no awkwardness at all. Bobby might be an actor, but she was very sure of one thing – he wasn't performing now.

Chapter Ten

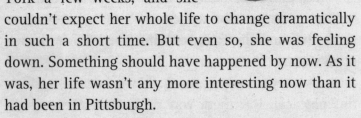

Pamela knew she should be patient. She'd only been in New York a few weeks, and she couldn't expect her whole life to change dramatically in such a short time. But even so, she was feeling down. Something should have happened by now. As it was, her life wasn't any more interesting now than it had been in Pittsburgh.

She *did* have friends here – that was an improvement, she supposed. But that wasn't really making much of a difference. Allison was now spending most evenings and all of her weekends with Bobby. Donna was always with her model friend. And Sherry had turned into a real career girl, staying late at the office and bringing work home. Nobody had any time for *her*.

Maybe she should think about trying to make new friends – but how? Working for a temp agency meant she moved from office to office, never staying anywhere long enough to strike up friendships. As for men – forget it. None of the jobs she'd been sent to so far had put her in proximity to anyone worth a little flirtation.

GL♥SS

She was back at *Modern Girl* now. This was the last day of a three-day job, and she still had no one to talk to or eat lunch with. No one had even bothered to learn her name. Even the executive she was working for kept calling her 'Miss . . .uh' as he dropped business reports on her desk in the bullpen for her to type.

It was noon, and all around her secretaries were turning off their electric typewriters and gathering in small groups to go down to the cafeteria. She considered calling Sherry or Donna – the Hartnell Building was just up the street, and maybe one or both of them could meet her for a bite. But she'd been warned about making personal calls, and besides, they probably weren't available.

Pamela was hungry, so she turned off her own typewriter, retrieved her handbag from the desk drawer and left to go downstairs. Once inside the cafeteria, she looked around, hoping someone might catch her eye and invite her to join a table. It didn't happen.

She did see one girl who looked vaguely familiar. She had distinctive straight, shiny black hair, and Pamela knew she'd seen her before somewhere outside of *Modern Girl*. But then the girl actually looked in her direction, and there was no sign of recognition in her dark eyes.

The thought of sitting alone in this place was just too, too depressing. Then it dawned on her – she had a whole hour to eat, and she certainly wasn't required to take her lunch in this cafeteria. She could go outside, buy a sandwich and a soda and take them to Central Park.

But once outside, she felt a few drops of rain. She'd have to find a coffee shop, where she'd sit at the counter and eat alone. She might as well have stayed in the cafeteria. At least that would have been cheaper.

On the other hand, there was always the possibility that some nice young up-and-coming businessman would be eating alone at the coffee-shop counter too . . .

Then the skies opened and it started to really pour so she ducked into the Eastside Coffee Shop. It was the first one she came to, but as she entered, she thought the name of the place rang a bell. The reason came back to her when she surveyed the place and recognized a man sitting alone in a booth. Larry Something, the guy she'd met on the Greyhound bus – the friend of her brother, Bud. He'd told her he always ate lunch here.

He saw her, and his eyes lit up as he beckoned to her. He might not be the man of her dreams, but she remembered that he was nice, and she was starved of human contact.

He rose as she approached. 'Pamela, hi! I was wondering if I'd ever see you again. Did you remember I always eat here?'

Uh-oh, now he'd think she was interested in him.

GL♥SS

'No, I just ducked in to get out of the rain. But it's nice to see you,' she added hastily.

'Sit down,' he urged, and she did. 'How are you? Are you working around here?'

'Just at a temp job,' she told him. The waitress came over, and beamed at Larry.

'The usual?' she asked.

'Absolutely, Marie.' To Pamela, he said, 'A grilled cheese-and-tomato sandwich, with a side of fries. Same for you, Pam?'

She wished she could see a menu and check out the prices, but maybe he'd pay. 'Sure, OK.'

'You won't be sorry,' he promised.

'How are *you*?' she asked when the waitress left.

'Good! Well, things are a little crazy at work.'

She realized she had no idea what he did for a living. 'Where do you work?'

'Around the corner – Crain, Livingstone and Blackwell. Advertising.'

'Oh.' Advertising made her think of Alex Parker. Not an appealing profession.

'Did you find a place to live?' Larry asked.

She nodded. 'I've got a place on Fifth Avenue and Seventy-third.'

He whistled. 'Wow. Temp work must be paying well.'

If she wanted him to pick up the check, she couldn't let him think she was making a ton of money. 'Actually, a friend of mine is subletting a place there for the summer and she's letting me stay.'

The waitress reappeared with the food. Pamela took a bite of her sandwich.

'Hey, this is really good!'

He grinned. 'Told ya! Stick with me, Pam, you'll have only the best sandwiches in town.'

He was joking of course, but she couldn't help remembering the restaurants where she had eaten with Alex Parker, the married man that she had an affair with last summer. Duck à l'orange, steak Diane . . . Well, at least Larry wasn't married. But she really hated being called 'Pam'. It sounded like a laundry detergent.

'So what's it like, living on Fifth Avenue?' he asked.

'It's nice. But like I said, it's only for the summer. I'll have to find another place before September. I hope I have a real job by then.'

'You're a secretary, right? There might be something at my company. I can check with personnel if you like.'

Pamela made a non-committal 'hmm' noise, mainly because she didn't know how to respond to such an offer. He was an awfully nice guy to want to help her, and it was clear that he was interested in her. But the feelings weren't mutual, and it would be cruel to encourage him. Besides, did she really want to find herself working in the same building as him?

Larry didn't seem bothered by her lack of enthusiasm.

GL♥SS

'Heard from Bud lately?' he asked.

She shook her head. 'My family's not great about staying in touch.'

'You're lucky,' he said. 'I get a call from my mother every week. And she always asks the same question. "Have you met a nice girl, Larry?"'

'Have you?' she asked brightly.

'I don't know,' he said. 'Maybe.'

He was looking at her with a question in his eyes. Time to change the subject, fast.

'You said your job is making you crazy. What are you working on?'

'Oh, it's this client I have. They make a furniture polish.'

'That's interesting,' she lied.

'They want to sponsor a TV show, and I'm looking for the right one to hook them up with.'

Now she didn't have to fake an interest. 'A TV show? Cool!' She considered the possibilities. 'You'll want something everyone watches so a lot of people will see the ads, right? How about a western, like *Bonanza* or *Gunsmoke*?'

He shook his head. 'No, I'm afraid that's outside their budget. We're thinking more along the lines of daytime TV. Soap operas, or a quiz show maybe.'

'Oh, I see.' Daytime TV – not as glamorous as prime time, but still kind of interesting. On school vacations she used to watch *As the World Turns* religiously. Also

The Secret Storm and *Search for Tomorrow*. And a few others . . .

He gave an exaggerated shudder. 'The worst part is that I have to watch these shows. I can't approach a producer without knowing something about his programme.'

She decided not to mention her soap-opera favourites. 'Quiz shows are really dumb,' she said. 'Like *The Price Is Right*. I mean, are you a genius because you can guess how much a refrigerator costs?'

'Have you ever seen *Queen for a Day*?' he asked. 'That's the worst. These women tell these unbelievably sad stories about their lives – sick children, out-of-work husband, you name it. And the one with the most depressing story wins.'

Fortunately Pamela had never caught this one. 'What does she win?'

'Oh, something that will change her life and solve all her problems. Something magical and fantastic. Something to turn her sad world around.' He paused. 'Like a combination washer-dryer.'

She couldn't help smiling at his sarcasm. Encouraged, he smiled back and continued.

'And the host of the show, he's unbelievable! The one time I watched it, this contestant was describing all the medical problems in her family. She had arthritis, her husband was in a wheelchair, one of her children was asthmatic and the other was allergic to everything. The host says, "You told us you have three children. How's the third one?" She says he's the only one who's never sick. And the idiot host beams at her happily and says, "Well, at least you have one healthy child!"'

This time Pamela actually laughed out loud. 'I'd go crazy if I had to watch this junk too. Maybe you should look for another job.'

He shrugged. 'It's not so bad usually. To tell you the truth, I'm not all that ambitious. As long as I like the folks I work with, and I can pay my rent, I'm content. It's not like I have expensive tastes.'

The waitress slapped a paper on the table, and before Pamela could even see what was written on it, Larry snatched it up.

'This is on me,' he said.

'Thank you.' She looked at the clock on the wall. 'Oh no, I'm going to be late getting back. I'd better take off.'

'Before you go . . .' He hesitated, and then plunged in with the question she was afraid he'd ask. 'Would you like to go out sometime?'

Now it was her turn to hesitate. He was a nice guy. But in the past hour he hadn't gotten any taller or more handsome. He wasn't a sophisticated Sean Connery or a sexy Steve McQueen.

On the other hand, she'd just spent an entire hour not feeling lonely. She didn't want to use him, but on the other hand – what would she be using him for? He didn't have expensive tastes – that meant no dinners at the Russian Tea Room or the 21 Club, no late nights at the Copacabana.

He wasn't her type, but he'd been good company for the past hour. So she scrawled Allison's number on a napkin and pushed it across the table.

'Thanks for lunch. See ya!' she said. And she left, feeling more cheerful than she'd felt in weeks.

But she was slightly alarmed at how happy *he* looked.

Chapter Eleven

Donna peered through the magnifying lens at the contact sheet and ticked off the ones that David wanted blown up. The extension phone beeped, and she answered.

'David Barnes's office.'

The receptionist spoke. 'Phone, Donna.'

'He's not here.'

'No, it's for you.'

Donna flinched, and hoped it wasn't Bonnie. There had been too many late nights recently, and she was so looking forward to a quiet evening at home. With a sigh, she pressed a button. 'Hello?'

'Donna? This is Jack. Jack Vanderwill.'

She caught her breath.

'Actually . . . I'm not sure I've got the right person,' he said. 'Is this the Donna I met at Rafe Bryant's?'

She swallowed, and found her voice. 'Yes. Hi.'

'I can't believe it – I tracked you down! I've been wanting to call you, and I didn't have your last name. But I suddenly remembered you said you worked at *Gloss*, so I got hold of one of my sister's magazines and checked the masthead. I was just hoping you're the only Donna there.'

'Yes,' she said. 'I'm the only Donna. I'm sorry you had to go to so much trouble.'

'It's OK, I found you. I'm happy!'

She knew she should say something along the lines of, 'I'm happy you called,' but the words wouldn't come. 'That's . . . nice.'

He didn't seem put off by her lack of enthusiasm.

'Would you like to get together?'

When she didn't immediately respond, he went on. 'It doesn't have to be a date, no major commitment. Just a drink?'

She was almost surprised at how quickly she responded. 'OK.'

'Great! When?'

'I don't know.' Now she knew she sounded cold, and she didn't want to. She had to make some effort. 'I mean, it doesn't matter. Anytime.' And now she probably sounded pathetic, as if she never had anything else to do.

'Well . . . OK, I'm going to take a wild chance. How about today? I know this is last minute, but what about a drink after work?'

'Yes. OK.'

'Where? You have a favourite place? You name it, I'll be there.'

Her mind went blank. It wasn't as if she frequented

the after-work bars. And the places she'd been to with Bonnie, they were always so loud and crowded. But she'd passed a place across the street that looked calm . . .

'Do you know Charlie's? It's across the street from the Hartnell Building on Madison.'

'I'll find it,' he said. 'Six o'clock?'

'Yes.'

It was only a drink, she thought as she hung up the phone. A simple drink, just one, that would last less than an hour. How much trouble could that bring? How much conversation could they really have? She could ask about his kid sister, the one who read *Gloss* – no, that wasn't a good idea. If she asked about his family, he could ask about hers. She needed to come up with topics that wouldn't lead to anything personal. Sports maybe. Guys could always talk about sports. This was baseball season; she'd check today's newspaper to see how the Yankees were doing.

Armed with the latest baseball statistics, she left the office a few minutes before six and went into the restroom, where she ran a brush through her hair and did a little repair work on her make-up. It was pure luck that she'd put on the yellow empire-waist dress this morning – it brought out the gold highlights in her brown hair and made her legs look miles long.

She had a feeling he was the type who would be prompt, and she was right. When she entered Charlie's, he was sitting at the bar. Taking a deep breath, she walked over to him.

He turned as she approached, and there was no mistaking the way his face lit up.

'Hi!'

She smiled. 'Hi.'

He indicated the stool next to him, and she sat down. The bartender came down to their end.

'What can I get you?'

Donna looked at the drink that rested on the bar in front of Jack. 'What are you having?'

'It's just a Coke,' Jack said, looking a little embarrassed. 'I'm not much of a drinker, and I'm bringing some work home to do tonight. Gotta keep a clear head.'

'I'll have a Coke,' Donna told the bartender.

'You sure you don't want a little rum in that?' Jack asked anxiously. 'I mean, just because I'm not drinking, doesn't mean you can't!'

'I know that. But I'm not much of a drinker either.' And I don't want anything loosening my tongue, she added silently.

'So . . . how are you?' Jack asked.

'Fine. How are you?'

'Fine. How's your job?'

'It's going well. How's work coming along for you?'

'Hectic, but good.'

And then they both smiled, as if they realized at

the same time how dull they sounded.

'Have you been back to the Electric Pig?' she asked.

'*No*,' he said emphatically. 'You?'

'No, thank goodness. It's really not my kind of place. I only went because of Bonnie.'

'I guess if you hang around with models, that's where you go,' he remarked.

She realized that she didn't want him thinking she was the discotheque type. Or that she normally lived in the glamorous world of models.

'Actually, Bonnie's my work assignment.' She explained how the managing editor wanted Bonnie to sign an exclusive contract with *Gloss*.

Jack grinned. 'I totally get it. I had to play golf to court a client. And I hate golf. We played at this snotty country club where he was a member. And he was the biggest snob around.'

'My job's not that painful,' Donna told him. 'Bonnie's very sweet. We just don't have the same interests.'

'What *do* you like to do?'

She thought about that. 'I like movies. And art. I go to museums and galleries. I don't know much about art, but I like looking.'

'I like art,' he said.

She knew that this was the moment when she should suggest that they go to a museum together, but she didn't.

'Do you like to read?' he asked.

She hesitated. 'Not that much.' And then, for some crazy reason, she actually told him about the problems she'd always had with reading.

His eyebrows shot up. 'That sounds like dyslexia!'

She nodded. 'Yes, that's what my high-school counsellor said.' Then she wanted to kick herself. Now he could ask where she went to high school.

But he didn't. Instead he looked almost excited. '*I* have dyslexia!'

She was surprised. 'But . . . didn't you say you went to Yale? How could you go to a university if you can't read?'

'Oh, I can read, but not very fast, and it's not easy for me. I was diagnosed when I was in elementary school. My parents sent me for therapy with a specialist, and I learned tricks that helped me make out the words.'

She remembered the school counsellor telling her that there were treatments for reading disorders. Of course Jack would have received those treatments. He came from a good family. He didn't have a mother who would prefer to spend what little money she had on booze. She had to change the subject before he could ask her why she'd never seen a specialist.

But before she could, he spoke. 'I'll bet you're from a small town. Where they didn't have reading specialists. It's a pretty new field, I think.'

She nodded again.

'Are you? From a small town?'

And now it was beginning – the personal questions. Surreptitiously she glanced at the clock over the bar. Had they only been here for fifteen minutes? How was she going to fill the rest of the time?

'I'd rather hear about you!' she said brightly. 'Have you always lived in New York?'

'All my life,' he said. 'My parents wanted to ship me off to boarding school in Connecticut, but I lucked out. The reading specialist said I'd do better at a private school right here in Manhattan.'

'Have you travelled much?'

'Not as much as I'd like to. When I was in high school my parents took us to Europe one summer. The usual tourist spots – London, Paris, Rome. And we went to Bermuda for spring breaks a couple of times. What about you?'

She wasn't going to be able to avoid the questions, she knew that now. And what would he say if she told him about growing up in a trailer park, an absent father, an alcoholic mother? Getting knocked up by a low-life boyfriend? Losing the baby, working as a cleaner, being abused . . .

'I'd love to travel,' she murmured vaguely, but he wasn't satisfied with that.

'No, I mean, tell me about you.'

Her mind was racing. She had to say something. And an image of Allison came to mind. Fortunately, even though she couldn't read well, she had a great memory for stories her friends told.

'I'm from Boston. Beacon Hill.'

'Brothers, sisters?'

Hadn't Allison once mentioned an older brother? But she didn't know anything about him. She'd have to improvise.

'No. Only child.'

'So you got all the attention. Was that a good thing?'

'No,' she said. 'I never got along well with my parents. They wanted me to go to college after I did the internship at *Gloss*, but I preferred to stay in New York and keep on working.'

'I guess they weren't too happy about that,' he commented.

She nodded. 'They're very . . . conventional. If you know what I mean.'

'Do I?' He whistled softly. 'My folks are totally stuck in their ways. And they judge other people by their rules. You have to go to the right schools, have the right jobs, join the right clubs. They're incredible snobs.' He paused. 'I admire you.'

'You do? Why?'

'You're a rebel! I always did what the parents wanted me to do.' He gave her an abashed smile. 'Now you'll think I'm a wimp.'

'Oh no,' she said quickly. 'Not at all.' She remembered something Allison had once said, when she was talking about how staid and conservative her older brother was.

'I think it must be harder for a son to rebel. Parents, they want their daughters to look nice, and behave properly, and marry well. So much more is expected from a guy.'

'I think maybe you're right,' Jack said. He smiled. 'Are you sure you never had any brothers?'

'No. No brothers.' She looked at the clock again. It was quarter to seven. And she'd finished her Coke. 'I should go.'

'I guess you've got something else to do,' Jack said. She nodded.

'Could we go out again sometime?' he asked. 'Like, on a real date? For a whole evening?'

Why did his eyes have to be so brown, so deep, so soft? Why did he have to look so sincere?

End it now, she told herself. Stop this, before you get in any deeper. Tell him you're busy, tell him you've got a boyfriend, tell him anything.

But what she said was, 'Yes. I'd like that.'

Chapter Twelve

Sherry picked up the phone and dialled three numbers. As she waited for a response, Liz Madrigal sauntered into her office. Sherry repressed an automatic frown and reminded herself that she really needed to start keeping her office door closed.

She heard a tinny voice on the phone. 'Information, what city please?'

'New York, Manhattan. Could I have the number for a Dr Naomi Cutler, please?'

'Office or home?'

'Office.'

Liz took a seat without waiting to be invited. Sherry would never have done that when she was an intern, and once again she was amazed and annoyed by the girl's nerve.

The operator recited a phone number, and Sherry jotted it down.

'Thank you,' she said, and hung up.

'Who's Naomi Cutler?' Liz asked.

None of your business, Sherry wanted to say. But Caroline wouldn't like that.

'She's a therapist who specializes in the problems of teenage girls.'

GL♥SS

'Oh, for the interview. About how women's roles are changing.'

Sherry nodded. 'That's right. Do you want something, Liz?' Silently she added, 'And no, I'm not leaving my job any time soon.'

'I was wondering if you needed any help with anything.'

'No, thank you. In fact, I'm going to the library now to do some research.'

'About what?'

'An idea for an article.'

'What kind of idea?'

She was so nosy! 'Actually, Liz, I don't have time to talk about it now. Don't you have something else you should be doing? Haven't you been assigned to an editor?'

'Mr Simpson.' She made a face, and Sherry could understand why. But she kept any expression of sympathy off her face and out of her voice.

'Well, I'm sure he has something that needs to be typed,' she said briskly.

'He thinks my typing is too slow,' Liz said.

Sherry ignored that. She got up and went to the doorway. 'I need to go now.' She remained standing there, to make it clear that Liz was expected to leave. Finally she did.

Sherry closed the door. To Gloria she said, 'If Caroline needs me, I'll be up in the library.'

Gloria nodded. Then she put her hand to her cheek and grimaced.

'Are you OK?' Sherry asked.

'Toothache,' Gloria said. 'I'm going to call my dentist now.'

'Need an aspirin?'

'I've already taken one,' Gloria said mournfully. 'Thanks anyway.'

Up in the library, Sherry once again sought the aid of the librarian. The woman gathered microfilm versions of major newspapers from the past year and showed Sherry how to use the reader.

Looking at the fuzzy images on the screen, Sherry turned the knob to move from page to page as she searched for information. Every time she saw photos of civil-rights demonstrations or marches, she squinted, and tried to see if any white people were present.

She spotted plenty of white celebrities. Even if she hadn't recognized them, their names were given in the photo captions: Charlton Heston, Marlon Brando, Paul Newman . . . a lot of famous people had come out in support of equal rights. But these weren't the people she was interested in.

She did spot unknown white faces, but the images were too blurry for her to tell if they might be young people, like the missing workers in Mississippi. After an hour poring over microfilms, she didn't have anything that would contribute to the kind of article

GL♥SS

she'd proposed to Caroline. She wanted to write about young people coming together for equality, but it seemed that library research wasn't going to provide the material.

Coming back down to her office, she found Gloria waiting for the elevator as she stepped out. The secretary looked as if she was in real pain.

'My dentist got a cancellation, so I'm going now,' she told Sherry. But as she got into the elevator, she stopped the doors from closing and groaned.

'I completely forgot – the budget reports from accounting came this morning and I was supposed to put them on Caroline's desk.'

'I'll do it,' Sherry told her. 'Where are they?'

'In a stack of papers on my desk. Thanks, Sherry.' She took her hand from the doors and let them close.

Back in the bullpen, Sherry went to Gloria's desk and began going through the papers. She found the budget reports, but when she picked them up, a paper under them caught her eye.

It was a mimeographed sheet, with the words 'EQUALITY NOW' in capital letters. Under that heading, she read:

If you're serious about working together for
civil rights, join us: the Alliance for Change.
Ferris Booth Hall, Columbia University.

This was followed by a time – seven o'clock – and a date. Today's.

Immediately Sherry realized that this was what she needed to write her article. A real experience, something she could get involved in personally instead of just reading about.

She could go to this meeting – clearly it was open to anyone. And it was being held at a university, which meant most of the participants would be young people. She could listen; she could find out for herself what was going on; she'd get ideas. Maybe meet some people she could interview.

She was excited, and she was nervous. Would she be the only white person there? Surely not.

Caroline wasn't in her office, but as Sherry put the budget reports on her desk she wondered if she should tell Caroline her plan. No, she'd rather wait till she had something of substance to show her, maybe an outline for the actual story.

So after work she took the subway up to 116th street, just by the entrance to the university, and started looking for Ferris Booth Hall. On Broadway, she asked a passing student, who told her it was just past 115th street. But it was hard to see the names on the buildings, and there weren't any signs.

She paused uncertainly before an imposing five-storey structure with a statue of Thomas Jefferson in front of it. She stopped another passing student.

GL♥SS

'Excuse me, is this Ferris Booth Hall?'

'No, that's the journalism school. Booth Hall is over there.'

'Thank you,' Sherry said, but she didn't move on right away. So this was the place Caroline had been talking about, and now she recognized it from the picture on the brochure the editor had given her. It looked serious, a place for serious students with serious ambitions.

She looked at her watch. She was early – it was six thirty, and the meeting wasn't until seven. She could walk into the journalism school now, look around, get a feel for the place.

But she didn't, and she wasn't sure why. Because she was happy with her life the way it was? Because she had other things on her mind? Or maybe because it was too intimidating . . .

Anyway, she was already a journalist, right? OK, maybe she was a lowly editorial assistant at the moment, but she was on her way to investigate a real story and write up a real article. She didn't need journalism school.

She moved on and found the right building. It turned out to be some kind of student centre, and there were a lot of young people milling about. On a bulletin board she saw notices and listings of meetings and events, and found the Alliance for Change.

It took more time to locate the room, and when

she finally got there it was a quarter to seven. The room looked like a cross between a classroom and a lounge – there were chairs in rows and a podium, but also a couple of sofas against the walls. Over at one end there was a long table with a coffee urn and a platter of doughnuts. About a dozen people, Negro and white, were there, standing or sitting in small groups, drinking coffee and talking.

They all seemed to be around her age, and she was relieved that she didn't stand out in any way. At least, no one was looking at her.

And then someone did.

She recognized him right away. It was Gloria's brother. She smiled at him.

He didn't smile back but turned away.

She knew he must have recognized her too. But he didn't seem to want to acknowledge her presence. She watched as he walked over to the table and waited in line to use the coffee urn.

She went over and stood alongside him.

'Hi,' she said.

He glanced at her, and his expression wasn't encouraging. Maybe he was shy.

'We met at *Gloss*,' she said. 'I work with Gloria.'

'Yeah, I know.'

'You're William.'

'Yeah, I know that too,' he said.

'I'm Sherry.'

It was his turn to get coffee. He picked up the disposable cup and held it under the spigot. He didn't offer to pour some for her.

She followed him as he moved away from the table. 'Most of the folks here, are they students?' she asked.

'Yeah.'

'Here at Columbia?'

He nodded. He was looking everywhere but at her. Still she persisted.

'Do *you* go to Columbia?'

He actually faced her. 'You ask a lot of questions.'

'I'm interested,' she replied.

'Yeah, I go to Columbia. Surprised?'

She blinked. 'Why would I be surprised?'

'That a big famous Ivy League university takes Negroes? Oh, wait – you probably call us "coloured people".'

She drew in her breath. She had no idea how to respond to that.

'Where are you from anyway?' he asked.

'I told you, I work at *Gloss*,' she said faintly.

'No, I mean, you're not a New Yorker. Where do you come from?'

She swallowed. 'Georgia.'

His eyes were so cold. 'What are you doing here? At this meeting?'

'Like I said, I'm interested.'

He repeated her words with an exaggeration of her

accent. 'Lahk Ah say-ed, Ahm innerested.'

A couple of people standing nearby heard him and chuckled.

Sherry could feel her face turning red. 'That wasn't nice,' she stammered.

He continued with his fake-Southern accent. 'Oh, excuse me, ma'am, so sorry if I offended you. Please, pretty please, don't tell master to whip me.'

Now her eyes were burning. More people were listening, and there was another chuckle or two. She wanted to turn and run out of the room.

You're a journalist, she told herself fiercely. A journalist doesn't run away from a story.

Miraculously she was able to hold back the tears. 'Look, I know there are bad people where I come from. Racist people. But we're not all like that. I believe in equal rights, civil rights, and I want to help.'

Now his voice became almost taunting. 'So we should be honoured by your presence?'

'No!' she declared, and she was startled to hear that she had just shouted. How shocked her mother would be if she could see and hear her right now. A lady never raised her voice – that was what Mama always said. But Mama had never been in a situation like this.

'No,' she repeated, just as loudly. 'I don't expect to be treated like I'm special. But you shouldn't try to make me feel like crap!'

She could almost see her mother fainting now.

One of the observers spoke. 'Wow, Scarlett O'Hara's getting feisty.'

She ignored that. 'The notice I saw, it said any person who was interested in working together could come to this meeting. Well, I'm interested. And I'm a person. I have every right to be here.'

She had kept her eyes on William as she spoke, and now she waited to see his reaction. He met her eyes, and his seemed to be shooting sparks. She could almost feel them stinging her.

A man went to the podium. 'Could everyone find a seat? I want to call this meeting to order.'

As the people standing around moved towards the centre of the room, Sherry was jostled and almost lost her balance. William grabbed her arm to steady her.

That was when she really felt the sparks. Only they were more like a surge of electricity passing through her. She stared at him, and he dropped her arm.

'Sorry,' he said stiffly.

He left her and walked to a sofa.

She followed him there. And she sat down next to him. He turned and looked at her, seeming almost alarmed to see her there.

> . . . like a surge of electricity passing though her.

But she didn't move away.

Chapter Thirteen

'King me!' Tommy shrieked.

Allison obliged, and placed a checker on top of his.

'I'm winning,' Tommy said happily.

'You always win,' Allison pointed out.

After almost two weeks of daily checkers games, she thought she could beat him on occasion if she tried. But the little boy's delight in winning was just too enjoyable to pass up. Although, given Tommy's sunny personality, he'd probably stay just as cheerful if he lost a game.

It was too bad she couldn't say the same about his sister. Allison could count on one hand the number of times she'd seen Karen smile.

But generally speaking, her days as a nanny were working out well. Tom Markham wasn't a very demanding parent, and he seemed pleased with Allison and her relationship with his kids. She was actually feeling close to Tommy, and at least Karen had stopped giving her nasty looks.

At that moment Karen was reading in her bedroom. In the morning, Allison had taken the children to the Museum of Natural History, where Tommy had been thrilled to see the huge dinosaur models. Karen, however, had spent most of the time sitting on benches reading *Charlotte's Web*. Allison hadn't had the heart to make her put the book away. She remembered how glued *she* had been to that story so many years ago.

They'd come home for lunch, and then while Karen did her piano practice, Tommy had his nap. Allison had planned to take them to the park afterwards, but it started raining and Karen had retreated to her bedroom.

'I won!' Tommy crowed. 'Let's play again.'

Three consecutive games of checkers was about all Allison could take. 'How about Lego?'

Tommy agreed to this, and she got out the box. As soon as he was happily involved in making a tower, she left his room to go check on Karen.

She rapped softly on the closed door. When there was no response, she turned the knob and opened it. Karen was on her bed, face down, and her body was trembling. The closed copy of *Charlotte's Web* was on the floor.

'Karen, what's the matter?'

The girl mumbled something.

'Karen, I can't hear you. Tell me what's wrong.'

She turned over and sat up. Her face was streaked with tears.

'She died! Charlotte died!'

Oh damn, Allison thought. Damn, damn, damn. She

mentally kicked herself. What kind of an idiot gives a motherless child a story where the maternal figure dies?

Tentatively she put an arm around Karen. The child didn't shrug her off.

Encouraged, Allison spoke. 'It's very sad, isn't it? But she lives on in Wilbur's memory.'

Karen whispered something.

'What?'

She spoke louder, almost fiercely. 'My mother died.'

'I know.'

'And she won't live on in Tommy's memory. He was only three years old. He doesn't even remember her!'

'But *you* do,' Allison said. 'She lives on in your memory.'

Karen sniffed and rubbed her eyes. 'What if I forget her?'

'You won't,' Allison said firmly. 'Besides, she lives on in your father's memory too, and he won't let you forget her.'

'But he never talks about her,' Karen cried out. There was a sudden fresh onslaught of tears. Allison grabbed a box of tissues from the nightstand.

'Maybe he doesn't talk about her because he's afraid it will make you too sad.'

'But I *want* to talk about her! So I can make sure I don't forget!'

'You can talk to me,' Allison suggested.

That earned her one of Karen's scornful looks, clearly evident even through tears. 'You didn't even know her.'

She was making a good point. 'That's true,' Allison admitted. She really couldn't talk to Karen about her mother. That was her father's job. And she wondered why he avoided it. Too painful for him probably.

Eventually Karen's tears subsided. She looked at Allison in a more friendly way than usual.

'Can we do something?'

'Sure!' Allison said. 'Anything! What would you like to do?'

'Make cookies.'

Allison winced. 'I don't know how to make cookies, Karen. I've never baked anything in my life.'

'We have chocolate chips with the recipe on the bag,' Karen informed her. 'You can read, can't you?'

Allison chose to ignore the sarcasm. They headed to the kitchen, where Tommy joined them, and went to work. Sure enough, the bag of chocolate chips held a recipe for cookies that was actually pretty easy to follow. Karen measured, Tommy mixed, they spooned the mixture on the baking sheet together, and Allison slid the tray into the hot stove. Ten minutes later, she was amazed to see what looked like real cookies emerge.

The three of them then played a game of Chutes and Ladders to give the cookies time to cool. Allison poured glasses of milk, and they sat down together at the kitchen table.

Watching the contented kids happily enjoying their cookies, Allison was aware of the oddest sensation. She realized she was more than fond of them both. For the first time in her life, she actually felt maternal, as if the kids were more important to her than just charges she was paid to watch.

Sugary treats weren't a normal part of the daily routine, especially not this late in the day when they'd be having dinner with their father in two hours. So she limited them to two cookies each, and hoped she could get everything cleared away before Tom got home.

Unfortunately Tom arrived early. And when he came into the kitchen, Tommy was quick to announce what they'd been doing.

'We made cookies, Daddy!'

'And they're really good,' Karen added. 'Do you want one?'

Tom's smile looked a little forced, and Allison worried that she'd broken a rule by feeding them cookies before dinner.

'No, thanks, honey. Hey, isn't it time for *Huckleberry Hound*?'

The kids left the table and ran into the living room to watch their favourite cartoon show. Tom opened a cabinet, took out a bottle of Scotch and poured himself a drink.

Allison watched him uneasily. 'I'm sorry.'

He sat down heavily at the table. 'About what?'

'Giving them cookies so soon before dinner.'

'That's OK. Once in a while it won't kill them.' He drank down his whisky in one gulp and then poured another.

She still felt the need to explain.

'It's just that . . . well, Karen was upset.' She hesitated, and then plunged in. 'She was talking about her mother.'

Tom looked at her sharply. 'Did she notice the date?'

Allison was confused. 'I don't think so. Why?'

'It was two years ago today that my wife died.'

Allison drew in her breath. 'Oh. I'm so sorry.'

He shrugged. 'To tell you the truth, I didn't realize it until I opened my agenda to write something down.' He finished the second drink and poured another. 'Can I offer you a drink?'

'No, thanks,' Allison said, watching him with apprehension. He caught her expression and gave her a brief smile.

'Don't worry, this is my last one. I won't get drunk.'

'How about some coffee?' Allison asked. 'And maybe a cookie?'

He shrugged. 'Sure. Why not?'

She made the coffee, put some cookies on a plate and sat down across from him.

'I know this is none of my business,' she began, 'but Karen says you never talk about your late wife. And I think she needs to talk about her with you.'

Tom was silent for a moment, staring down into his steaming mug of coffee. He raised it, took a sip and then he spoke.

'When my wife was killed in that car accident . . . she wasn't alone.'

Allison nodded politely. 'Oh?'

'She was with another man. Her lover.'

Allison could only respond with another 'oh'.

He began breaking up a cookie into little pieces and paying a great deal of attention to it. 'Sometimes I wonder which was the greater shock, finding out she was having an affair or . . .'

'You didn't know?' Allison asked.

He shrugged. 'Oh, I suppose I suspected. Things weren't going well between us. Then she was dead, and I found out about the other man. I didn't know how to feel.' He raised his eyes and looked directly at Allison. 'You love someone. Then she dies, and you find out she didn't really love you.'

Allison tried to think of something to say. 'It's complicated.'

'Yes. And maybe that's why I don't talk to the kids about her.' Another brief smile crossed his face. 'Actually I think this is the first time I've talked about her at all. You're a good listener, Allison.'

Personally Allison thought it was the three whiskies that had made it easier for him to speak. But she was touched by the way he was confiding in her.

She couldn't imagine why a woman would leave a man like Tom Markham. He was warm, generous, handsome . . . and open with his feelings. How very hurt he must have been.

'I'm keeping you overtime,' he said suddenly. He reached in his pocket and took out a wallet.

'No, no, you don't have to pay me extra,' Allison told him. 'This wasn't work, talking to you.'

'Well, I'm sure you've got things to do,' he said, rising. 'And I'd better get dinner started.'

Allison rose too. And to her surprise, he leaned over and kissed her on the cheek.

'Thanks for listening,' he said. 'See you tomorrow.'

She grabbed her bag, said goodbye to the children and left. She had to hurry to get ready for the evening.

. . . he leaned over and kissed her . . .

Pamela was in the apartment when she got home, and she was already primping for *her* evening. She made room for Allison in front of the large bathroom mirror.

'You going out tonight?' Allison asked.

Pamela nodded. 'With Larry.'

'Again?' Allison was impressed. 'Is this getting serious?'

Pamela leaned forward to apply a heavy dose of mascara to her lashes. 'No, he's not my type. But he's fun. Hey, is it OK if I bring him back here after dinner?'

Allison raised her eyebrows and grinned.

'No, not for *that*,' Pamela said quickly. 'There's a ball game on TV, and his set's broken.'

'Sure, of course you can bring him back here. Maybe I'll finally get a chance to meet him.'

'Are you going to bring Bobby back here?'

'I doubt it. We're having dinner at his grandmother's in Queens, where he's staying. He has to be on the set at eight in the morning, so he'll want an early night.'

It took her an hour on the subway to get there. She'd brought a book to read, but she couldn't concentrate. All she could think about was what Tom Markham had told her. How did that happen to a couple? she wondered. How could they be in love, and then stop loving? That photo on the mantelpiece in the apartment – they looked so happy there. Suddenly she felt depressed. And she was anxious to be with someone whose love for her was solid.

She'd had dinners at Bobby's grandmother's several times before, and they were pleasant evenings. Mrs Dale was a fabulous cook, and the atmosphere was always happy and cosy. The last time she visited, Allison was instructed to call her 'Nana', like Bobby did, and that made her feel she was special and accepted. Plus the older woman always discretely retired to her room after dinner, giving Allison and Bobby some alone time.

Once off the train, she practically ran the rest of the way. Dinner was supposed to be at six thirty and it was almost quarter to seven.

But when she arrived, Bobby's grandmother wasn't even there.

'She just called. She's been visiting a friend in the hospital,' Bobby told her. 'She's on her way home now.'

Allison was relieved. She hated being late, and now she and Bobby could have a few minutes alone.

Only they weren't alone. Sitting on the sofa in the living room was Beverly Gray.

'Allison, you remember Beverly, right?'

Allison forced a smile. How could she forget? Much as she'd have liked to . . .

'Hi, Beverly.'

'Hi,' Beverly chirped. 'Hope you don't mind – Bobby and I are going over the script. He's been a very naughty boy, you know.'

'In what way?' Allison asked stiffly.

'He hasn't learned his lines!'

'I don't know why I'm having so much trouble,' Bobby said. 'I could always remember song lyrics.'

'Maybe you should try singing your lines,' Beverly suggested.

Bobby picked up the script. To the tune of his last hit, 'Let Me Love You', he sang, 'Where have you been, Marcia? I've been looking all over for you. Do you have any idea what time it is?'

Beverly burst out in giggles, Bobby laughed along with her and Allison forced yet another smile.

Beverly sang out her line. 'Oh, John, you don't own me. I can go anywhere I please.'

This time Allison's smile was sincere. Her singing voice was so terrible Allison couldn't even recognize the tune. After Beverly left, she and Bobby could have a good laugh over that.

At that moment Bobby's grandmother walked in.

'Allison, so good to see you!' she said. 'Come give me a hug.'

Allison was happy to do so. Partly because she was very fond of the woman, but also because it showed Beverly that *she* belonged here.

Then Bobby introduced Beverly to his grandmother. Personally Allison thought it was a little pushy, the way Beverly immediately embraced the older woman.

'Bobby is always talking about you, Mrs Dale,' the actress gushed. 'This is such a thrill for me!'

Allison thought Nana would see right through Beverly's theatrical behaviour, but she actually seemed pleased.

GL♥SS

'Why, thank you, my dear. Aren't you the sweetest thing! So pretty too!'

'Well, I guess I should be off,' Beverly said. 'It was very nice to meet you, Mrs Dale.'

'Why don't you stay for dinner,' Mrs Dale asked.

'Oh no, I couldn't impose.'

'But you must. I've got a gorgeous beef brisket in the slow cooker, and there's more than enough. And Bobby's told me so much about you.'

'And if you haven't tasted Nana's brisket, you haven't lived,' Bobby added.

Allison stared at him in wonderment, but his eyes were on Beverly, who simpered sweetly.

'Well, I do want to go on living, so I guess I'd better stay! Thank you, Mrs Dale.'

'Now, now, none of that Mrs Dale business. All Bobby's good friends call me Nana.'

Allison couldn't believe it. How many visits had she made before she was invited to call her Nana?

It was a sumptuous meal. Along with Nana's melt-in-your-mouth tangy beef, there were home-made noodles and a fresh-green-bean salad. But although everything looked delicious, Allison wasn't very hungry. And for once Bobby's grandmother didn't urge her to eat more. She was too engrossed in Beverly's descriptions of filming on location in Rome.

'Nana's always wanted to see Rome,' Bobby said.

'I've promised her, as soon as I get some time off, I'll take her there.'

'Oh, Nana, you must go to Rome!' Beverly declared. 'It's so beautiful!'

'Did you go to the Trevi Fountain?' Mrs Dale wanted to know. 'I saw that movie *Three Coins in a Fountain* three times. You're supposed to throw in a coin and wish that you'll come back to Rome.'

'I did that!' Beverly told her. She lowered her eyes demurely. 'Only I added a little something. I wished that the next time I saw Rome, it would be with my own true love.'

Allison wanted to gag. She shot a quick glance at Bobby, hoping to exchange a private look that would assure her he was having the same reaction to this garbage. But he wasn't looking in her direction. And Nana was completely taken in.

'Oh, that's so romantic!' she sighed.

When Beverly finally finished talking about Rome, she went on to entertain them with tales of Hollywood scandals and celebrity gossip. Again Allison tried to share a look with Bobby. She knew he hated that movie-magazine junk as much as she did. But he actually looked interested in what Beverly was saying.

He's just being polite, Allison told herself. Beverly's a guest in this house, plus he has to work with her. He's got to fake a good relationship. But it occurred to her that he was getting awfully good at this faking.

Beverly was totally dominating the conversation and no one else seemed to mind. What was even worse was the fact that Allison couldn't compete. What could she possibly contribute? Her thrilling trip to the Museum of Natural History? Some cute little comment that Tommy had made? How could that stack up against the rumours of Rock Hudson's love affairs?

It was at times like this that she was almost grateful for her proper-young-lady upbringing. Somehow she managed to keep her face from reflecting how neglected she was feeling.

Allison was picking at her cherry pie when Beverly looked at her expensive gold watch and let out a little squeaky noise which was supposed to convey alarm.

'Oh no, look at the time! We've got an early call tomorrow, Bobby.'

Did she have to make that 'we' sound so intimate?

'It's only ten o'clock,' Allison pointed out.

'Yeah, but I've got a car picking me up at six thirty,' Bobby said.

'Why so early?' Allison asked. 'I thought you didn't have to be on set till eight.'

'You wouldn't believe how long it takes to get into Manhattan during rush hour,' Bobby replied.

These were pretty much the first words he'd spoken directly to her all evening. Naturally Beverly had to jump into the conversation.

'Bobby, I know how lovely it must be for you to

GL♥SS

151

stay with your grandmother, but maybe you should think about staying in Manhattan while we're filming. It would make life a lot easier for you. At least you'd get more sleep.'

There was no way Allison was going to let her think she was the first to come up with this idea.

'That's what I told him ages ago. I've got a place on Fifth Avenue, and I thought he should live with me while he was making the movie.'

Even as the words left her mouth, she knew this wasn't a proper-young-lady thing to say. Bobby's grandmother turned to her with a shocked expression. Bobby looked embarrassed.

'I have two bedrooms,' she added weakly, but the harm was done. Now Bobby was embarrassed, and his grandmother thought she was a slut. She wanted to die. And it didn't help when she saw the small smile on Beverly's face.

Bobby stood up. 'I'll clear the table, Nana.'

'And I'll help,' Beverly said, and picked up a glass.

Nana took the glass from her. 'Nonsense, my dear, you're a guest.'

Allison got up and started gathering plates. Nobody stopped *her*.

'Nana, may I use your phone?' Beverly asked. 'I need to call for my car to come get me.'

'Maybe you could drop Allison off on your way to the hotel,' Bobby suggested.

So she wouldn't be having any private time at all with Bobby tonight. And how in the world would she be able to stand the long drive back to Manhattan in the car with Beverly?

When they said their goodbyes, Bobby kissed Allison on the cheek. Well, it wasn't as if he could give her a real soulful kiss in front of his grandmother and Beverly. But what really bugged her was the way he planted the exact same kiss on Beverly's cheek.

At least she didn't have to make conversation in the limousine. From her handbag Beverly extracted a transistor radio, stuck the little plug in her ear, closed her eyes and leaned back. She didn't say a word during the entire ride, which was a relief – but it also left Allison with too much time to brood over the evening.

When they arrived at her building on Fifth Avenue, Allison turned to Beverly.

'Thanks for the ride,' she muttered.

Beverly opened one eye, gave her a wretchedly smug smile and wiggled her fingers in a sort of wave. It was too bad the chauffeur opened the door for Allison. She would have loved to slam it shut.

All she wanted to do now was put on her pyjamas, crawl into bed and pray for sleep to come quickly so she could stop thinking. She'd completely forgotten that Pamela was bringing her friend Larry home.

Pamela and Larry were there, snuggled on the sofa in front of the TV. They weren't paying too much attention to it. When they heard the door close, they both jumped up.

Pamela's lipstick was smeared, and Allison could see pink traces of it on the boy's white shirt. His face was almost the same colour.

'Hi! Allison, this is Larry.'

Allison shook hands with him, and she was surprised to see how good-looking he was. The way Pamela had described him, she'd expected someone a little more frog-like. He was very pleasant, too.

'It's nice to finally meet you,' he said. 'Pamela talks about you all the time.'

It was pretty much what Beverly had said to Bobby's grandmother, but Larry sounded a lot more sincere.

'It's nice to meet you too,' she replied.

'I hope you don't mind that I'm here so late,' he said. He nodded towards the TV. 'The game went into extra innings.'

'What's the score?' Allison asked.

Pamela and Larry looked at each other. Then Larry gave Allison a sheepish grin.

'Oops.'

Despite her bad mood, Allison had to smile. Obviously they hadn't been paying too much attention to the game.

'Stay as late as you like,' she said. 'I'm going to bed.'

'Did you have a nice evening?' Pamela asked.

GL♥SS

'Absolutely,' she lied.

She was just crawling into bed when she heard the front door close. Seconds later, Pamela rapped lightly at her door.

'Allison? Are you still up?'

'Yeah.'

Pamela came in and sat on her bed. 'So, what did you think of Larry?'

'He's nice.'

Pamela nodded. 'I just wish he was taller. And better-looking.'

'He's not exactly ugly, Pamela!'

'Yeah, but he's no Steve McQueen.'

'What kind of work does he do?'

Pamela made a face. 'Advertising. But he's got connections in television. Maybe he could get me a job there.'

'What kind of job could you do in television?'

'I don't know. Just be a secretary, I guess. But maybe I'd have the chance to meet celebrities.'

Allison rolled her eyes. 'Celebrities aren't so great, Pamela. Beverly Gray was with us tonight.'

Pamela's eyes widened. 'Ooh, what's she like in person?'

Allison made a face. 'She was flirting with Bobby.'

'Do you think he's interested in her?'

'Oh no, not at all,' Allison said quickly. 'But he has to be nice, because they're working together.'

'Beverly Gray,' Pamela said thoughtfully. 'She's really beautiful. He's gotta be tempted.'

'Pamela!'

'Come on, I'm being realistic. He's only human. You know what I think? Maybe it's time for you to step up your game.'

'What's that supposed to mean?'

'Make yourself more desirable.'

'And how am I supposed to do that? Have a makeover? Dye my hair blonde, start wearing falsies?'

'Not necessarily. Maybe you should start playing more hard to get, not so available. Tell him you're too busy to see him sometimes. Make him think there's another guy in your life.'

'Make him jealous? That's ridiculous. We don't play those kinds of games.' She yawned. 'And I have to go to sleep.'

'Nighty-night,' Pamela sang out as she left.

Make him jealous? Typical Pamela-speak, Allison thought as she rolled over. That wasn't even worth contemplating. She put her friend's advice out of her mind.

Even so, she had a hard time getting to sleep that night.

Chapter Fourteen

D r Naomi Cutler was not an easy person to reach. Sherry had tried calling the therapist several times, but she'd only been able to get through to a service that took appointments. She'd tried leaving a message, but Dr Cutler hadn't called back.

But that morning she was in luck. The doctor herself answered the phone.

'Dr Cutler.'

'Hello, Dr Cutler, my name is Sherry Forrester and I'm calling from *Gloss* magazine. We were wondering if you'd be interested in doing an interview with us.' Sherry went on to explain the idea they'd had, but before she could go into any detail, the woman interrupted her.

'I'm sorry, what magazine did you say you're from?'

'*Gloss*. We're a monthly magazine for teenage girls.'

'Oh! Well, that's strange. I've just accepted an invitation to do an interview with another magazine. Let me see, what was the name . . . ?'

Sherry could hear papers rustling, and then the therapist spoke again.

'Here it is. I'm scheduled to be interviewed by *Modern Girl*.'

Sherry's heart sank. '*Modern Girl*?' she repeated.

'Yes, I believe it's also a magazine for teenage girls. This is quite a coincidence.'

'It certainly is,' Sherry said glumly. 'Thank you anyway.'

She hung up the phone and frowned. Yes, it certainly was a coincidence, and a pretty strange one. It wasn't as if changing roles for girls was some hot, new topic that everyone wanted to write about, like the Beatles. Caroline was not going to be happy when she heard about this.

With a sigh she left her office and headed next door, but Caroline wasn't there.

'She's in a meeting,' Gloria told her.

'OK. Hey, do you have today's paper?'

'Right here,' Gloria said, and handed the rolled paper to her.

Sherry opened it, and a photo on the front page caught her eye. Surrounded by a group of men in suits, President Lyndon Johnson sat at a desk with a pen in his hand. The headline read 'LBJ signs Civil Rights Act into Law.'

'Wow!' Sherry exclaimed. 'Did you see this, Gloria?'

'What?'

Sherry showed the secretary the front page.

'Yes, I've seen it,' Gloria said. She took her handbag

out of her drawer. 'I'm going to the restroom. Would you listen for the phone?'

'Sure.' She looked after the secretary in surprise. She would have expected more of a reaction.

Leaving her door open so she could hear the phone if it rang, she sat back down at her desk to peruse the article. When she glanced up a moment later, she saw a figure standing at Gloria's desk.

With the newspaper still in her hand, she went back into the bullpen.

'William. Hi.'

Gloria's brother turned. 'Oh, hi. I was looking for my sister.' He indicated the wallet in his hand. 'She left this at our mother's last night.' He placed it on her desk.

'She'll be right back.' After a moment, she said, 'You must be feeling pretty good today.'

He raised his eyebrows.

'About the signing of the Civil Rights Act,' she said.

He nodded.

Again she was surprised by the lack of enthusiasm. 'I think it's wonderful.'

'Do you?' he asked. A small and not-very-warm smile played around his lips. 'Why?'

'*Why?* Because . . . Because it's a good thing!'

Gloria returned and saw the wallet on her desk. 'Oh, thanks, William. I've been looking all over for that.'

'Sherry and I were talking about the Civil Rights

Act,' he said casually. 'She thinks it's wonderful.'

Again Gloria didn't react. She sat down at her desk and began rolling a sheet of paper into her typewriter.

'And I was asking her why *she* thinks it's wonderful.'

Sherry was perplexed, and now she was getting a little annoyed. His tone was undeniably sarcastic.

'I think it's wonderful because I don't believe in segregation. You *know* that, William.'

Gloria lifted her head from the keyboard and looked at them both in surprise. 'Am I missing something here?'

'Sherry came to the meeting at Columbia Monday,' William told her.

Gloria turned to Sherry, and Sherry almost took a step backwards. She'd never seen such a cold expression on the woman's face. It only lasted a second, and then the secretary turned back to her work without saying anything.

Sherry was completely confused. Shouldn't Gloria be pleased that Sherry supported civil rights? William too – why did he have that smirk on his face, as if he was laughing at her?

'It seems to me,' she said, 'that y'all should be celebrating.' Oh damn, she thought. Why did that 'y'all' have to slip out just then? It only reminded them where she came from.

'I mean, we should all be celebrating,' she added quickly.

GL♥SS

William studied her with amusement in his eyes. 'Do you really think the Civil Rights Act is going to make a difference?'

'Of course it will! Now it will be against the law to discriminate.'

'And everybody always obeys the law, right?' he countered. 'That's a little naive.'

She put the newspaper down on Gloria's desk and pointed to the photo. 'Look. There's Martin Luther King, Jr., standing right behind the president. *He* looks happy.'

'The *Reverend Doctor* Martin Luther King, Jr.,' William said, emphasizing the titles. He turned to his sister. 'I'm getting together with some of the folks from Monday's meeting tonight. Gloria, you want to meet us at Gino's for pizza?'

'Maybe,' Gloria said, her eyes still on her work.

Sherry wasn't sure where the impulse came from, or where she found the courage to speak. But she actually heard herself asking, 'Can I come too?'

Even though Gloria's back was to her, she could see the woman stiffen. But William just shrugged.

'It's a free country. You know Gino's, in the Village?'

She nodded.

'See ya. Bye, Glo.'

The secretary waved a hand in the air, and William strode off.

'Your brother's nice,' Sherry said.

Gloria didn't respond, and Sherry went back into her own office.

She didn't get it. It wasn't as if she and Gloria had been chummy, but they'd always had a pleasant relationship. Sherry got the feeling that she had somehow offended the secretary, but she didn't know why.

She couldn't brood about that now. She'd rather think about tonight.

She wondered who else would be at Gino's. She'd met some nice people at that meeting. They were all students, of course. In fact, she got the feeling she was the only non-student there. Even though they were all in the same age range, she felt older. Maybe it was the way she was dressed, in her proper little going-to-work clothes, while the others looked much more casual.

The meeting had been interesting. There'd been a lot of talk about the three missing men in Mississippi, and demonstrations going on throughout the Southern states. There was discussion about the likelihood of the Civil Rights Act being passed, how it would end racial segregation and unequal voter registration requirements that had kept many non-white people from voting. A committee was established to look into charges of police brutality in the shooting of a Negro boy in Harlem. A collection was taken up to rent a bus that would bring students down to

Alabama, to help with voter registration.

Despite what William said, Sherry felt she wasn't all that naive. She read newspapers, she knew what was going on in the world. But she'd never heard topics like this discussed so openly. Back home, no one ever spoke about these things. Opinions weren't shared. Sherry couldn't remember any of her friends expressing *support* for racism and segregation. They just didn't question it.

Sherry didn't say much at the meeting, she didn't even ask any questions – she was too afraid of the reaction to her accent. She listened. And the more she heard, the more ashamed she felt. Not that she blamed herself for the attitudes of the South, but she was horrified because she'd never considered how terrible it was. The only Negro she'd ever known growing up was the woman who came to her home every day, to watch the children when they were younger and to clean the house. Sarah Jane. It was with shame that she realized she'd never known Sarah Jane's last name.

There were only white people living in her neighbourhood, and all her classmates at school were white. The others had their own neighbourhoods, their own schools . . . Why? It was a small town, with plenty of room in one high school for all the teenagers there.

Now, sitting in her office, a memory from childhood came to her. She couldn't have been more than five because she wasn't able to read yet.

She was in Atlanta with her mother, at one of the big department stores. While her mother was chatting with a saleslady, little Sherry Ann was suddenly thirsty. She spotted water fountains against a wall. Two water fountains, with a notice above each one.

She'd assumed one was for boys and one was for girls. At kindergarten there were two restrooms right next to each other. One had a picture of a boy on the door and the other had a picture of a girl. She remembered wishing these department-store water fountains had pictures over them instead of words she couldn't read.

She was relieved when she saw a woman go up to one of the fountains, turn the spigot and drink some water. As soon as the woman walked away, she made a beeline for that same fountain. But just as she put her hand on the spigot, a saleslady grabbed her arm and pulled her away.

'No, no, sugar, you don't want to drink out of that fountain!' The woman steered her towards the other fountain.

Did the saleslady think she was a boy? In horror she forgot her thirst and ran back to her mother.

She realized later that the lady who drank from the first fountain was a Negro. And it wasn't much later before she could read the words that had hung over the fountains, the words she would see over many, many fountains and on many restroom doors for

GL♥SS

years to come: WHITE and COLOURED.

And she'd just accepted that this was OK.

As she polished her nails at the dining table early that evening, she called out to Donna. 'Were there Negroes at school with you when you were growing up?'

'Sure,' Donna called back. She was in the bedroom they shared, getting ready to go out.

'Were you friends with them?'

'No. But not because they weren't white. I didn't have *any* friends.' She came out into the main room, and Sherry gasped. She was used to seeing Donna all dolled up in samples-closet clothes for her evenings with Bonnie-the-model, but this was a whole different story. Her roommate was clad in a long blue sheath trimmed in gold braid, and her hair was up in a sleek French chignon.

'Wow! Where are you going tonight?'

'Some benefit dinner.'

'And Bonnie's not taking a date?'

Donna shrugged and looked down at her white ballet-style slippers. 'These are so wrong. But the shoes in the samples closet are too small for me.'

'I've got some light gold heels,' Sherry declared, and went into the bedroom. Way in the back of the closet, she dug out the shoes that had been purchased a year earlier to go with a wretched bridesmaid dress for her brother's wedding. She hadn't worn them since.

Donna tried them on. 'They're a little big.'

'I'll get some cotton balls,' Sherry said.

Once the toes were stuffed with the wadded-up balls, Donna pronounced them wearable.

'Thanks. What are *you* doing tonight?'

'I'm meeting some people who were at that civil-rights thing I went to.'

Donna nodded. 'Oh, right, for that article you want to do.'

Sherry paused in the middle of applying the top coat to her nails. How strange . . . She hadn't even been thinking about the article! But of course, maybe she could pick up some useful information tonight.

'What's going on with you and Jack? Are you going to see him again?'

'Maybe.'

Sherry looked at her with interest. Donna wasn't much of a talker, but she'd been particularly secretive about this guy. 'Is it getting serious?'

Donna smiled and picked up the little gold clutch bag, another samples-closet item. 'See ya.' She started towards the door, but as she was passing the phone, it rang and she picked it up.

'Hello? One minute, please. Sherry, it's for you!'

Sherry took the phone from her and waved as Donna left the apartment.

'Hello?'

'Hey, darlin'!'

'Hey, Mama, how are you?'

'Just fine, sugar, how are you?'

'I'm good. I'm getting ready to go out.'

'How nice! Where to?'

'I'm meeting some friends for pizza.'

'Well, I won't keep you long, Sherry Ann. I wanted to tell you, cousin Melanie's engaged!'

As her mother went on to tell her about Melanie's fiancé and her wedding plans, Sherry kept her eye on the time and only half listened. Then something occurred to her. And as soon as her mother paused to take a breath, she broke in.

'Mama, there's something I've been meaning to ask. How do you and Daddy feel about this Civil Rights Act?'

'Why, what does that have to do with cousin Melanie? She's not marrying a Negro!' Her mother laughed merrily.

'It's just that, well, it was signed into law today, and everyone's talking about it. So I was wondering . . .'

'Well, of course, we're in favour of equal rights. You know we're not racist, sugar. But . . .'

'But what?' Sherry prompted.

'You know that nice Mr Hawkins, who runs that lovely seafood restaurant down on South Main? I was talking to him the other day, and he's not happy about this at all.'

'Why not?'

'It's the federal government poking its nose in his business! Mr Hawkins owns that restaurant, and he thinks he should have the right to decide who he'll serve at his tables. And I have to admit, sugar, he has a point.'

'Mama, I gotta run. Tell cousin Melanie congratulations for me, OK?'

So maybe William was right, she thought as she walked to Gino's. Laws could be passed, but that didn't mean people would obey them.

Inside Gino's, she spotted the group immediately. They were sitting around the large round table in the centre of the noisy, crowded restaurant. There was William, of course, and three other guys she recognized from the meeting. And a girl she remembered too – Denise had been sitting on her other side on Monday and had introduced herself. Hoping she looked more nonchalant than she felt, she headed to the table.

Denise spotted her first, and her smile was encouraging.

'Hi! Sherry, right?'

'Yes, hi, Denise.'

William looked up, and for the briefest moment she thought she saw a smile cross his face. It disappeared so fast she couldn't be sure. She stood there uncertainly.

'Aren't you going to sit down?' Denise asked.

'She's waiting for an engraved invitation,' William murmured.

GL♥SS

She ignored that and took a seat. One of the other boys flagged a passing waitress.

'Could you change that order to an extra-large?'

Another boy grinned. 'C'mon, Matt, she doesn't look like she'll eat all that much.'

'No, but I will. And she's my excuse. What's your name? I remember seeing you at Columbia.'

'I'm Sherry.'

'Matt.' He nodded towards each of the others at the table. 'Peter, Barry, William. Wait, you already know William, right? Weren't you with him at the meeting?'

'No, she was just sitting next to me,' William said.

A waiter appeared with a tray bearing five glasses of beer and began setting them on the table.

'You want a beer, Sherry?' Matt asked.

'No, thanks.'

'Maybe she'd prefer a mint julep,' William said. 'Isn't that what you drink, you folks way down south in Dixieland?'

Sherry fought back the temper rising inside her. 'I've never had a mint julep in my life,' she said. It wasn't much of a comeback, but it was all she could think of to say.

The only other white person at the table, the boy named Barry, spoke. 'Are you really from the South?'

There was no point in lying. A 'y'all' would slip out sooner or later.

'Born and bred,' she replied lightly.

'You sure you don't want anything to drink?' Matt asked.

'Maybe some water,' she said.

William indicated the glass of water near him. 'You can have mine. I haven't drunk from it.' His eyes met hers, and she could see the challenge.

She met it. 'It wouldn't matter to me if you had.' She took the glass, started to raise it to her lips, then put it back down and gave him a suspicious look. 'Unless you've got a cold.'

He actually gave her a smile. A real one. 'No cold.'

'How do they feel about the Civil Rights Act down South?' Matt asked.

She kept her eyes on William. 'It's like you said. You can pass laws but you can't make people keep them.' She recounted to the group what her mother had told her about Mr Hawkins and his restaurant.

Denise nodded. 'It's going to take time. This is just a beginning.'

The waitress returned with an enormous pizza. The next few minutes were taken up with distributing slices.

Matt took a huge bite and then moaned in satisfaction. 'Best pizza in New York City. This is why I go to New York University instead of Columbia. It's closer to Gino's.'

'Ha!' Peter said with a grin. 'You're at NYU because you couldn't get into Columbia.' He turned to Sherry.

'Hey, hope I'm not offending anyone. Are you at NYU or Columbia?'

'Neither,' Sherry said. 'I'm not a student. I work for a magazine – *Gloss*.'

'I remember *Gloss*!' Denise exclaimed. 'It was my Bible when I was a teenager.' Her smile drooped a little. 'Not that I could ever completely relate to it.'

'Why not?' Sherry asked.

Denise gave her a reproving look. 'None of the models in the pictures looked like me.'

'Oh.' She was absolutely right. All those girls in *Gloss* magazine, all those lovely girls showing off the fashionable shorter skirts, wearing this season's new cherry-pink lipstick, presenting costume jewellery and handbags and frilly flannel nightgowns . . .

'All the models are white, aren't they?' she said in wonderment. Why had she never even noticed that before?

Denise nodded. 'It's as if the rest of us aren't expected to be interested in fashion and beauty.'

'As if you don't exist,' Sherry murmured. 'Oh, this is wrong! This is so wrong!'

She didn't realize how her voice had risen until she saw how the others were looking at her. And she wasn't embarrassed at all – because they were looking at her with approval. Even William.

'Maybe you can talk to the higher-ups at *Gloss*,'

Matt said. 'Get them to start using some models who aren't white.'

'I will,' Sherry said. 'I work for the managing editor, and I'm going to ask her about this.'

'Good for you,' Denise said.

Peter was less enthusiastic. 'That's going to be your big contribution to civil rights? Getting a Negro girl into a teen magazine?'

William spoke up. 'Hey, don't knock it. Little things like that, they're important. This is how attitudes start changing.'

Sherry smiled at him. He smiled back. With a surge of pleasure, she felt as if they'd made some sort of connection.

Then, almost too quickly, he looked away and spoke to Matt. 'You still thinking about making a run for student-government president?'

The conversation veered off into a discussion of campus politics at Columbia, with Barry offering some comparisons to student elections at NYU. It moved on from there to talk of the student newspapers, and an editorial that Peter was planning to write about the drive for voter registration in Mississippi. Denise talked about her student-council committee, which was allocating funds to bring prominent Negro speakers to campus.

It was all so incredibly exhilarating for Sherry. Even though she wasn't a part of that world, she could thoroughly enjoy listening to talk that had nothing to do with fashion and beauty. Their lives seemed so full, so varied.

'We need to get another meeting scheduled,' William mentioned at one point. 'To organize the Wall Street event.'

'What's the Wall Street event?' Sherry asked.

'We're planning a demonstration on Wall Street in a few weeks,' William told her. 'To protest the lack of Negro employees in finance and banking.'

They started talking about meeting dates and getting publicity started. Then Denise announced she had to leave.

'Eight o'clock class,' she explained.

Matt called for the check, and everyone started tossing in their contributions. Peter and Barry left to go uptown with Denise, and Matt said his goodbyes a moment later.

Sherry found herself alone at the table with William. At the table next to them, there was a loud burst of drunken laughter from two boys who were calling for another pitcher of beer. Sherry glanced in their direction.

'They look awfully young to be drinking,' she commented.

'Yeah, I don't think they check IDs here,' William said. 'Hey, there's a slice left,' he noted, with a nod towards the remains of the pizza.

'Take it,' she urged.

'No, you take it,' he said.

Sherry shook her head. 'No, thanks.'

'You don't like the pizza?'

'Are you kidding? I love pizza. It's my favourite food.'

'Yeah? Mine too.'

'But I can't eat another bite,' she said.

'Neither can I,' William said. Then he grinned. 'We'll split it.' He took a knife and divided the pizza. Then he pretended to examine the pieces carefully, to make sure they were the same size. He frowned.

'I think that one's bigger.'

Sherry reached out and grabbed it. He laughed.

'Is that any way for a Southern belle to behave?' Then he put his hands up in a defensive mode. 'Just kidding!' He took the other piece. 'Besides, I was lying. *This* is the bigger piece.'

They ate in silence. When she had finished her piece, Sherry said, 'I meant what I said, about talking to my boss about putting Negro models in *Gloss*. Maybe Gloria would want to talk to Caroline with me. Caroline's her boss too.'

William shook her head. 'No.'

'Why not? She supports civil rights, doesn't she?'

'Of course she does.' He hesitated, as if he was trying to decide what to say next. Then he plunged in. 'The thing is, my sister . . . she doesn't trust white people.'

Sherry was taken aback. 'But she works with white people!'

'She's OK working with them, but she doesn't want things to get too . . . familiar. She'd rather keep a certain distance.' He studied her for a moment. 'I don't know if you can understand this, Sherry. We come from different worlds, we have different histories. I used to be like Gloria. I didn't know any white people and I didn't want to. Going to Columbia changed that for me. I met white people I could actually connect with. Gloria hasn't had that opportunity.'

'She's been acting different with me lately,' Sherry told him. 'Ever since I tried to talk with her about the Civil Rights Act.'

William nodded. 'Don't take it personally. It just makes her uncomfortable, when white people get too close.' He smiled. 'I'll talk to her. I'll tell her you're OK.'

'Thank you,' she said simply.

There was another moment of silence, which William finally broke.

'Well . . . I've got a morning class too.'

'And I have to go to work,' Sherry said.

He looked around for the waitress. 'I'll go up to the cash register and pay the check.' He gathered the money.

Sherry waited there at the table. One of the drunk teenagers at the next table caught her eye.

'Hey, honey, whatcha doing with him?' he called

out loudly. 'You're cute enough to get a white boy to date you.'

William returned and stared at the boy. 'What were you saying to her?'

'It's nothing,' Sherry said. 'Let's go.' She stood up, but William didn't move. He was still looking at the boy. And now a few people from other tables were looking too.

'Please, William,' she said quickly, and in her urgency she took his arm.

He shot one last hostile glare at the boy, but he started walking with her to the door. When they got outside he asked, 'What did he say to you?'

'It was just something stupid.'

'*What?*'

She hesitated, then gave in. 'Oh, something about how I should date a white guy.'

He shook his head wearily. 'Jerk.' Then he looked at her thoughtfully. 'Didn't you tell him I wasn't your date?'

She looked up at him.

'No.'

Chapter Fifteen

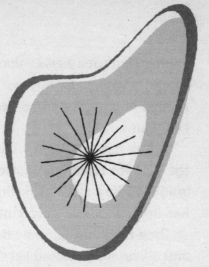

'You look beautiful,' Jack said. Donna smiled. 'So do you.'

'I'm glad to hear that.' Jack ran a finger inside the stiff white collar of his shirt. 'Because if I'm going to have to be this uncomfortable all evening, at least I'll know I look good.'

Donna squeezed his hand. They were in the back seat of a taxi, on their way to the Metropolitan Museum of Art to attend a grand benefit evening, and Jack did look incredibly handsome in his tux. She believed him when he said she looked beautiful. Because Jack never told lies. Not like she did.

And not just to Jack. She'd lied that afternoon, when she asked for the key to the samples closet, and let Caroline think she was doing something with Bonnie. She'd lied to Sherry about that too. And with Jack she was living a lie.

But at least she looked the part. Her gown was beautiful. She couldn't remember the name on the label, but she was pretty sure it came from a famous

French couturier. Earlier that day she'd watched very carefully while a hairdresser put a model's hair into a twisted bun, and she had been able to do it with her own hair.

Before turning the key back in, she'd gone back to the samples closet and picked up some accessories – gold dangling earrings, a thin gold chain for around her neck, the little gold clutch bag. And as she was stuffing the items in a tote bag, a memory came back. Just a year ago, she had been stealing things from this very closet to sell on the street for money to survive.

This was why the closet was kept locked now. She'd managed to return the items without being caught. But even so, she was still little more than a common thief. As well as trailer trash. What would Jack think if he knew he was dating a girl like that?

She'd been with him almost every night since that cocktail at Charlie's. Fortunately Bonnie now had an admirer whom she was seeing more regularly, so she'd been making fewer demands for Donna's companionship. Jack had taken her to the movies, to nice restaurants, to a Broadway play. Somehow she'd managed to avoid speaking too much about herself, her past. But occasionally she'd been forced by their conversation to throw in a titbit or two. So now Jack believed she'd been to Italy on a vacation with her parents. Having once seen a movie set in Venice, that became the town they'd visited.

GL♥SS

And she'd overheard the fashion editor at *Gloss* talking about a recent trip to Boston, where she'd splurged on an expensive dress at a store called Jordan Marsh. So that became the place where her mother used to take her shopping.

'I hate these things,' Jack said suddenly. 'I hate having to get all dressed up and sit at a table with people you don't even like and talk about stuff that doesn't interest you.'

'Like what?'

'Money. High finance, the stock market, banking.'

'But isn't that what you do?'

'Yeah. But I don't like talking about it.' He was silent for a moment. 'Did I ever tell you what I really wanted to be?'

'No.'

'An archaeologist. When I was about twelve I read a book about archaeologists digging up ancient civilizations in faraway places. And I thought, That's what I want to do someday.'

'Couldn't you have studied for that at the university?'

'Sure,' he said. 'But I didn't. Because my family is in banking. And I was expected to go into banking.'

For a moment, Donna almost felt as if she'd been lucky. No one had ever had any expectations for her.

'So, if you don't want to go to this thing, why are we going?' she asked.

'It's for my parents. They're big contributors,

and they couldn't come tonight so I'm supposed to represent the family.' He sighed. 'You must think I'm one helluva wimp – doing everything my parents want me to do.'

Donna patted his arm. 'You're not a wimp. You're a good son.'

He gave her a half-hearted smile. 'I'm sure you're a good daughter too.'

A good daughter who didn't even know where her mother was, Donna responded silently. A good daughter who rarely spoke to her father. Martin Peake really wasn't such a bad sort. True, he'd walked out on the family when she was only fourteen, but he'd eventually come back to rescue her younger brother and sister. And he'd sent Donna money so she could get by until she started making a salary at *Gloss*. But when Donna called to talk to little Kathy and Billy, she could barely think of anything to say to her father. How could someone like Jack ever understand relationships like that?

They'd arrived uptown, where cabs and limousines lined Fifth Avenue in the vicinity of the Met. The museum was closed to regular visitors, so all the people climbing the stairs at the front of the massive building were there for the benefit. Walking up to the entrance with Jack, she admired the beautifully dressed people around her and knew she'd blend in. On the surface, at least.

Inside, they followed the crowd and found themselves in a magnificent ballroom, dazzling with ornate mirrors on the walls and dripping chandeliers. It was a huge room – there had to be at least fifty round tables dressed in fine white tablecloths and covered in crystal and silverware.

For now, though, they were ushered into a side room, where uniformed waiters were circling with trays of champagne flutes. Jack took two and handed one to Donna.

'Do you see anyone you know?' she asked him.

He looked around. 'There are some familiar faces,' he admitted. 'Mostly friends of my parents.'

She lowered her voice. 'Well, there's one person who definitely knows *you*. She's heading this way.'

She was a woman in her forties, with frosted blonde hair, wearing a designer dress and making a beeline in their direction. Jack turned to see who Donna was talking about, and his brow furrowed.

'What's *she* doing here?' he muttered under his breath.

The woman came closer. 'Jack, dear,' she cooed.

'Hello, Mother. I thought you weren't coming. You said Father was sick.'

'It's just a nasty cold, dear. The servants can take care of him. I decided to come along with the Mayfairs. Now, aren't you going to introduce me to your companion?'

'This is Donna Peake, Mother. Donna, my mother.'

Donna could feel the stiffness in her own smile, and she could actually see it in the smile of Jack's mother.

'How do you do, Mrs Vanderwill?'

'A pleasure to meet you, dear. That's a lovely dress you're wearing.'

'Thank you.'

'Givenchy?' she asked.

Donna couldn't recall what the label said. 'I'm not sure.' Then, 'My mother bought it for me,' she added rapidly.

'Well, your mother has excellent taste. Did she get it at Bergdorf's?'

Jack broke in. 'Donna's family is in Boston, Mother.'

Donna remembered the name of the fancy department store. 'Yes, she bought it at Jordan Marsh, I believe.'

'Really? I didn't know Jordan Marsh carried Givenchy. Whereabouts in Boston is your family living?'

She could answer that easily. 'Beacon Hill.'

'Very nice,' Mrs Vanderwill said. 'It must have been lovely growing up so close to the Common.'

Donna didn't know what 'the Common' was, but she nodded.

'Where on Beacon Hill?'

Donna looked at her blankly.

'What street, dear?' the woman asked.

GL♥SS

She had no idea; she'd never seen Allison's actual address. But if the area was called Beacon Hill, maybe there was a street called . . . 'Beacon Street?'

She realized that this had come out more as a question than a statement, and the keen, penetrating expression in the woman's eyes was making her very uncomfortable. She felt as if she was lying on an examination table in a doctor's office.

At least it seemed there *was* a Beacon Street on Beacon Hill. 'What a coincidence!' Mrs Vanderwill exclaimed. 'I have very close friends on Beacon Street. Do you know the Gilberts, Donna? Muriel and Frank?'

'I'm afraid not.'

'Well, I'm sure your parents do. Muriel Gilbert knows everyone! And Frank has been president of the Beacon Hill Residents Association for years! Surely the name rings a bell?'

Donna's hands were beginning to feel clammy. 'Maybe,' she said vaguely.

'I must tell the Gilberts we met. What are your parents' names?'

She swallowed. 'Shirley and Martin,' she whispered.

'Shirley and Martin Peake,' Jack's mother said loudly. 'I'll remember that. You know, the Gilberts have a daughter about your age. Cordelia Gilbert?'

Donna shook her head.

'Where did you go to school, dear? Winsor? Dana Hall?'

Suddenly she began to feel dizzy. She must have swayed, because Jack put an arm around her. 'Are you all right?'

'I . . . I'm feeling a little faint. I think I need some air.'

'Excuse us, Mother,' Jack said hurriedly, and began leading Donna out of the room, then through the lobby and finally outside the museum. She sank down on the stairs, and he sat next to her.

'Take a deep breath,' he ordered her.

She did.

'Do you feel better?'

She nodded. 'I'm fine.'

He grinned. 'That's what I thought. Thank you.'

'For what?'

'You were faking, right? To get us out of there?'

She smiled. She really was feeling absolutely normal now. 'Maybe.'

'I'm really sorry about my mother putting you through the Spanish Inquisition.'

Donna didn't know what the Spanish Inquisition was, but clearly it had not been a good thing. 'She asks a lot of questions.'

'No kidding. And I just let her interrogate you like

that. You must think I'm an awful coward.' He sighed. 'Maybe I am. I've always had a hard time standing up to her and my father.'

'I don't think you're a coward,' Donna assured him. 'Parents – they can make us feel so . . . so . . .' She couldn't come up with the right word.

But Jack understood. 'Tell me about it,' he agreed. He shook his head ruefully. 'My mother's the worst. She's paranoid, positively obsessed with the idea that some gold-digger is going to seduce me, trick me into marrying her, for the family money.' He uttered a humourless laugh. 'Which is ironic, in a way. I'm pretty sure that's why she married my father. Unfortunately, he figured that out too late. People like us don't get divorced. Which is too bad, because they really hate each other.'

She gazed at him in wonderment. So even wealthy, so-called normal families could be miserable too.

A guard standing outside the museum was looking at them oddly, and Donna stood up.

'It's beautiful out tonight. Let's walk through the park.'

Holding hands, they walked down the rest of the steps, went a little way along Fifth Avenue and then turned on to a pathway that would take them deep into the park.

'Was your mother poor when she married your father?'

'Not poor exactly. More like decayed aristocracy. She was from an old family, but her father had lost everything in the stock-market crash of 1929. They still had a nice home and all that, but she wanted a lot more.'

'Jack . . . ?' she hesitated.

'What?'

'I'm not interested in your money.' As she spoke, she realized this was probably the first honest thing she'd ever told him about herself.

His grip on her hand tightened. 'I know that,' he said simply.

But of course he could believe that, she thought. He believed she came from plenty of money herself. Why would she be after his?

She stumbled on a rock, and he steadied her with his hand. 'Hey, you only had half a glass of champagne,' he joked. 'Don't tell me you got tipsy on that!'

'It's these shoes,' she said. 'I guess they're not meant for walking.'

'Let's sit for a minute,' he said, indicating a nearby bench.

They sat down, he put his arm around her, and she rested her head on his chest. 'I don't want to get any make-up on your shirt,' she said softly.

'It doesn't matter.' He lifted her face towards his, and they kissed. She could feel the warmth of his lips soak into her skin, move through her body. She put her arms around him and tried to pull him even closer, though it wasn't possible. Suddenly it was as if every cell in her body was calling out for his touch . . .

'Let's go back to my place,' he whispered in her ear.

Back to his place . . . where they could have privacy, and a bed. For a moment there was nothing she wanted more. But should he be asking this of her so soon? Did he suspect she had a past? And what would he think of her for giving in so easily?

She pulled away. 'No, not tonight. I can't.'

She could see the disappointment on his face, but he nodded. 'OK.'

'I'm sorry, I'm really sorry.'

'Don't be. I shouldn't have been so pushy.'

'No, you were fine, you were more than fine! I'm just . . . I'm just not ready.'

'I understand,' he said. 'I respect that.'

'Really?'

He nodded. 'We don't have to rush things. We haven't been together that long.' He smiled. 'Even though I feel like I've known you forever. Maybe that's because I've been looking for you for so long.'

Her heart was beating so hard, so fast, she felt sure he must be able to hear it. 'What do you mean?'

'The girls I meet, they're so shallow. They think they're sophisticated, but they're so boring and superficial. You're sweet; you're not spoilt like they are.'

Oh, Jack, she thought sadly. You have no idea how spoilt I am. In a very different sense of the word.

'You look a bit pale,' he said.

'I'm a little tired,' she admitted.

'Come on. I'm taking you home. To *your* home,' he added quickly.

'You can just put me in a cab,' she said as they started walking back towards the avenue.

'Are you kidding? You're much too precious for that. I want to see you all the way to your door.'

She looked up and smiled at him, but it wasn't easy. Any girl would feel wonderful hearing words like this, she thought. But she felt terrible.

Because her heart was full, and now she knew the worst had happened. She was falling in love.

Chapter Sixteen

At eight forty-five in the morning, in her pyjamas, Allison opened the door to the apartment just enough to snatch up the daily newspaper that was always left there. She took it into the kitchen, put the kettle on to boil and sat down.

Pamela came in and grabbed a stale doughnut out of the box on the table.

'How are you feeling?'

'Much better,' Allison replied. She'd been hit with a nasty cold on Friday, and she'd spent the weekend in bed. But she'd been up for thirty minutes now and hadn't sneezed or coughed once.

'Are you going to work today?'

Allison shook her head. 'Tom, the kids' father, called last night. Now *he's* got this cold, so he's staying home with the kids and I've got a day off.'

'And what are you going to do with your precious day off?'

'I think I'll go to the film set and surprise Bobby. I haven't seen him since Thursday.' She smiled. 'It's funny, you know? I used to go for weeks, sometimes months, without seeing him. But now three days apart seems like a really long time.'

'That's true love for you,' Pamela said. 'You guys just can't get enough of each other.'

'And I've never seen him as an actor,' Allison continued. 'He told me I could come any time, but I was afraid I'd make him nervous. But he gave me a copy of the shooting schedule, so I guess it's OK.'

'Gee, I'd love to see a real movie being made.' Pamela cocked her head thoughtfully. 'Maybe I could call the temp agency and tell them *I've* got a cold. They'd believe me – there's something going around.'

Allison looked at her sternly. 'Pamela, you don't get sick days working as a temp. If you don't work, you don't get paid. And weren't you just telling me yesterday about some fabulous shoes at Saks?'

Pamela sighed. 'That's true. I really want those shoes.' She brushed crumbs from the doughnut off the front of her dress. 'I'd better go.'

'Where are you working today?'

'I'm back at *Modern Girl*. It's boring, but at least I'll be able to have lunch at the coffee shop with Larry.'

Allison nodded with approval. 'Can't get enough of him, huh? He must be growing on you.'

'He'll do,' Pamela said lightly. 'Until someone better comes along.' She grinned. 'And he always pays for the lunch.' She blew a kiss at Allison and hurried out.

The water was boiling. Allison fixed herself some tea and sat back down to skim the newspaper. A photo on the society page caught her eye – some la-di-da benefit at the Met. It wasn't a very clear photo, but she could have sworn she could see Donna there, with a very handsome man. Her friend was certainly coming up in the world.

Allison's eyes drifted down to the gossip column. She always felt a little embarrassed reading celebrity nonsense, but checking out the silly-but-sometimes-juicy titbits had become a sort of guilty pleasure.

This time, however, the column didn't bring any pleasure at all. It was with a shock that she read a passage:

Seen at the Peppermint Lounge Saturday night – pop idol and future film star Bobby Dale with his Tangled Hearts *co-star Beverly Gray, looking very happy together as they twisted the night away.*

In disbelief, she read the line again.

He'd offered to come over Saturday night and pay a sick call, but she'd refused. She didn't want him catching her cold, and she wasn't feeling up for conversation, or anything else, for that matter.

So this was what he had done instead. He'd gone dancing with Beverly Gray. When Allison had spoken to him on the phone yesterday, he hadn't said a word about it. So it was something he'd decided to hide from her.

For the next few minutes she sat there, too stunned to move. Why would he do something like this? Was he so desperate to go out that he called Beverly? Or did Beverly call him? But why would he agree to go out with her? Bobby didn't even like to dance.

Maybe her worst fears had come true – seeing each other more frequently had killed the romance. Did familiarity truly breed contempt?

Well, she wasn't going to sit there and brood; that wasn't her style. She forced herself to get up and get into the shower.

She dressed with a little more care than usual and examined her reflection critically. Two days in bed had left her a little pale, and she actually considered raiding Pamela's cosmetic bag. No, Bobby always said he liked that she didn't wear make-up, that she always looked so natural.

But maybe he'd changed. Maybe this thin redhead with her boyish figure and clean skin had become less appealing to him. Maybe now he wanted a voluptuous blonde who painted her face.

She checked the shooting schedule he'd given her to see where they were filming today. Then she left the apartment and took the subway downtown.

Leaving the train at Twenty-third Street, she saw that two of the exits were closed. When she finally found an open one and came out of the tunnel, she realized why. Across from the station, a whole street had been blocked off with bright red wide ribbons strung between poles. Outside the barriers were large vans.

Within the blocked-off area there were huge lighting fixtures, and cameras set up on rolling platforms. People were moving around, sweeping sidewalks and pushing garbage cans aside. There were people outside the barriers too, curious onlookers trying to see what was going on or catch a glimpse of a celebrity.

Then she saw Bobby, coming out of one of the vans. Despite her anxiety, she almost laughed. He was wearing a formal tuxedo, something so unlike what he'd normally wear that it looked to her like a Halloween costume. At the same time, he *did* look handsome. Almost like a real movie star.

She started towards him, but her view was immediately cut off by a gaggle of girls waving autograph books. Before they dispersed, a couple of burly men rescued him, hurried him under the ribbon and into the street. He didn't even see her.

She moved closer to the barrier, but as she was about to lift the ribbon another burly man grabbed her arm.

'Sorry, no visitors on the set.'

'It's OK, just ask—'

'No exceptions. Move along!' he bellowed.

Then she saw Beverly coming out of another van. She looked unbelievably glamorous, in a black floor-length gown and a fur stole. Allison had to wonder what kind of scene was being shot, with both the characters in formal clothes so early in the morning and outside on a city street.

She had no desire to speak to the girl, but Beverly could get her past the guard.

'Beverly!' she called.

The actress turned and looked directly at her. Then she kept right on walking.

There was no way she hadn't seen Allison, but Allison knew she shouldn't be surprised by Beverly's reaction. The girl was after Bobby; of course she wouldn't want Allison around.

Desperately she circled the area, looking for someone – anyone – who could get her closer to Bobby. And finally she spotted a man she'd met at that party. It had been a while since then, but maybe he'd recognize her. She couldn't remember his name or what he did – lighting, maybe?

'Excuse me?'

He looked up and she was immensely relieved to see a glimmer of recognition in his face.

'Oh, hi. You're . . .'

'Allison,' she supplied.

'Right. Bobby's girl.'

For once she wasn't going to argue with that.

'Yes, he told me I could come watch a scene being shot.'

'Sure, no problem. Come with me.'

With whoever-he-was by her side, she had no

problem passing the barrier. He led her behind some cameras and equipment and brought her to a spot on the sidewalk, just by a tree.

'They're shooting the other side of the street, so you should get a good view from here.'

She thanked him and he left her there. She looked around. There was no sign of Bobby or Beverly. People with an air of self-importance were scurrying about, some with headphones over their ears, others speaking into walkie-talkies. No one paid any attention to her.

Then, when some massive piece of equipment was moved, she saw Bobby and Beverly standing at the corner of the street. A woman was dabbing their faces with what looked like a powder puff.

She heard a loud voice coming from somewhere, calling, 'OK, everyone, quiet on the set! This is a take.'

The area went suddenly silent.

'Places, John and Marcia!'

Bobby and Beverly moved to the opposite sidewalk. A man darted forward and did something to Beverly's hair, then jumped back. Another man went over and stood in front of them with some kind of little chalkboard in his hand.

'*Tangled Hearts*, scene eight, take one.'

Bobby and Beverly walked, hand in hand. Then Beverly broke free and skipped in front of him.

'What a night,' she cried out. 'Oh, John, I could have danced till dawn.'

'You did,' Bobby said. 'It's way past dawn, Marcia. Look, the sun is up.'

Her blonde hair cascaded down her back as she gazed skyward. 'Why, so it is!'

'You're not tired?' he asked.

'Not at all! In fact, I still want to dance. Dance with me, John.'

'But there's no music, Marcia.'

'Yes, there is. Just listen.'

'I don't hear anything.'

She came closer to him and took both his hands in hers. 'Darling, when two people are in love, there's always music.' Then she dropped his hands and stepped back. 'Or maybe you're just not in love.'

Bobby stepped closer and gripped her arms.

'Not in love? Marcia, I've been in love with you since that first day I laid eyes on you. Remember? You ran by me on the beach. You kicked sand in my face.'

'Sand in your face? But that wasn't very nice.'

'It was magic,' Bobby said. 'Like fairy dust. And I knew at that moment, I would love you forever.'

Watching, Allison felt sick, but she couldn't look away. The words might have been corny, but she was too intent on Bobby's face to really hear them. She knew that expression; she knew it so well. It was how he looked at *her*, when they were alone, when they were in each other's arms.

Then Bobby put his right hand on Beverly's waist,

and she put her left hand on his shoulder.

'I do hear music,' Bobby said. They began to dance, a slow, silent waltz on an empty street.

'Cut!' the voice bellowed. 'Beautiful, kids! We'll do one more take, just to be safe.'

Allison wasn't going to watch this again. She moved swiftly, behind the cameras and the lights and the equipment and the people. And once she was outside the barrier, she ran across the street and down the stairs into the subway station, all the while willing herself not to cry.

Bobby had told her he was no actor. She had believed him when he said that, and she believed him now. What she'd just seen wasn't acting. She knew that face, that smile, that voice so well. He'd meant everything he'd said to Beverly. Allison couldn't breathe.

Once on the train, she was only dimly aware of the passing stations. It was so strange, how she'd always just assumed they'd be together forever. Funny, she'd never thought of herself as a wildly romantic person. She liked to believe she was down-to-earth, realistic. True, she'd lapsed a year ago, when she thought she was madly in love with Sam. Now she was doing it again. Apparently she didn't know herself as well as she'd thought she did.

She was so caught up in her misery that she missed her stop and got off at the next one. Once out of the station, she started walking down the street, but then she stopped.

Allison didn't want to go back to the apartment. She didn't want to be alone.

She supposed she could go wander around in shops, go to a bookstore and browse, any place where there would be people, but she'd still be alone with her thoughts. She needed a friend. But her friends in New York – Sherry, Donna, Pamela – they were all at work. They wouldn't even be able to talk on the phone for long. Who else did she know in New York?

No one to whom she could pour her heart out. But there was someone who might be able to take her mind off her problems.

She walked to the nearest phone booth, put a dime in the slot and dialled a number.

'Hello?' croaked a male voice.

'Tom, hi, it's Allison. I wanted to know how you're feeling. And if you need any help with the kids.' She heard a sneeze, and then the hoarse voice returned.

'Oh, we're all fine. I'm not too bad.' But he barely got the words out before issuing a hacking cough that went on for about ten seconds.

'Well, you sound terrible. Are you taking anything for that cough?'

'No . . . In fact, I was just looking in the medicine cabinet. There's some children's cough medicine here. Maybe if I took a double dose . . .'

'No, you need something stronger,' Allison declared. 'Look, I'm near your place. I'm going to run into a pharmacy and get something for you. I'll bring it right over.'

'You don't have to do that . . .' he began, but Allison didn't let him finish.

'See you in about ten minutes,' she said, and hung up.

She went to the closest pharmacy and picked up some heavy-duty cough medicine. Next door was a bakery, and she remembered how, in the past, sadness had been eased a little by chocolate. She ducked inside, bought half a dozen brownies and then walked directly to the Markhams' building. Just having something to do made her feel a little better.

Karen opened the door. 'Hi, Allison! I'm halfway through *Beezus and Ramona* and nobody's died yet.'

'And nobody will,' Allison assured her.

In the living room, stretched out on the sofa in a terry-cloth robe, Tom Markham raised bleary eyes and gave her a smile.

'This is really nice of you, Allison,' he rasped.

He looked pretty awful – unshaven, red nose, red eyes, a box of tissues resting on his chest. Little Tommy, sitting on the floor with a box of toy soldiers, looked up at Allison.

'Checkers?' he asked hopefully.

'Let me fix your dad some medicine,' Allison

told him. She went into the kitchen for a teaspoon. Remembering how nasty cough medicine could taste, she also poured a glass of orange juice.

Back in the living room, she carefully poured the medicine into the spoon.

'Sit up so you won't choke,' she instructed Tom. 'Now, open wide.'

Tom obliged, took the medicine and made a face. Allison quickly handed him the glass of orange juice.

'You'd make a good nurse,' he croaked.

'She can't be your nurse,' Tommy declared. 'She's our nanny.'

Tom sank back on to the sofa. 'Well, today she has to be my nanny too.'

'I'm hungry,' Tommy complained.

Karen looked up from her book. 'Me too.'

Tom struggled to sit back up. 'I guess I can drum up enough strength to open a box of cereal.'

Allison shook her head. 'I think I can do better than that.'

'Open a can of soup?' Tom asked.

She grinned. 'Didn't Karen tell you? We're way beyond that now.' She went into the kitchen, took a book off a shelf and brought it back out to show him.

'I bought this for us – *The I Don't Know How to Cook Book*.'

Tom was impressed. 'You learned how to cook?'

'No. I learned which cans to open and mix together.'

Karen looked up. 'Casserole surprise?'

'You got it.' She turned to Tom. 'I find whatever leftovers you have, mix them up with a can of cream-of-mushroom soup, sprinkle breadcrumbs on top, stick it in the oven, and that's all there is to it!'

'I don't want to trouble you,' Tom called out weakly as she left them.

It was a relief to be busy. In the refrigerator she found leftover chicken. She could do an excellent casserole surprise with this.

Karen and Tommy joined her as she was chopping an onion.

'Can I do that?' Tommy asked.

'No, chopping is a grown-up job. Karen, can you get the seasonings? We need salt, pepper and garlic.'

'I want to do that!' Tommy declared.

'You can't read the labels,' Karen told him.

Tommy's face began to pucker up, and Allison spoke quickly.

'Tommy, I need you for stirring.' She dumped everything in a bowl, added two cans of the soup, put it on the kitchen table and handed Tommy a big wooden spoon.

'And you can preheat the oven too,' she told him. 'You know your numbers. Turn the dial to three-five-zero.'

Turning, she saw Tom standing in the doorway.

'You're great with them,' he said, with real admiration in his voice.

Allison smiled and shrugged. 'It's easy to be great with great kids.' She was amazed at how convincingly cheerful she sounded.

After sprinkling the breadcrumbs on top, she put the casserole into the oven, and then cut up lettuce and tomatoes for a salad.

'OK, who's going to help set the table? And since your father's here, let's eat at the *real* dining table.'

While rummaging for placemats, she discovered a box of candles and remembered there were candlesticks on the sideboard in the dining room. Candles on the table might be a little strange for lunch on a summer's day, but they would make the table look special.

'Whose birthday is it?' Tommy asked when he saw the candles.

'Nobody's,' Allison replied. 'But if you clean your plate today, you can make a wish and blow them out after lunch.'

As she was putting the meal on the table, Tom reappeared. He'd changed into some khakis and a white shirt.

'I'm feeling so much better I decided to dress for dinner,' he announced.

Karen frowned. 'It's not dinner, daddy, it's lunch.'

Tom waved a hand in the air. 'That's semantics, sweetie. Let's eat!'

GL♥SS

He hadn't just changed his clothes, Allison noticed. He'd shaved and combed his hair. Was that for me? she wondered. His eyes were less red too.

He's a nice-looking man, she thought as she served the casserole. And she wondered how old he was. Surely no more than thirty-five. Maybe as young as thirty-two. Which was only thirteen years older than she was. And widowed.

Good-looking, smart, nice . . . Pamela's advice came back to her. *Make Bobby jealous.* She pushed the words away, but they hovered in the back of her mind.

'Earth to Allison: come in, Allison.'

She looked at Tom blankly.

He smiled. 'I was asking you what you're majoring in at Radcliffe.'

'Oh, sorry! I haven't decided yet. Probably English.'

'You already speak English,' Karen pointed out. 'You could take French. Or Spanish.'

'When we say "English" like that, we mean English literature,' Allison told her.

'Literature,' Karen repeated. 'That's like books, right?'

'Exactly.'

Karen nodded and turned to her father. 'I'm going to major in English too.'

Tommy looked at Allison curiously. 'When you come to stay with us, who stays with *your* children?'

'I don't have any children,' Allison told him.

'How come?'

'Well . . . I'm not married.'

Tommy's brow furrowed. 'Daddy's not married and *he* has children.'

'He *used* to be married, dummy,' Karen said.

'No names at the table,' Allison reprimanded her. 'Or anywhere else, for that matter.'

'When you get married, are you going to have children?' Tommy asked.

'I might.'

'What kind of children?' he wanted to know. 'Boys or girls?'

'You know what I think?' Tom interjected. 'I'll bet she wants to have children just like you and Karen.'

Allison met his eyes and smiled. What was he really saying? she wondered. Was she reading too much into this?

'Yes,' she found herself saying. Her eyes darted between the two kids. 'Just like you.'

Chapter
Seventeen

'You know it's just a stupid game show,' Larry reminded Pamela as they turned on to West 67th Street.

'I don't care,' Pamela said. 'I've never seen a TV show in real life before. It's exciting!'

When Larry had learned that his furniture-polish client wanted him to be more familiar with the TV show they might sponsor, he'd wangled two 'privileged guest' tickets to a taping of the show. Pamela had happily told the temp agency she wouldn't be available today.

'I talked to my mother last night. She's thrilled. She wants to know when the show is going to be on.'

'I'll get the date,' Larry promised her.

'Do I look OK?' she asked anxiously.

'Better than OK. You're gorgeous as usual. But what are you worried about? You're not going to be on TV, you're just going to be in the audience.'

'Have you ever actually *seen What's That They Say?* The camera pans the audience sometimes.'

Larry smiled at her. 'Maybe some important movie maker will be watching. He'll spot you in the audience and think, She could be my next star!'

Pamela sighed. 'If only.'

'Well, you never know, Pammy. You'd definitely stand out in a crowd.'

She looked at him fondly. She didn't even mind him calling her 'Pam' or 'Pammy' any more. He was so sweet, and he so obviously adored her. He was generous, he treated her like a princess and he could make her laugh.

He had nice friends too, and he seemed proud to introduce her to them. They were all pleasant, regular people, down-to-earth and friendly.

If only he was more, more . . . *something*. More handsome, rich, famous – something. Still, she was ashamed when she recalled telling Allison he was better than nothing. Larry was better than – well, any other ordinary nice guy.

When they arrived at the television studio building, there was a long line of people, mostly women, waiting at the door. They were all clutching tickets for *What's That They Say?* and talking excitedly.

'Wait here,' Larry instructed her, and hurried to the front of the line. Seconds later, he came back and beckoned to her.

'We're privileged guests, remember?' he said, and they proceeded to the entrance while the people standing on line gaped at them.

'They think we're famous,' Pamela whispered, and she loved that.

At the door they were met by a uniformed man, who ushered them inside and then down a long corridor, where he opened double doors. Pamela recognized the set of the game show – the podium where the host always stood, the counter behind which the four contestants sat, the board where the words appeared, and the area covered by a gold curtain. Behind the curtain were the prizes the contestants could win.

They were led down to their seats – third row, in the centre.

'I could put you up closer,' the usher confided, 'but then you'd have to lean back and look up to see. These are really the best seats.'

'These will be fine,' Larry assured him.

Pamela admired the way he spoke so confidently to the usher. For an ordinary guy, Larry could actually be pretty classy.

The other audience members were coming in now, all giggling and yakking in shrill voices, so obviously thrilled to be here. Then, just in front of her, a woman wearing a huge flowered hat sat down.

'Oh no,' Pamela moaned.

Larry quickly assessed the situation. He leaned forward and tapped the woman lightly on the shoulder.

'Excuse me, ma'am, your hat is beautiful, but would you mind removing it?' he asked sweetly. 'My girlfriend can't see.'

'Of course,' the woman said, and took off the hat.

Again Pamela was impressed by how smooth he was. But something else in his words stood out.

He'd referred to her as his girlfriend.

It occurred to her that no one had ever called her that before. She'd been a date, of course. And for a brief time last summer she was a lover. But a girlfriend? It sounded so permanent. She wasn't sure how she felt about that.

The lights in the theatre dimmed, and a man she'd never seen before came out on the stage.

'Hello, folks, I'm Joe, and I'm here to warm you up!' He proceeded to tell some very corny jokes. Pamela and Larry rolled eyes at each other, but the less sophisticated people in the audience actually laughed. Finally, when the man must have figured they were appropriately warmed, he announced, 'And now, ladies and gentlemen, the star of the show, your host, Dominic Dupont!'

That got the audience shrieking and clapping wildly. Even Pamela had to admit she'd been looking forward to seeing the game-show host. On TV he always looked very dapper and refined, but not so much in person, she thought. Sitting so close, she could see how much shorter he was than he appeared on TV, how thick the make-up had been applied to his face. And that glossy brown wavy hair – it looked too perfect.

Larry must have read her mind. 'It's a toupee,' he whispered.

GL♥SS

Dominick Dupont waved to the audience, and then the warm-up guy yelled, 'And here she is, America's game-show sweetheart, Tippy Turner!'

Larry leaned towards her. 'Does everyone in show business have alliterative names? Or just on game shows?'

She smiled, and made a mental memo to find out what 'alliterative' meant later. That was something else she had to admire about Larry – he was smart.

The blonde bombshell who came on to the stage *did* look as good as she looked on TV, with her curvy figure and masses of platinum hair. Pamela would have killed for the dress she was wearing – a long baby-blue gown covered in sparkling rhinestones. How wonderful to be able to dress like that in the middle of the afternoon, she thought.

The applause from the audience was almost as deafening as the applause that had greeted the host. As it died down Pamela murmured, 'She's so pretty!'

'Are you kidding?' Larry asked.

'You don't think she's pretty?'

'Not when I'm sitting next to the most beautiful girl in the world.'

How amazing, she thought. Other guys would say a line like that, and you knew they were only trying to get into your pants. Larry sounded sincere.

But as her eyes moved from the fabulous dress to the woman's face, she realized that maybe she wasn't so gorgeous. Her nose was a little long, Pamela decided. And her lips were very thin. She could even see how the make-up artist must have used a lining pencil to make them look more full. Pamela wouldn't have needed that. And if *she* had a professional fussing with her hair every day, hers would look just as good.

She couldn't help noticing that Tippy was wobbling in her stilettos, and she even seemed to be swaying a bit. She staggered over to the host and clutched the podium as if to steady herself.

'Hi, everyone!' she called out in her famous squeaky voice.

Dominick Dupont looked at her with some alarm. He left the podium and spoke to someone off to the side. Then he shrugged and returned to his post. Tippy Turner left the podium and lurched back offstage. The host nodded to someone, and the lights went down on the audience and up on the stage.

From somewhere unseen, a voice boomed out.

'Ladies and gentlemen – what's that they say?'

The familiar theme song played, and a spotlight hit the host.

'Hello, folks, Dominick Dupont here, and welcome to the show. This is how we play the game.'

Pamela didn't have to listen to the explanation; she knew the rules. A famous saying or proverb would appear on the board with most of the letters missing. Contestants started off with a certain number of points. They had to guess what the words were, and whenever they guessed wrong, they lost points. The first to guess the saying correctly won the game. After all three games, the scores were tallied, and there were first place, second place, and third place winners.

'Let's meet our contestants. First, all the way from Chicago, Illinois – Kathleen Prendergast! Hi, Kathleen, good to see you. Tell us, what do you do in Chicago?'

'I'm a librarian, Dominick.'

'A librarian! I guess that means you read a lot. Which means you must know a lot of famous sayings!'

'Why yes, Dominick, I believe I do.'

'And here's our next contestant, from Maplewood, New Jersey – Leo Chapman!'

It went on like this, with the host exchanging a word or two with each of the four contestants.

'Now, let's play What's That They Say?!'

Some letters and blanks went up on the board, and the game began.

Pamela wondered if maybe she should apply to be a contestant. The first one was easy – 'An apple a day keeps the doctor away ' – and she figured it out even before the librarian did.

After the first game Dominick said, 'Let's take a look at what our contestants can win today. Tippy, will you show the folks at home the prizes?'

Tippy tottered back out on stage and tugged on a

rope. Part of the gold curtain fell. revealing an upright clock.

'For our third-place winner, an authentic replica of an antique grandfather clock!' the host declared, and Tippy pointed to it.

'For our second-place winner . . .'

Tippy had remained by the clock, staring at it as if she'd never seen one before.

'Um, Tippy, would you draw the second curtain?'

Tippy giggled and minced over to the next rope.

'A combination washer and dryer!' the host bellowed.

Standing by the machine, Tippy lifted the lid of it. Then she let it drop, and it made a resounding bang. The audience tittered, and Pamela could see the host's lips tighten.

Tippy made her way to the third rope.

'And for our first-prize winner . . .'

Tippy pulled the rope.

'A complete three-piece living-room suite!'

It actually looked pretty nice, Pamela thought – a sofa and two easy chairs. Tippy tripped over to one of the chairs and sank into it.

'Ooh, it's comfy!' she squealed. And she started bouncing up and down.

Now Dominick Dupont was grimacing.

'I don't think she's supposed to do that,' Pamela whispered to Larry.

GL♥SS

'*I* think she's loaded,' Larry whispered back. 'And my client won't like that.'

'It's just a taping; they won't show it on the air,' Pamela said.

Sure enough, someone yelled, 'Cut!'

Some people went up on the stage, conferred in hushed voices and one of them led Tippy off. The show started up again.

The second famous saying was 'Every cloud has a silver lining', and the third was 'A stitch in time saves nine'. The librarian from Chicago won all three rounds. She cried, she got a hug from Dominick Dupont, and the show was over.

The audience began leaving.

'I have to talk to the producer,' Larry said. Pamela walked with him over to a harried-looking man.

'Hi, Larry Taylor from Crain, Livingstone and Blackwell. This is—'

But before he could introduce Pamela, the man spoke. 'Yes, I heard you were coming. We have to talk,' and he pulled Larry aside. Larry shot Pamela an apologetic look, and she smiled back and shrugged. Then she wandered over to the other side of the set, near the display of prizes, where Dominick Dupont was talking to another man. Maybe she could get his autograph for her mother.

'I'm telling you, she's a disaster!' the host was saying. 'I can't work with her! I don't care if she's

"America's Game-Show Sweetheart" – it's her or me!'
And he stalked away.

The man left behind muttered a four-letter word under his breath.

'Oh dear,' Pamela said.

He turned and looked at her sharply. 'Who the hell are you?'

'I'm Pamela Mackle. I'm a privileged guest.'

The man immediately adjusted his expression. 'Oh, how do you do? I'm Bret Styles, the director. How did you like the show?'

'Very much,' she said. 'It's a shame about Tippy Turner though.'

The man looked uneasy. 'What do you mean?'

Pamela affected a look of sincere reluctance. 'Well, I shouldn't really say . . .'

'No, tell me what you think,' the man said.

Pamela looked to the right, then to the left, as if to make sure no one was nearby. Then she lowered her voice and moved in closer to Bret Styles.

'It seemed like she'd been drinking.'

The man groaned. 'It was that obvious, huh?'

Pamela nodded solemnly. 'It was the way she moved. Like when she pointed at the grandfather clock. I think she should have done it more like this.' And she waved her arm gracefully towards it, curving her hand delicately, like a ballerina. Thank goodness she'd polished her nails that morning.

'Yeah, exactly,' Bret Styles said.

'And I would have shown the furniture suite like this,' she continued. She strolled over to the sofa, and she could practically feel him watching her hips in action. She stroked the arm of the sofa, and slightly closed her eyes as if overcome by the feel of the fabric.

'Very nice!' the man declared.

'Thank you, Mr Styles.'

'Call me Bret.'

She smiled and went into one of her best moves – cocking her head to one side and giving him a sidelong look.

He was impressed, she could tell. 'And what do *you* do, young lady?'

'Well, at the moment . . .' she hesitated. 'Secretary' sounded so bland. 'I'm in fashion.' It wasn't really a lie – she was currently typing at a fashion magazine.

He nodded with approval. 'Yes, I can believe that. You've got the look. You're a model?'

She didn't answer that. 'But what I'd really like to do is get into television.' She hit him with another sidelong look.

'Really?' He moved in closer, and she recognized the expression on his face. If they weren't in a room with other people, she'd have been a little nervous.

'Maybe I could help you with that,' he said in a very suggestive voice. He gave her body the once-over, and his eyes settled on her chest. 'Are those real?'

'What do *you* think?' she asked.

He reached out, and he would have touched her if Larry hadn't suddenly appeared by their side.

'Hey, what do you think you're doing?'

Bret Styles glanced at him. 'Back off, pal.'

'No, *you* back off!'

Pamela gasped as Larry actually shoved the man so hard he fell down. The producer came running over.

'What's going on here?'

'This jerk was making a pass at my girlfriend,' Larry declared.

The producer glared angrily at the man on the floor, and then turned to Larry. 'I'm so sorry. He can be a little pushy. I hope this won't be a problem for the sponsorship.'

'We'll be in touch,' Larry said stiffly. He put a hand on Pamela's arm. 'Let's go.'

And she gazed at him in utter confusion as they walked towards the exit. Had Larry really defended her honour? That was so romantic.

But on the other hand – had he blown her chance of a job in television?

Chapter Eighteen

With her elbows on her desk and her chin cupped in her hands, Sherry looked up to see her boss standing in the doorway to her office.

'Daydreaming?' Caroline asked with a smile.

Sherry smiled back. 'I call it thinking.'

'Same difference,' Caroline said. 'How's the civil-rights piece coming along? What's your angle, by the way? Can white and Negro people work together?'

'That's the general idea,' Sherry said. 'But I want to go beyond that. I want to stress how important this is; I want to encourage readers to get involved.' She paused. 'Or would that be too controversial? I know our policy is not to take political stands. And there are Southern readers who could take offence.'

Caroline looked at her steadily. 'Well, that's just too bad if they do. It's the law now.'

Sherry nodded. 'That's what I think too.'

'Good luck,' Caroline said, and moved on to her office.

Sherry really had been thinking about the article – sort of. Last night she'd gone to another meeting at Columbia, a planning session for the upcoming Wall

Street demonstration. This time she'd been more comfortable there. She knew people, and they'd welcomed her, which made others there seem to accept her. Even though she wasn't a student, and even though she was from the South.

They'd all talked about making flyers, getting them distributed, designing signs to be carried on the march, establishing the time, the route . . . there were a million things to be worked out and jobs to be assigned. Some were boring details, but she enjoyed every minute of the discussion, of just being with all these interesting, smart, caring people.

But one particular person dominated her thoughts. William – was his intensity, his passion for the cause, so much more intriguing than anyone else's? Or was there another reason why she couldn't stop seeing him in her mind?

Resolutely she pushed him out of her head. She shouldn't even be thinking about him. It was . . . unseemly. That was what Mama would say.

'Hi. Am I disturbing you?'

Now Gloria was standing in her doorway, and she was holding the newspaper.

'No, not at all,' Sherry said uneasily. For the past week the coldness hadn't lifted. But now she thought she saw emotion in the secretary's face. And it was definitely in her voice when she spoke again.

'They found the bodies.'

She lay the paper on Sherry's desk. There they were again – the three missing civil-rights workers. Only this time the story was different.

The bodies of Michael Schwermer, Andrew Goodman and James Chaney were found buried in a dam near Philadelphia, Mississippi . . .

The news didn't come as a surprise. The three hadn't been seen for almost six weeks. But even so, having the worst fears confirmed was a blow.

Gloria saved her from having to read the entire article. 'Some Ku Klux Klan guy gave the authorities information in exchange for immunity.'

'So the police know who killed them?'

Gloria nodded. 'But no one's been arrested.'

That didn't surprise Sherry either. But the awfulness of this was overwhelming. Three young men, in the prime of life, murdered for doing the right thing. Trying to make the world a better place. And their killers wouldn't even be punished.

Her eyes burned with unshed tears. Or maybe she was shedding them, because Gloria came closer and spoke.

'You really care, don't you?'

'Of course I care!' Sherry exclaimed. 'Look, I know where I come from, but that doesn't define me!'

'I know,' Gloria said. 'William . . . He says you're OK.'

OK. William thinks I'm OK. That was something, she supposed.

From her desk, she could see Caroline out in the bullpen, clearly looking for her secretary.

'We're in here,' Sherry called out.

Caroline came to the door, and she must have been able to see from their faces that something was wrong.

'What's going on?' she asked.

The phone on Gloria's desk started ringing, and she ran out to answer it. Which left Sherry to tell Caroline the news about the civil-rights workers.

Caroline sighed deeply, closed her eyes for a moment and shook her head.

'Well. That puts *my* bad news in perspective.'

'What's your bad news?'

Caroline had a magazine in her hand, and she put it on Sherry's desk. 'This came out today.'

It was the August edition of *Modern Girl*. And on the front cover, with its list of feature articles, were the words: 'The Beatles: Fab or Fad?'

'That's *our* title!' Sherry cried out. 'I came up with that!'

'I know,' Caroline said. 'At least there's time for me to alert the writer to change it.'

'This is too weird,' Sherry declared. 'First, they get Dr Naomi Cutler before I can reach her. Now they've got my title . . .'

'That's not all,' Caroline said. 'Turn to the last page.'

Sherry did. Then she drew in her breath so hard and fast that her gasp became a soft shriek. Right there, under the heading 'Coming next month in *Modern Girl*': 'Can White and Negro Teenagers Work Together for Civil Rights?' It was the third feature listed, after 'What to Wear This Fall' and 'How to Flatten Your Tummy in 10 Minutes a Day.'

'I can't believe it!' Sherry moaned.

'Neither can I,' Caroline said flatly.

'But how could this happen?' Sherry wondered. 'Another coincidence?'

Caroline's expression was grim. 'There have been just too many coincidences as far as I'm concerned. Sherry . . . I think there's a spy in our midst.'

'A *spy*?'

'Someone's telling *Modern Girl* about our plans.'

'But *why*?'

'I don't know. Maybe they're getting paid for information.' Then she shook her head. 'I doubt that though. *Modern Girl* may be our competition, but it's run by professionals. I can't imagine anyone there would be into bribery. No, it has to be someone with a vested interest in *Modern Girl*. Or who's got a problem with *Gloss*.'

'You mean, someone who wants revenge?' Sherry considered this. 'Has anyone been fired lately?'

'No. But listen, Sherry – I want you to think about who you've talked to about our forthcoming articles. Consider whether any of them might want to hurt us.'

'I will,' Sherry promised.

'Meanwhile, I still want you to write our article about civil rights. Just try to come up with a different angle, or a twist on the subject.'

'I think I've already got one,' Sherry told her. She tapped her finger on the *Modern Girl* page. 'This article asks if white and negro teens can work together. Well, I already know they can. What I'd like to suggest is that it's not a question of "can", it's "should", and the answer is yes. Because it's not simply a question of helping Negroes get their rights. It's for everyone; it's for the common good.'

'Equality. It will make the world a better place for all of us.'

'Exactly.'

She got the nod of approval from Caroline.

All morning Sherry worked furiously. Scribbling pages and pages of notes, she was unaware of time passing and didn't even take her usual coffee break. It wasn't until she heard a familiar voice out in the bullpen that she was distracted.

She got up and walked out to Gloria's desk, where William was standing.

'Hi.'

He smiled, and it was a *real* smile, a glad-to-see-you smile. 'Hi, how are you?'

'OK. Sad though, about the news.'

She didn't have to tell him what news she was referring to.

'Yeah. It's bad.'

Gloria picked up her handbag. 'We're going to lunch.' She looked at her brother with a question in her eyes. It must have been silently answered, because she turned to Sherry. 'Would you like to join us?'

'I'd love to!' Did she sound just a little too enthusiastic? She didn't care, and she hurried back into her office to grab her bag.

Outside the Hartnell Building, Gloria asked, 'What do you want? Burgers? A sandwich?'

Sherry and William looked at each other and responded in unison. 'Pizza.'

Gloria rolled her eyes. 'Oh, Sherry, not you too! It's all my brother ever wants to eat.'

Sherry smiled happily. She liked very much the fact that she and William had something in common. Even if it only involved dough, tomato sauce and cheese.

'There's a little place a couple of blocks from here,' William said.

Gloria gave in, and in a few minutes they found themselves in a cute, cosy Italian restaurant, the kind with red-checked tablecloths and candles stuck in bottles with wax dripping down the sides. They found a little table by a window. The waitress appeared, and they ordered a large pizza to share.

'That was a good meeting last night,' Sherry remarked.

'What happened?' Gloria asked.

William recounted the discussions, and Gloria listened with interest.

'Why don't you come to the meetings?' Sherry asked her.

Gloria hesitated for a minute before responding. 'I'm taking night classes. In accounting.'

'Wow,' Sherry commented. 'You work all day and you go to school at night? That's impressive.'

Gloria smiled. 'It's exhausting. But listen, Sherry . . . I'd appreciate it if you wouldn't mention this in the office.'

'Why not?'

Gloria and William exchanged glances before Gloria went on. 'People might think I'm trying to rise above myself.'

Sherry was puzzled. 'I don't understand.'

'Come on, Sherry,' William remonstrated. 'You know there are people who think we should know our place. What do they call us down South? Uppity Negroes? Only they use a different word that begins with the letter 'n'.'

Sherry knew the word he was referring to. And she knew people back home who used it.

'But here, in New York? At *Gloss*?'

'The South doesn't have a monopoly on racism,' William said.

Sherry considered this. 'It's a question of roles, isn't it? And expectations.'

Gloria nodded. 'We're supposed to be maids, janitors. Not accountants.'

'Or lawyers, or doctors,' William added. 'I should be shining shoes, not attending an Ivy League university.'

'According to some, I should be thrilled to have my job as a secretary,' Gloria told her. 'Do you know how many secretaries work for Hartnell Publications? One hundred and twenty-four. Do you know how many are not white? Twelve.'

Sherry nodded. She understood, maybe even better than they thought she would. She knew what it was like to have a role you were supposed to play. Of course, for her, rebellion was easier . . .

The waitress reappeared with their pizza, and the conversation shifted to something else.

'What do you think?' William asked. 'As good as Gino's?'

'Almost,' Sherry conceded. 'I needed this. It's been a rough morning.'

'I heard about the Beatles article,' Gloria commented. 'That's awful.'

'What are you talking about?' William asked.

'Another magazine came out today with an article that has the same title we were planning to use,' Sherry told him.

'Did you already write the article?'

'Oh no, I'm not writing it. I just came up with the

title. I've only written a handful of small pieces for the magazine.'

'I remember that little article you wrote about the Miss Teen Georgia pageant,' Gloria commented. 'I liked that.'

William shook his head in exasperation. 'I still can't believe you actually watch the Miss America pageant.'

Sherry laughed. 'So do I. I know it's stupid, but it's fun. I can never decide which talent I like best – the baton twirlers or the ventriloquists.'

Now Gloria was laughing too. 'My friends and I used to make mock ballots and take bets on who would win.'

'We did that too!'

But William was still shaking his head. 'I've never watched, but I can't imagine there's much variety among the contestants' colour.'

'True,' Gloria admitted. 'I can't say I could ever relate to any of them.'

'Times are changing,' Sherry declared. 'Who knows? Maybe in the not-too-distant future, we'll see a Negro Miss America.'

William snorted. 'I think we can aim a little higher than that.'

'OK,' Sherry said. 'How about a Negro President?'

'Let's not get delusional,' William muttered.

'Getting back to the Beatles,' Gloria said. 'Do you really think there could be a spy at *Gloss*?'

'I don't know,' Sherry replied. 'It could be, I suppose. Like Caroline said, there have been a lot of coincidences. *Modern Girl* has an article about civil rights coming next month.'

'What's wrong with that?' William asked.

'Nothing,' Sherry said. 'Except that they're taking the same approach I've been planning – how white and Negro young people are working together.'

William put down the last bit of pizza that he had been about to pop into his mouth and looked at her strangely.

'You're writing this article?'

Sherry nodded happily. 'I came up with the idea and Caroline's letting me write it. It will be my first feature article, and . . .' She stopped. William's expression had changed. He looked *angry*.

'What's the matter?' she asked.

'So that's why you got involved with us. To get information for your story.'

'No, not exactly, but . . .'

Now he was shaking his head in disbelief. 'Boy, did I have you wrong!' Suddenly he stood up, reached in his pocket and took out some bills that he threw on the table. And walked out of the restaurant.

'What . . . ?' Sherry stared after him and then looked at Gloria. She shrugged.

Sherry jumped up and ran out after him.

'Wait!' she called. 'William, wait!'

He stopped, turned and let her catch up. But his expression had gone beyond anger now. He was clearly furious.

'I should have known,' he said.

'You should have known *what*?'

'That you had ulterior motives. That you weren't to be trusted.'

She was utterly and totally bewildered. 'I don't understand.'

'Why would a pretty little white girl from the Deep South suddenly feel the need to fight for civil rights? You really had me fooled, you know. I believed you cared.'

'But I *do* care!' she cried out.

'Sure you do,' he snapped. 'You care about writing an article, getting your name in print. Making your reputation in journalism on our backs. Using our cause to get a story!'

'That is not true! Don't you think I want to change the world too?'

He uttered a short, humourless laugh. 'Right. You want to change the world that you control.'

'That *I* control?' Now she could feel the anger rising in *her*. 'You think a girl like me controls anything? You don't know anything about me! You don't know the rules I'm supposed to follow, the expectations—'

He snickered again. 'You're asking me to feel sorry for you?'

'No, I'm asking you not to put me in a box. Yes, I'm white, yes, I'm from Georgia, but that doesn't tell you everything about me! Can't you see me as an individual?'

She hadn't realized how her voice had risen, until a man, some passing stranger, paused and spoke.

'Lady, is this fellow bothering you?' He looked at William with blatant hostility.

'No, he's my friend! We're having a discussion.'

The man shrugged, shot William one more suspicious look and moved on.

William's lips tightened. Then he started to walk away.

'Don't turn your back on me!' she yelled.

More passers-by glanced in their direction. She ignored them and grabbed William's arm. He turned back, and now he looked surprised.

She couldn't blame him. She was surprised at herself. This wasn't like her, to make a scene, to be so aggressive. But she couldn't stop herself; it was as if some demon inside her had killed all inhibitions.

At least she managed to lower her voice. 'And yes, if you want to know the truth, I did have an ulterior motive. Not what you think though.'

'Yeah? What was it?'

'You. I wanted to know *you*.'

And then it was as if some magnetic force took hold

of them both, pulling them closer together. He looked down, she looked up. And their lips met.

And their lips met.

She had no idea how long it lasted. Time seemed to stand still. And she wasn't sure who backed away first. But then they were both staring at each other, and she knew his expression reflected her own. They were both stunned.

Then, abruptly, he turned and walked rapidly away.

For a moment Sherry stood there, frozen. She watched William's retreating figure. He didn't look back, and then he disappeared in the distance. Finally she started back towards the restaurant.

Gloria was standing outside, holding Sherry's handbag as well as her own. When Sherry reached her, Gloria didn't say a word. She didn't have to. Clearly she had seen what had just transpired, and her reaction was written across her face. Disbelief. Shock. Maybe even horror.

Silently she held out Sherry's bag, and Sherry took it. Then she looked up and met Gloria's eyes. Gloria shook her head.

'We should be getting back to the office,' Sherry murmured.

Gloria gazed at her steadily and eventually spoke. 'I have errands to run.'

Sherry watched her go, and wondered if that was

GL♥SS

true, or if Gloria wanted an excuse not to walk back with her. To avoid making conversation about what she'd seen. In a way, Sherry was relieved. She wouldn't know what to say either.

Back at *Gloss*, she could feel her face burning and her body trembling. Nobody else seemed to notice, but even so, she was glad to be in her own office. And this time she made sure to close the door.

As usual, this being August, the air conditioning was on full blast, but she was still hot; she could feel the perspiration on her forehead. From somewhere she heard her mother's voice . . . *Southern girls don't sweat, Sherry, they glow.*

No, this was sweat, pure and simple. She went into her bag and searched for tissues. She found them, and something else too. Maybe this was why she'd heard her mother's voice. She took out the sealed letter from Mama that she'd received at home that morning.

Tearing open the envelope, she extracted the familiar delicate sheets of pale blue stationery.

Hey, honey, hope everything goes well for you. We're just dandy here. Your little sister had her first date this weekend! Of course Daddy thinks she's too young to be going out with a boy, but Beth is thirteen now, and as I recall, wasn't that when you first went out with Johnny?

Sherry sighed. Mama could never resist an opportunity to mention her high school sweetheart.

She couldn't give up the hope that Sherry would get back together with him.

Most of the letter contained the usual chit-chat – a movie her parents had seen, a new recipe she'd tried and how everyone in her bridge club had raved about it, her plans to re-cover the sofa in the den.

And now, some BIG news! Daddy and I are coming to New York! We've decided it's about time we saw how our little girl is living in the Big Apple. Now, don't you worry, we're not about to cramp your style! We'll stay at a hotel. But we just can't wait to meet your roommate and all your friends and get a real first-hand look at what you've been up to!

Like kissing a Negro man on the street? Sherry shuddered.

She took out her pocket calendar and jotted down the dates. Then the phone on her desk rang. William . . . ?

'Hello?'

'Hi, it's me.'

She tried not to reveal any disappointment in her voice. 'Hi, Donna.'

'I wanted to tell you – I'm at a shoot downtown with David, so I won't stop by for you. I'll meet you guys at Charlie's.'

She'd completely forgotten. They'd organized this a couple of days ago – the four former interns were meeting for a drink after work at the bar across the street. Maybe that was a good thing. She could tell them about what happened to her today. Or maybe not. It wasn't so much that she was worried about their reaction. It was the retelling that would be hard. Right now, it all seemed so unreal. Maybe it was better to keep it that way.

On her desk she found a stack of articles Caroline had left with a note, asking her to proofread them. She was pleased – proofreading was something that required concentration. She needed to keep busy.

She skipped her coffee break again, and only left her office once that afternoon, to use the restroom. Gloria looked up as she passed. Then she looked away.

She concentrated on her work, grateful for something that kept her from daydreaming, and the next time she looked at her watch, it was after five. By the time she'd straightened up her desk and left the office everyone in the bullpen – including Gloria – had left.

When she arrived at Charlie's the others were already there in a booth, and their drinks were being served.

'And a Coke for our friend, please,' Allison told the waiter as Sherry joined them.

'No, I think I'll have a real drink,' Sherry said. 'Um . . . a gin and tonic, please.'

The others looked at her in surprise, and Sherry gave them a nonchalant shrug. 'I need it today.'

'Ooh, does that mean you've got a story to tell?' Pamela chirped.

'Just a headache,' Sherry murmured, which was actually the truth.

Pamela didn't hear her. 'Well, you'll have to wait till I've finished mine. So, get this, girls. Larry hauls off and slugs the man!'

Donna gasped. 'He actually hit the director? Right there in the studio?'

Pamela nodded. 'Well, it was actually more of a push. But the guy fell down!'

'That's so romantic!' Allison exclaimed.

'Very manly,' Pamela added happily.

'What is she talking about?' Sherry asked Donna.

Donna brought her up to date with the story of how Larry had taken her to a game-show taping where the director had made a pass at her.

'Wow, Larry must be crazy about you,' Sherry commented. 'How do you feel about him?'

'He's OK,' Pamela said carelessly. 'Well, better than OK. But this is what I'm really excited about. The girl who works on the show – she's terrible. I could do that job! All you have to do is look beautiful and point to prizes!'

'You could do that,' Sherry agreed. The waiter returned with her drink. She took a sip and tried not to make a face.

'OK, your turn, Sherry,' Pamela declared.

'No, someone else go next,' Sherry said. She was going to have to choke down this whole drink before she'd have the courage to talk.

Pamela turned to Donna. 'You're seeing someone, right?'

Donna looked about as eager to talk as Sherry.

'Er . . . yes. His name's Jack.'

'And . . . ?' Pamela prodded.

'He's nice,' Donna said.

Pamela and Allison looked at her in exasperation. 'Come on,' Allison said. 'Give us more than that!'

'He's *very* nice,' Donna said lamely. 'OK, this is the deal. He's from a kind of high-class family. And he doesn't know about me.'

Pamela and Allison looked sympathetic.

'Hasn't he asked?' Pamela wanted to know.

Now Donna looked nervous. 'Yes, but . . . I change the subject.'

'Well, it's going to come out sooner or later,' Allison said. 'You should just tell him.'

Pamela agreed. 'If he really loves you, it won't make a difference.'

Sherry noticed with some surprise that she'd managed to finish her gin and tonic. She broke into the conversation.

'Y'all want another drink?'

Allison grinned. '*Y'all.* I can't believe you still use that word.'

Sherry managed a small smile. 'Well, like I told you before, you can take a girl out of the South, but you can't take the South out of the girl.' She waved to the waiter.

Was that really true? she wondered, after he had taken their orders. Was this why she felt so completely lost and confused? Because she was a girl from the South, and a nice Southern girl didn't fall in love with a Negro man?

That small pain in her head began to pound.

Now Allison was talking, bringing them up to date on her situation with Bobby. Something about how he was fooling around with his co-star. Her words seemed to be floating over Sherry's head.

The waiter placed their drinks on the table, and this time Sherry didn't sip. She took a long gulp. For medicinal purposes. There were aspirins in her bag, but she thought this would ease the pain more quickly.

Vaguely she was aware that Pamela was talking now. Complaining about her job this time . . .

'. . . and believe me, *Modern Girl* is even more boring than *Gloss* . . .'

Somehow the words penetrated her brain, and Sherry looked up sharply. *Gloss* . . . *Modern Girl* . . . Pamela had worked at both since she'd been in New York.

'Can we get the check?' Donna asked. 'I have to go

home and change. And before you ask, yes, I've got a date with Jack tonight.'

'And, yes, you're going to tell him about your past,' Allison said.

'Maybe,' Donna said lightly.

Sherry moved out of the booth to let Donna pass. 'Can I borrow your red clutch bag?' Donna asked.

'Sure,' Sherry said, not really hearing her. Her mind was on Pamela. Hadn't Sherry told her about the articles she was working on during a coffee break together?

A few moments later, Allison announced she had to leave. 'Gotta babysit my kids tonight,' she said. 'Their father has a meeting. I want to get there early so I can chat with him.'

'Why?' Pamela asked.

'Oh, he's interesting. See you guys.'

Now it was just Sherry and Pamela, alone. And Sherry's mind was suddenly racing. Pamela . . . she loved drama and gossip. She loved being in the know. She loved feeling important.

'Why are you looking at me like that?' Pamela asked.

'It was you,' Sherry blurted out.

'What was me?'

'You told someone at *Modern Girl* about the stories I was working on.'

It dawned on her that she was having a hard time

focusing on Pamela's face across the table, but she could imagine the guilty look.

'What are you talking about?'

'You told someone we wanted to set up an interview with Dr Naomi Cutler.'

'Who?'

'And the Beatles article – you gave them my title.'

'Sherry, I don't know what you're talking about.'

'And my civil-rights story . . . It had to be you, there's no one else! You're the spy. You gave them my ideas!'

'Are you crazy? I don't even remember you telling me about your stories.'

'What did you get for the information, Pamela? A dress from their samples closet? You sold me out, didn't you? Don't deny it!'

'I can't believe you're accusing me of–'

But Sherry wouldn't let her finish.

'I told you stuff in confidence, and you just went on your merry little way and blabbed everything to the competition. Do you realize what you've done to me?'

'No. But I realize I don't have to sit here and listen to this.' Pamela slid out of the booth. 'I don't know what's gotten into you, Sherry, but when you're normal again, call me. No, I take that back. Call me when you're ready to apologize.'

Alone in the booth, Sherry picked up her drink

and saw that the glass was empty again. The waiter reappeared.

'Can I get you something?'

Sherry thought about this. Nice Southern girls didn't sit drinking alone in bars. She touched her glass and looked up at the waiter.

'Yes. I'll have another.'

Chapter Nineteen

At the children's playground in Central Park, Allison sat on one of the benches where all the nannies were sitting. She didn't know any of them, though she recognized a couple from previous visits to the playground, and they would always nod and smile at each other. Most of them were chatting to each other in Spanish, so she couldn't join in any of the conversations. Which was OK with her – she was content to just sit there in the sunshine, watch the children and think her own thoughts.

She hadn't seen Bobby in well over a week. He'd called of course. Many times, in fact.

Allison wished there was some way of knowing who was calling when a phone rang. But since there wasn't, she always had to answer. The call could be from a friend, her parents, Tom Markham . . . someone who would worry if she didn't respond. So she'd been forced to speak with Bobby, but she'd kept it brief. Each time she made an excuse – she was just leaving the apartment, she was late for an appointment, she had visitors and couldn't talk. She would promise to call him back. Lies, all of them.

And what she really wanted to say, to shriek,

was, 'You broke my heart, Bobby!'

Was he worried? she wondered. Did he realize she must have found out about him and Beverly? She didn't know, and she told herself she didn't care.

After the first few days it got easier. Tom Markham had joined some kind of political action group that was meeting almost every night, and he'd asked Allison to babysit. She didn't mind at all – she'd be making more money, and the job got her out of the apartment and away from the phone.

Plus there was the pleasure of having more time with Tom. When he came home from his meetings, they always had a cup of tea together and chatted about various things . . .

'Tommy, stop!' she yelled.

Tommy had seen some other child go down the slide head first, and he seemed determined to try this himself.

'I said *no*, remember? That's dangerous!'

Tommy pouted, but he proceeded to sit down at the top of the slide and go down normally.

Fortunately she didn't have to keep such an eagle eye on Karen, who was sitting on a swing and reading.

They were really great kids, she thought. Having never considered herself to be the maternal type, she was pleasantly surprised at how well she'd adapted to her role as nanny. She was beginning to suspect that her feelings towards Karen and Tommy were stronger than the ordinary feelings of a babysitter towards her charges – the two had found a real place in her heart. She could actually imagine herself mothering a pair like them. No, not *like* them. *Them.*

Was she crazy to be thinking this way? Maybe, maybe not. Her relationship with their father had certainly moved beyond nanny and employer. Not in a romantic way, but they'd become real friends, she believed. They had proper conversations, intense ones sometimes, and not just about the children. What he'd told her about his late wife – surely that was something he didn't share with just anyone.

He didn't treat Allison like a servant, or even like a teenager, a student. He talked to her like she was his peer, his equal. Yes, they were *friends*, there was no question about that. Friends of the opposite sex. And didn't all romances start off that way?

Plus, other than age, they were so suited to each other! They were both great readers, seriously into good literature, but at the same time harbouring a guilty passion for detective novels. They both loved old Hollywood movies, anything with Humphrey Bogart or Bette Davis or Joan Crawford. He even liked folk music, almost as much as she did. He'd gone to Harvard; she went to Radcliffe, Harvard's sister school. He loved his children, she was beginning to love them too . . .

A sudden cry from the playground ripped into her

GL♥SS

daydreams. Leaping up, she ran to the slide, where Bobby had finally succeeded in going down head first. And now lay wailing on the ground, with blood streaming down the side of his head.

She scooped him up in her arms. A nanny from the benches came running over with a clean cloth diaper in her hand. Allison took it and pressed it against the cut.

His wailing had actually drawn Karen away from her book. The little girl looked at the bloody cloth in horror.

'Is he going to die?'

'No!' Allison declared. 'Come on, we're taking him to the hospital.'

They hurried out of the park, and she was able to hail a taxi on Fifth Avenue. It was just a short ride to the hospital on Seventy-seventh Street. By the time they were inside the emergency room, Tommy's sobs had escalated to screams – which was actually no bad thing, since this got him seen by a nurse right away.

The nurse took one look, replaced the diaper with another cloth and announced that he would probably need stitches.

'Could you call his father for me?' Allison pleaded, and gave the nurse the Markham number. Thank goodness Tom had been planning to work at home all day.

She was holding Tommy's hand while the doctor

finished the stitching when Tom arrived. She left the treatment room so he could confer privately with the doctor. Moments later, he joined her and she explained what had happened.

At that point, her concerted efforts to remain calm in front of the children gave way, and she burst into tears. Tom wrapped his arms around her tightly.

'It's OK, it wasn't your fault,' he said. 'These things happen. Kids fall down. The doctor says there's no concussion, and the cut won't even leave a scar. You dealt with the situation perfectly, and Tommy's going to be fine.'

His words were comforting, his embrace even more so. She could have stayed in his arms longer, but he released her.

'Now, I want you to go home and relax,' he instructed her.

She fumbled in her bag for a tissue to wipe her eyes, and noticed the time on her watch.

'It's only four thirty,' she said.

'That's OK,' he said. 'I'll take the kids home.'

'Shall I come back tonight and babysit?' she asked.

'No, I'm going to stay home.' Then he smiled. 'I tell you what – why don't you come over for dinner?'

'For dinner?' she repeated stupidly.

'Yeah! I've been looking through that cookbook you bought. And if you're willing to take a risk and eat something I prepare . . .'

GL♥SS

'I'm willing,' she said.

'Great! Around eight?'

Walking home, she found herself feeling more cheerful than she'd felt for ages. Despite the fact that she was still upset about Tommy's accident, she was exhilarated by Tom's invitation. A dinner together – and if it was going to be at eight o'clock, that meant the children wouldn't be eating with them. It would be her and Tom, alone.

And that hug he gave her . . . It was meant to be comforting, but even so, she'd felt very nice pressed against his body like that. She knew she shouldn't read anything into it, but maybe it was a hint of things to come.

At the corner of Seventy-fifth, she passed a boutique that had a 'Sale' sign in the window, and on a sudden impulse, she went inside. Flipping through the rack, a sleeveless green dress with a full skirt caught her eye. From back when she was at *Gloss*, she remembered fashion articles that recommended the colour green for redheads. Since she rarely wore any colour besides black, she never paid much attention to the advice, but she took the dress off the rack and went into the dressing room to try it on.

She had to admit, the colour worked for her. She'd never worn a full-skirted dress before, but it made her boyish figure look curvier, more feminine. And it was on sale, fifty per cent off.

Paying for it at the counter, the salesgirl showed her a cute bangle bracelet with white and green stones. She bought that too.

She was swinging her shopping bag and smiling as she turned the corner on to Fifth Avenue, but the smile faded when she saw Bobby standing out in front of her building. He was a few feet away from the awning, where the doorman kept glancing at him suspiciously.

Bobby waved as she approached, but she didn't wave back. She didn't smile either.

'What are you doing here?' she asked. 'Aren't you filming?'

'I'm not in the scene they're shooting today,' he said.

'Oh. But you didn't answer my first question. What are you doing here?'

She could hear how aggressive she sounded, and she was almost pleased to see him take a small step back. 'I wanted to see you. I've been standing out here since five, so I could catch you when you came home from work. Allison, what the hell is going on?'

'Excuse me?' she asked.

'You won't talk to me on the phone, you don't return my calls. Why are you avoiding me?'

He looked so innocent, so concerned and perplexed, that she almost felt sorry for him. Almost.

'Oh, come on, Bobby. Did you really think I wouldn't find out?'

'Find out *what*?'

'For crying out loud, Bobby, the picture was in the paper!' She tried to recall the exact words of the caption. '"Bobby and Beverly, all cosy together, twisting the night away at the Peppermint Lounge."'

'Oh. That.'

'Yes. That.'

'It was a publicity thing! The press agent from the company called and asked me to take Beverly there. He knew there would be photographers at the disco, and he thought it would be good public relations, get people talking about the film. They do this kind of thing all the time, for publicity. It doesn't mean a thing. Like, you know all those pictures you see about Rock Hudson and his latest girlfriend? He's *gay*!'

'So that's showbiz, huh?'

'Exactly.'

'Oh, *please*. Bobby, I went to the set the next Monday. I saw you and Beverly filming in Chelsea.' She mimicked the scene. '"Oh, John, don't you hear the music of love?" . . . "Oh, Marcia, my darling, I hear it, I've been in love with you forever."'

Now he looked incredulous. 'Allison, that was in the script! I was acting!'

'You can't act, Bobby. You've said so yourself.'

'I'm getting better.' Bobby shook his head. 'Allison, there is absolutely nothing going on between me and Beverly.'

He *was* becoming a good actor. She could almost believe him. But she didn't.

He went on. 'You want another reason I came over here today? I have to go to a movie premiere tonight, some big spy flick. There's going to be a lot of press coverage, so the publicity guy told me to take Beverly. But I told him no, I wouldn't. Because I'm taking you.'

'You're taking me,' she repeated. He'd said it like it was a certainty.

'Yes. It's at Radio City Music Hall, at eight. So I'll pick you up at seven thirty, and we'll–'

She wouldn't let him finish. 'I'm busy tonight.'

'What?'

'I can't go to the premiere with you. I've got other plans. So why don't you just go ahead and make the press agent happy? And yourself too. Take Beverly.'

With that, she turned her back on him and went into the building.

Inside her apartment, she was relieved to find it empty. She was in no mood to talk.

So it was over between her and Bobby. They were finished. Just like that, in a five-minute conversation on the street. The enormity of it all was too much to contemplate – and she didn't have time to think about it anyway. She had well over an hour before she needed to leave for dinner, but suddenly there was a lot she wanted to do.

First she went into Pamela's room and pored through

her toiletry case. In her time working at *Modern Girl*, Pamela had managed to become the recipient of a multitude of beauty samples. Allison found a face masque that claimed it would make her radiant. A hair conditioner guaranteed an unbelievably brilliant shine. She gathered up all the creams and lotions. Pamela wouldn't mind – she was always telling Allison to help herself.

She raided Pamela's cosmetic bag too, and found a green eyeshadow that matched the dress. She also picked out some coral lipstick and a matching nail polish. While the masque rested on her face for the required fifteen minutes, she painted her fingernails. Of course, when she scrubbed off the masque, she smeared the nails. Then the stuff she put on her hair didn't make it shine at all – it looked greasy, so she had to wash it out, and then sit with the hair-drying bonnet on with the heat turned up full blast. Which only made her want another shower.

Maybe this was why girls spent so much time preening and fussing and messing about with their appearance, she thought as she reapplied nail polish. It kept you occupied, took your mind off thinking about other things.

She'd never spent so much time or concentrated so hard on her appearance. But all the preening and fussing did produce results, she thought as she examined her reflection in Pamela's full-length mirror. In her new dress, with her carefully applied make-up, she had to admit she looked very nice. She doused herself with Pamela's precious Chanel No. 5, and borrowed a little white clutch bag that would go with her own white ballerinas.

She left early and took her time walking back to the Markhams', not wanting to arrive all sweaty. And her efforts paid off – when Tom opened the door, he whistled.

'Well, don't you look lovely!'

'How's Tommy?' she asked as she came into the living room.

'He's fine. The doctor gave him something for the pain, and he conked out an hour ago. Karen's still reading in bed though, if you want to say goodnight.'

Karen looked up when Allison entered. 'I'm almost finished,' she said, showing Allison where she was in the book. 'But you know what? Sometimes I don't like to finish a book. Because then, you know . . . it's all over.'

'I know,' Allison said. 'It can be sad when something's all over. But there are lots more books to read.'

Karen nodded. 'Tommy's not going to die.'

'I know.'

'It's good you were there when he fell. You were just like a mother.'

Allison smiled. 'Thank you,' she said.

She heard the doorbell to the apartment ring. Had

Tom invited others tonight? Was he nervous about being alone with her? Or maybe his culinary efforts hadn't panned out, and this was the pizza delivery man.

She hugged Karen. Leaving the bedroom, she saw Tom emerge from the kitchen with a drink in his hand. As she passed the dining room, she saw that the table was set for three.

In the living room, he was handing the drink to a woman sitting on the sofa.

'Allison, I want you to meet Joan Lester. Now, Allison, what would you like to drink?'

'Just water, please.'

'Water coming up. *And* some appetizers!'

When he left the room, the woman smiled at Allison. 'I'm guessing the so-called appetizers will be potato chips with sour-cream-and-onion dip. What do you think?'

Allison smiled back. 'You're probably right. I don't think he's reached the level of pigs-in-blankets.' She sat down on a chair facing the sofa. 'Do you work with Tom?'

'No, I'm in real estate.'

Tom returned with Allison's water in one hand and a tray in the other. 'Ta-da!'

'Spinach dip!' Joan exclaimed. 'That's impressive, Tom.'

'I found the recipe in your cookbook, Allison,' he said.

Allison beamed. But her smile faded a bit when he sat down on the sofa, very close to Joan Lester.

'Tom tells me you're a wonderful nanny,' the woman said.

'Well, like I've told Tom, it's an easy job with children like Karen and Bobby. They're great kids.'

'I haven't met them yet,' Joan said, and gave Tom what Allison thought was a meaningful look.

'Actually, that's something I thought we could talk to Allison about,' he said. 'Allison, you've gotten really close to the kids. Maybe you could help us out.'

Allison was confused. 'Help you out? With what?'

'Well, Joan and I have been seeing each other for some time now. And . . .' he paused and took Joan's hand, 'it's getting serious. I'm worried about how the kids will react. Karen especially. She remembers her mother.'

'We were hoping you could help us prepare them,' Joan said.

'Prepare them?' She knew she was sounding like a parrot, repeating their words. But she was too taken aback to think of anything else to say.

'For the inevitable,' Tom said, and Joan punched him lightly on the shoulder with her free hand.

'That's a terrible way of putting it,' she said, laughing.

He grinned at her. Then he held up the hand he was holding, and Allison saw the sparkling

GL♥SS

solitaire diamond on her ring finger.

'You're engaged,' she said flatly.

The rest of the evening was a blur. Allison went through the motions, congratulating the couple, complimenting Joan on her ring, complimenting Tom on his beef stroganoff, making small talk. And even in the fog of disappointment that encircled her, the cloud of despair that planted itself firmly on her head, she saw it all – the way Tom's eyes followed Joan as she moved around, the special smiles he bestowed on her, which were nothing like the smiles he gave Allison. When he held out the chairs for the two women at the table, his hand caressed Joan's shoulder as she sat down.

She learned how they had met – through mutual friends – and how he'd suddenly become interested in her political leanings, to the point of joining her social-action group.

She really didn't want to know all the details of their romance, they didn't matter to her. All she knew was that on this one dreary day, not only had a relationship died, but so had a fantasy.

Somehow she made it through the evening, ending it with promises to help prepare the children for meeting Joan, and even a promise to come back to New York for the wedding in November.

She wanted to walk home, but it was late and Tom insisted on seeing her into a cab. He even gave the driver money for her ride. Allison protested weakly, but ultimately gave in. After all, this was what kind bosses did for their employees. And that's all she was to him – an employee.

At home, once again she was relieved to find the apartment empty so she wouldn't have to explain her mood to Pamela. She wasn't really sleepy yet, so she put the TV on, turning the channel dial in hope of landing on an old movie. She found nothing, and settled for the last ten minutes of the nightly news.

'And at Radio City Music Hall tonight, the stars came out for the premiere of *Darker Skies*, the new spy thriller.' The voice went on to name some of the celebrities seen walking up the red carpet to the entrance of the majestic theatre.

'And here come pop idol Bobby Dale and starlet Beverly Gray, who co-star in the upcoming release *Tangled Hearts*. And it looks like they may be co-starring in real life too!'

They certainly did, moving arm in arm, smiling at each other.

'And now, let's find out what tomorrow's weather is going to be like.'

Allison was dimly aware of a voice reciting highs and lows and the possibilities of precipitation. But she was too busy crying her heart out to listen.

GL♥SS

Chapter Twenty

It promised to be a quiet, uneventful day at work for Donna, and she appreciated that.

'We don't have any shoots scheduled,' David told her when she arrived at the office. 'I'm spending the day in plastic surgery.'

Donna knew what that meant. He'd be in the darkroom, retouching and airbrushing negatives. He would be taking out any visible dark shadows under the models' eyes, erasing any lines on their faces, removing any trace of a double chin. Upper arms would be slimmed, a large nose would be made smaller. It was amazing what a talented photographer could do. Sometimes Donna wondered what readers would think if they knew that models weren't quite as perfect in real life as they appeared to be on the pages of *Gloss*.

So Donna planned to spend her day cleaning off her desk, filing a huge stack of contact sheets, sending invoices for hairdressers and make-up artists down to the billing department. Boring, easy work that required minimal concentration and very little communication. She was way too tired to do much else.

She'd been with Bonnie Bailey at the model's apartment the evening before. Bonnie had just had her heart broken by some fellow she'd been seeing for all of two weeks, and she needed a friend to hear her tale of woe. It was all pretty silly, Donna thought. By now she'd learned that Bonnie was constantly falling madly in love, and these love affairs rarely lasted longer than a week. Donna suspected the model enjoyed the drama of it all.

But Donna had done what *Gloss* expected her to do. She'd sat up with Bonnie, listened to her and comforted her. And Bonnie had kept her there, listening and comforting, till two in the morning.

Donna was actually glad that Jack was out of town on business and wouldn't be back for at least two more days. She needed some quiet time, and a lot of sleep.

Sleep hadn't come easy to her lately, and not only because of late nights with Bonnie. She would lie in bed with her eyes open, thinking about Jack. And when she forced herself to close her eyes, she saw his face. She was so crazy about him, she was in love with him, and yet she was lying to him. It was getting harder and harder. She couldn't keep avoiding his questions, and she was constantly afraid she'd slip up and contradict something she'd told him before.

There had been an awkward moment just a few evenings before. She'd seen Allison that day, and Allison had complained about having lunch with her boring brother's boring wife at some expensive French restaurant called La Côte Basque. During the evening with Jack, he mentioned a dinner with a client.

'We went to La Côte Basque,' he said. 'Have you ever been there?'

'Yes, once. With my brother's wife.'

He'd looked at her in confusion. 'I thought you were an only child.'

She recovered as best as she could. 'Did I say "brother"? I meant, my cousin's wife. This cousin, he's always been like a brother to me.'

It was a pretty weak recovery, but Jack didn't press it.

She knew it wasn't just the fake stories themselves that were causing her the sleepless nights. It was simply the fact that she was lying to him, that she was deceiving the man she loved. And it couldn't go on forever.

Sometimes she almost wished the relationship would die a natural death. They'd start boring each other. Or one of them would fall in love with someone else. Or he'd transfer to a different university, so that when the summer was over he would move far, far away, and it would be out of sight, out of mind.

The receptionist appeared in the doorway. 'Phone call for you, Donna.'

She went out into the hall and picked up the receiver.

'Hello?'

'Is this Donna?'

'Yes.'

'Hello, Donna. This is Lucille Vanderwill. Jack's mother.'

Donna could literally feel her stomach turn over.

'Oh. Hello, Mrs Vanderwill. How are you?'

'Very well, dear. And you?'

'I'm fine.'

'I was wondering if you could have lunch with me today.'

A large lump suddenly appeared in Donna's throat. She swallowed, but it was still there.

'Lunch? With you? Today?'

'Yes, dear, that's what I said.'

'Well . . . yeah. Sure.' Oh, she sounded so low-class. 'I mean, yes, I would like that.'

'Good. Meet me at the Colony Restaurant at one o'clock. You do know the Colony, don't you?'

'Actually, no, I don't.'

She could have sworn she heard something like a chuckle at the other end.

'It's at Sixty-first and Madison.'

When she hung up, Donna looked at the clock. Eleven thirty. She had plenty of time – it wouldn't take more than ten minutes to get there – but then she remembered what she was wearing. A shirtdress that needed ironing, scuffed flats . . .

GL♥SS

She fled to the elevator and took it down to the editorial floor. Panic must have been all over her face, because Sherry looked at her in alarm when she came into her office.

'What's the matter?'

Donna slumped into a chair. 'Jack's mother just called me. She invited me to come to lunch with her. Today.'

'That's good, isn't it?'

'I don't know . . . The only time I met her, she wasn't very nice. She was practically quizzing me.'

'Well, you must have passed the quiz.'

Donna wasn't so sure. 'I guess. I'm meeting her at some place called the Colony.'

'Wow!' Sherry exclaimed.

'You know it?'

'I know *about* it. It's very high society.'

Donna moaned. 'What am I going to do?' She indicated her wrinkled dress. 'I can't wear this, and there's not enough time to go home and change.'

'Maybe you can find something in the samples closet.'

Donna was doubtful. 'I don't think Caroline would consider this to be *Gloss* business.'

'It doesn't matter. Caroline's not in the office. She's in meetings till after lunch.'

Donna slumped deeper into the chair. 'Oh, great. The keys to the samples closet are in her office.'

Sherry grinned. 'And I just happen to have keys to that office. Come on.'

The samples closet held the perfect two-piece outfit – a boxy, buttoned-up blouse and a straight skirt. The sample shoes were too small for Donna's feet, so she'd have wear her own ballerinas, but Sherry was able to locate some shoe polish to cover the scuff marks.

'And you'll need a hat,' Sherry said.

'I never wear hats!'

'But the ladies who lunch do. What about this?' Sherry showed her a bejewelled beret. But even though she didn't wear hats, Donna could still use her styling skills and selected something that worked better with the outfit – a simple straw derby with a ribbon that complemented the blouse.

She wouldn't say she was feeling confident, but at least she thought she looked OK when she entered the Colony. She could see into the main dining room, where there seemed to be only women at the tables. Nicely dressed, of course, and most of them wore hats.

'Yes? May I help you?'

'I'm meeting Mrs Vanderwill.'

'This way, please.'

The man led her through a room lined with tall glistening mirrors to a red plush banquette. Mrs Vanderwill looked up as they approached, and offered a thin smile.

'Hello, Donna. Do sit down.'

Donna did. 'It's very nice to see you again,' she said.

The woman continued to look at her with that brittle smile and didn't say anything. A waiter paused by their table.

'May I bring you and your guest a cocktail, Mrs Vanderwill?'

'Yes, Horace, I'll have a vodka gimlet,' Mrs Vanderwill said. 'Donna? What would you like to drink?'

'Um, just water, please.'

'You wouldn't like a beer?' the woman asked.

Puzzled, Donna shook her head. 'No, thank you.'

'I thought that might be your drink,' Mrs Vanderwill murmured. 'Oh, excuse me a moment. I see someone I must speak to.'

She left the table and walked across the floor to a table where four women were dining. Donna was still wondering why Jack's mother would think she'd want a beer. She never drank beer with Jack, and Jack knew she didn't like it.

The woman returned. 'Did you recognize whom I was speaking with?'

'No.'

'That was the Duchess of Windsor.'

'Oh.'

'You *do* know who the Duchess of Windsor is, don't you?'

'I've heard of her,' Donna managed weakly.

'You know, her husband was the King of England. He was in love with her, but since she'd been divorced, she wasn't permitted to become his queen. He gave up the throne to marry her.'

The waiter placed the cocktail in front of Mrs Vanderwill and water in a crystal glass in front of Donna. Mrs Vanderwill took a dainty sip and set her drink down.

'My son is not going to do that, Donna.'

Donna was completely confused. 'Do what?' She picked up her glass.

'Give up his place, his role in society, to be with a girl like you.'

Donna set her glass down without taking a drink. Her hand was trembling; she was afraid she wouldn't be able to lift the glass to her mouth.

'You see, Donna, I know all about you. I could tell, when we met at the museum benefit, that despite your nice dress, you are not one of us. Beacon Hill . . .' she shook her head in amusement. 'Have you ever even visited Beacon Hill?'

Donna didn't respond. She remained very still, aware of little else but her rapid heartbeat.

'I hired a private detective, Donna. To investigate your background. And he confirmed my suspicions. Raised in a trailer park by an alcoholic mother. High-school dropout. Pregnant at sixteen.'

'Seventeen,' Donna murmured, but the woman continued as if she hadn't spoken.

'Married to some low-life. And then you ran away from him. Are you still married, Donna?'

'He died. In an accident.'

'I see. My sympathies. Well, that doesn't really make much difference, does it?'

The waiter reappeared with large menus in his hand. Mrs Vanderwill waved him away. 'Not now, Horace.'

She turned back to Donna. 'You know, my dear, you would have been found out sooner or later. I presume you were hoping to marry Jack before that happened.'

Donna shook her head, but the woman went on.

'And then, when he discovered your deception and demanded a divorce, you would hire a lawyer and walk away from the marriage with a sizeable sum of money.'

Again Donna shook her head, and again the woman ignored this.

'Now, I considered offering you a bribe to leave my son alone, but I really don't think that's necessary. Because now that I know the truth about you, so will he. And once he's learned how you lied, he won't want you.'

Donna's mouth was so dry she absolutely had to have some of that water. Somehow she was able to get the glass to her lips and then back on to the table without spilling any.

'But I'm not a cruel or vindictive person,' Mrs Vanderwill said. 'I am giving you the opportunity to end this gracefully and without bringing any shame on yourself. You will break up with my son, on some pretext – I don't care what you tell him. And you will never see him again. Do you agree to this?'

Dumbly, Donna nodded.

The waiter came back with the menus.

'Shall we order now?' Mrs Vanderwill asked Donna.

Donna took a deep breath. 'I'm . . . I'm afraid I'm not very hungry. Excuse me.'

She was surprised to find her legs were strong and steady enough to carry her out of the restaurant. A wave of nausea engulfed her, but fortunately she hadn't eaten anything. She just kept moving, up the street to the Hartnell Building.

Once inside, she went directly to her office and changed back into the clothes she'd worn to work. Then she sat down at her desk.

Strange, how she didn't feel like crying. Maybe she was relieved; maybe it was all for the best. It couldn't have gone on like this, with lies, lies and more lies. She'd spent so long dreading the inevitable. Now it had arrived, and there would be no more dread. No more lies.

. . . no more dread. No more lies.

Well, just one more.

She took out a sheet of plain

white paper and a pen, and she started to write.

Dear Jack . . .

How easy it was! A little story that just popped into her head, and it was completely believable. An old boyfriend from years ago. The first love of her life, and she'd never gotten over him. He'd moved here to New York, they got together and rekindled their love. So sorry. Goodbye.

She folded the paper carefully, put it into an envelope and addressed it. Then she took it out to the receptionist's desk and dropped it in the outbox. The mail boy would be picking up the mail at four thirty, and it would go out in the morning post. Two days, maybe three. It should be waiting for Jack when he returned from his trip.

While she was standing there, the phone on the desk rang and the receptionist picked it up.

'It's for you, Donna.'

Now what? She took the phone.

'Hello?'

'Donna, it's Caroline. Could you come down to my office right away?'

Was it possible for her heart to sink any further? Caroline must have found out that she had taken items from the samples closet without permission.

She went into her office, carefully placed the outfit on its hanger and carried it with her down to the editorial floor. As she was approaching

Caroline's office, she heard a loud pop.

Caroline, Sherry and Belinda from fashion were in the office, and Caroline was pouring champagne into plastic cups.

'What's going on?' Donna asked.

'Bonnie signed with *Gloss*!' Caroline announced. 'We've got her exclusively for an entire year! And we owe it all to you, Donna!'

She handed Donna a filled cup. 'Let's raise our glasses for a toast.'

'To Bonnie Bailey,' Belinda said.

'And to Donna Peake!' Caroline added.

Donna took a sip. The bubbles from the champagne tickled her nose. She smiled at the others and thought to herself how remarkably easy it was to look alive when she was dead inside.

Chapter Twenty-One

'Hold the elevator!'

Sherry did, and she was immediately sorry. Pamela stepped into the lift. The girls took one look at each other and then stared straight ahead.

They hadn't spoken since that evening at Charlie's, over two weeks ago, when Sherry had accused her of passing on *Gloss* ideas to *Modern Girl*. The door opened on the floor that was home to the business offices of the magazine, and Pamela stepped out. Sherry went on up to her own floor.

She had a lot of work to do, and she needed to come up with a good excuse to leave the office an hour early. This was the day of the Wall Street demonstration, and she would be meeting William there.

William. She'd only seen him once since that fateful lunch. This past Sunday she'd gone to another meeting at Columbia, where she'd joined a dozen others to make signs for the march. They were back in the lounge room where they'd met before, but all the furniture had been pushed against the wall to make workspace. Jars of paint and brushes were strewn about. It was a lively, noisy, cheerful meeting as people came up with slogans and traded coloured marking pens.

William was pleasant – he greeted her nicely, but that was all. It was as if that kiss on the street had never happened.

At one point, one of the boys started singing a gospel song.

Rock my soul in the bosom of Abraham, rock my soul in the bosom of Abraham . . .

Others joined in. Looking around, Sherry could see that all the Negro members knew the words. William was belting it out with gusto.

It was just a song, but even so, it made Sherry think about the differences between herself and William. The history, the culture, the way of life . . . would she ever be able to understand? From across the room, she saw him looking at her. Was he thinking the same way? Was it possible to even contemplate coming together?

She wandered over to where he was in the process of lettering a sign. All it said at this point was WALL STREET.

'What do you think?' he asked her. 'Wall Street Stinks? Wall Street has to hire Negroes?'

'How about this?' She took a black marker pen and put a large X through the word 'Wall'. Above it, she wrote 'White'.

He nodded slowly and smiled. 'Not bad.'

When they'd finished making the signs, someone with a car was assigned the job of bringing them on the day of the demonstration, and people began to leave. Sherry looked for William, wanting to at least say a personal goodbye, but he was deep in conversation with a couple of other guys. She lingered for a while, until practically everyone had gone, but William was still occupied. So she gave up and left.

She was only half a block away when she heard the ominous rumble of thunder. It had been raining earlier and she'd brought an umbrella, but she realized she'd left it open to dry just outside the meeting room. She hurried back to retrieve it.

Through the open door, she could see that William was still there. He was stacking the signs in a corner of the room, alongside the sofa, and he was alone. He looked up when Sherry came in.

'I left my umbrella,' she said.

He nodded.

'Can I help?' she asked.

'I'm about finished,' he said. 'Thanks anyway.'

'I've been thinking about you,' she blurted out.

He very carefully placed the last sign on the stack.

'Do you ever think about me?' she asked.

He stood there, with his back to her. But she heard what he said.

'Yes.'

She came closer, and finally he turned to face her.

'Is it wrong?' she asked. 'Gloria thinks it's wrong. She thinks it can never be.'

'Gloria doesn't know everything,' he said.

'It doesn't *feel* wrong,' she said. 'Not to me. Does it feel wrong to you?'

He shook his head. She reached out and took his hand. Together they fell back on to the sofa.

She couldn't remember ever before in her life feeling such a need to touch, to be touched. She'd held on to her virginity, and it hadn't been that difficult since she'd never felt really tempted. But now it was as if touching, feeling, could open a door, build a bridge, connect them in a powerful and meaningful way. She'd been through the motions with other boys, but this was different, this was real; she'd never wanted someone this much.

Their bodies seemed to have found a harmony on their own, they seemed to meld. And as they both lay there, holding each other on the sofa, she could only think that if bodies could come together like this, why couldn't minds, and hearts, and souls?

She was thinking something else too, and William gave voice to her thoughts.

'What are we going to do about this?'

'I don't know,' she replied.

Silently they rose and straightened their rumpled clothes. It seemed very natural to walk together hand in hand, down the stairs to the front door. William touched the door handle.

'Oh no.'

GL♥SS

'What?' she asked.

'I forgot. The building gets locked at six on Sundays.'

Sherry gasped. 'You mean, we're trapped in here till they open it in the morning?'

'I guess so.'

They stared at each other. And then they both burst out laughing.

It was funny until Sherry became aware of another sensation, and the fact that she'd been too nervous about seeing him to eat lunch that afternoon.

'I'm hungry.'

William grinned. 'Come on.'

He led her down to the basement floor, which turned out to be a big snack bar lined with machines. Sherry pored through her handbag, William emptied his pockets, and between them they came up with enough coins to purchase a meal – sort of. Potato chips, cheese crackers, some rather deadly looking dried sausage and plenty of candy bars. They piled it all on a table and sat down.

'Tell me about yourself,' Sherry said. 'After what we've been doing, I feel like I should know you a little better!'

He laughed. 'Well, I grew up in Harlem. My dad was a jazz musician. He died when I was ten – tuberculosis.'

'How terrible for you.'

'Yeah. Anyway, my mother's a librarian, and she raised Gloria and me on her own. There are a lot of aunts, uncles and cousins, so my life has mainly been family, church and Harlem. Growing up, I rarely went below 125th Street.'

'Church,' Sherry mused. 'Are you religious?'

'Not really. It's mainly just part of the culture.' He smiled. 'If you were expecting some kind of hard-core ghetto story, I'm sorry to disappoint you.'

'I'm not disappointed,' Sherry said. 'But maybe you'll be disappointed to know I didn't grow up on a cotton plantation with a mammy.'

He raised his eyebrows and affected a look of astonishment. 'No?'

'Dad's a doctor, my mother's a homemaker. I've got an older brother and a younger sister. And none of them are members of the Ku Klux Klan.'

He grew more serious. 'But what would they say if they saw us together? What would your friends say?'

She thought about how her parents had always supported equal rights. But she also remembered how Mama had defended the restaurant owner who didn't want to serve Negroes.

As for her friends . . . she had no idea. They'd never spoken about these things.

'I don't know,' she said finally. 'Maybe they'd react the way Gloria did.'

A noise in the hall made them jump. They went out there and saw a man with a bucket and a mop.

'What are you kids doing in here?' the janitor barked.

He escorted them to the door, unlocked it and let them out. It was raining again – not a downpour, just a soft, steady, light drizzle. And Sherry had left her umbrella again.

She wasn't about to bang on the door and ask the janitor to let her back in so she could get it. William didn't have an umbrella either. It didn't matter – she couldn't even feel herself getting wet, and she suspected he couldn't either.

For a moment they stood there, looking at each other, all the unanswered questions still in their eyes.

'Well,' William said finally, 'I'm supposed to take my mother to church tonight, so I'd better head uptown.'

'And I'm going downtown,' Sherry said.

Were those symbolic statements, Sherry wondered. Uptown, downtown . . . opposite directions?

William shrugged and smiled. 'There's always midtown.'

They kissed, a very long kiss, with a passion that echoed their time on the sofa. And then they went off in their opposite directions.

The memory of that kiss was still with her as she sat at her desk that morning, still trying to come up with a good excuse to leave work early that day. There was a knock on her door.

'Come in.'

It was Liz Madrigal. 'Caroline wants to know if you have the corrected galleys for the Beatles article.'

'I gave them to Gloria,' Sherry said, and got up. She could see from her office that Gloria had gone on her coffee break, and she didn't want to give Liz any opportunity to poke around in the papers that might be lying on the secretary's desk. Maybe that was when the glimmer of a suspicion started growing in her mind. Liz, who was constantly asking what Sherry was working on. Liz, whom Sherry had discovered looking at papers on *her* desk. But what reason would Liz have to spy? Especially if she was coveting Sherry's job?

She searched for the article – now entitled 'We Want to Hold Their Hands' – on Gloria's desk. While she was looking, Pamela came into the office area. Sherry averted her eyes.

She was surprised when Pamela paused as she passed. 'Oh, hi!' Looking up, she saw that her former friend wasn't addressing *her*.

Liz suddenly appeared oddly tense. 'Hello,' she murmured, and looked away.

'What are you doing here?' Pamela asked her.

'I'm an intern.'

'Here are the galleys,' Sherry said.

Liz took them and scurried back into Caroline's office. Sherry turned to Pamela.

'Do you need something?'

'I'm supposed to give this folder to Belinda Collins.'

'She's in her office,' Sherry said, nodding in that direction, and went back into her own office.

A few moments later, Caroline appeared at her door.

'This is getting ridiculous,' the managing editor fumed. 'Bonnie Bailey just called me. She told me she's had an offer for an exclusive contract from *Modern Girl*.'

'But she's already signed with us!' Sherry exclaimed.

'Yes, and she told them that,' Caroline said. 'She's not leaving us. But I'm getting sick of this. Get me the name of their managing editor. I'm going to write a letter.'

Sherry dug out the issue of *Modern Girl* that was still sitting in a pile of magazines and newspapers on her desk and turned to the masthead. She found the name of the managing editor, but another name caught her eye.

Assistant Editor, Features. Janet Madrigal.

Madrigal. An unusual last name. And a familiar one.

Back out in the bullpen, Sherry saw Pamela coming out of the fashion editor's office. She waved to her.

'Now what are you accusing me of?' Pamela demanded to know. 'Are there clothes missing from the samples closet?'

'That girl you said hello to, the one with the black hair. How do you know Liz Madrigal?'

'Who?'

'The girl you said hello to.'

Pamela shrugged. 'I don't know her. I just saw her a couple of times at *Modern Girl*.'

'At *Modern Girl*,' Sherry repeated.

'Eating lunch with one of the editors in the cafeteria.'

It was all coming together.

'Oh, Pamela. I'm so sorry.'

Pamela sniffed. 'You should be.' Then she looked confused. 'Wait a minute. What does this have to do with that girl?'

'She was the spy!' She showed Pamela the masthead of Modern Girl. 'See? Same last name. I'll bet this is the editor you saw her having lunch with. They have to be related. Liz has been telling her what we were doing at *Gloss*. I was so wrong to accuse you.'

'No kidding. Did you honestly think I would do something like spy on *Gloss*?'

'Not really,' Sherry admitted. 'That time at Charlie's, I'd had a lot to drink. And I was upset about something else.'

'Oh yeah?' Pamela looked interested. 'What? A guy?'

Sherry smiled slightly. 'Sort of.'

'OK, spill it! What's been going on with you?'

'It's a long story.'

'Then we need another get-together,' Pamela declared. 'There's lots of news. Allison broke up with Bobby, you know.'

'Donna broke up with Jack.'

'Really? I thought she was so into him.'

'What about you and Larry?' Sherry asked.

'Oh, we're still hanging out. But that might not go on for much longer.'

'You've met someone else?'

'No . . . but I just might. Things could be changing for me.'

'How do you mean?'

Pamela grinned. 'It's a long story. Like I said, it's time for a get-together. See ya.'

Sherry gazed after her fondly. She was very, very lucky that Pamela was so quick to forgive.

Caroline's door was slightly open, and she could see that Liz was still in there. Sherry rapped lightly and went in.

Caroline looked up. 'Did you get the name for me?'

She went around to Caroline's side of the desk, set down the copy of *Modern Girl* and pointed to the name on the masthead.

Caroline's brow furrowed, and she looked up. 'Liz, who is Janet Madrigal?'

The intern went pale.

'My cousin.'

Caroline gazed at her steadily. 'I think we need to have a little talk. Sherry, could you leave us?'

This time, back in her own office, Sherry made sure to keep her door open. She wanted to see Liz leave.

And before another minute passed, she did.

A moment later, Caroline was in her office. The normally cool-and-confident managing editor actually looked embarrassed.

'Well, I *did* tell you to keep your eye on her,' she said. With an sheepish smile, she added, 'Though not for that reason.'

'So she was really spying on us?'

Caroline nodded. 'It was her cousin who talked her into applying for the internship, so she could pass on to *Modern Girl* what we were doing. I don't know if we would have ever caught her if you hadn't seen that masthead.'

'But I wouldn't have looked there if you hadn't wanted to write a letter,' Sherry said. 'And thank goodness her last name wasn't something like Smith.'

'Even so,' Caroline said, 'I owe you one.'

Sherry remembered those words later in the day, when she was still trying to come up with a reason to leave early. The demonstration was gathering at four o'clock, and it would take her at least a half-hour to get down to the financial district. By three o'clock, she still hadn't come up with an excuse. She supposed she could have invented a toothache or something like that, but she'd never been very good at lying.

But Caroline had said she owed her one, and maybe this was the time to collect on the favour. She saw her boss at Gloria's desk, and went out there.

'Caroline, I was wondering . . . There's going to be a civil-rights demonstration on Wall Street in an hour. And I'd like to go.'

'Is it for the story you're working on?' Caroline asked.

'Well . . . yes.' That was only a little white lie.

'Then of course you should go.'

She was clearing her desk when Gloria tapped on the door frame.

'Come in,' Sherry said.

Gloria entered and closed the door. Sherry examined her expression apprehensively. The secretary looked very serious.

'It's not just for the story, is it?' she asked, in a tone that told Sherry she already knew the answer.

'No.' Sherry faced her squarely. 'I believe in equal employment opportunities.'

'I'm sure you do,' Gloria said quietly. 'I don't doubt your sincerity, Sherry. But I know that's not the only reason either.'

Sherry bit her lip. 'No, it's not.'

'Sherry, I don't know how serious you and my brother are. He doesn't confide in me about, well, matters of the heart. But I have a feeling something's going on.'

'And you don't like it,' Sherry said.

'I'm afraid,' Gloria said simply. 'For William. *And*

for you. This is a dangerous game you're playing.'

'It's not a game,' Sherry said, and she could hear how sharp she sounded.

'Whatever it is, it's still dangerous. You know, Negro men have been lynched for messing about with white girls.'

'This isn't Mississippi, Gloria.'

'It doesn't have to be.'

'People don't get lynched in New York City.'

'Not literally,' Gloria retorted. 'But there are other ways of punishing people. William could get himself in a lot of trouble.'

Sherry didn't know how to respond to that.

Gloria continued. 'And I can't imagine your people would be too thrilled about the situation either.'

'We can deal with that,' Sherry said.

'Can you?' Gloria shook her head. 'For an intelligent girl, Sherry, you can be awfully naive.'

Sherry sighed. 'Look, Gloria, I can understand how you feel.' Then, seeing the scepticism on her face, she added, 'OK, maybe not exactly. But this is between William and me.'

'Did you know that in some states it's illegal for a Negro and a white person to marry?'

Sherry rolled her eyes. 'We're not talking about getting married, Gloria.'

'Then where is it leading?'

Once again, she couldn't answer.

'If you really care about him, Sherry, you'll let him go.'

Sherry picked up her handbag and tossed it over her arm. 'I can't, Gloria.' And she left the office.

Sherry had forgotten to look at a subway map, and she'd never been in the financial district before. So she splurged on a taxi to Wall Street.

'Trinity Church, please.'

That was where she and William had arranged to meet, in front of the old church just down the street from the Stock Exchange.

But as the taxi started moving, she realized that this splurge might have been a mistake. It wasn't yet rush hour, but there was plenty of traffic, and the cab was creeping downtown. She kept looking at her watch, and then out the window, to see how far they'd progressed.

Gloria's words rang in her ears. *It's dangerous, Sherry. It's dangerous.*

Surely she was exaggerating. Maybe she'd be nervous walking side by side with a Negro man down South. But here the races weren't separated. People of all races went to the same schools, used the same bathrooms, drank from the same water fountains. They ate in the same restaurants. People weren't segregated here.

And then she remembered the nasty drunk teenager at Gino's.

The taxi driver turned his head. 'You want to get out here and walk the rest of the way, miss? There seems to be something going on, and I don't know how much closer I can get.'

Sherry looked out the window, and she could see groups of people, some dragging signs. It dawned on her that this might be a really big crowd. Flyers and posters had been distributed all over the city.

'Yes, I'll get out here.'

There was a look of concern on the driver's face. Because she was white and the majority of the people walking by were not?

'Are you sure?'

'Yes, I'm sure.' She paid him and got out of the car.

It was a short walk to Trinity Church. When she arrived, she felt positively exultant. The steps leading up to the church and the sidewalk in front were packed with people, and many carried signs which blocked her view.

We Want Jobs on Wall Street.

March for Equal Opportunity.

I Have a Dream to Work on Wall Street.

Way up on the stairs, she spotted a sign she recognized. Where the word 'Wall' had been crossed out and replaced by the word 'White'.

As she manoeuvred her way up the steps, she was pleased to see so many happy, excited faces, mostly Negro, but plenty of white people too. It felt like a

GL♥SS

party. And when she finally reached William's side, his broad smile made her feel very sure she'd been invited.

'There you are!'

She raised her face, expecting a kiss, but all he did was hand her a sign. She wasn't offended – lots of guys weren't into public displays of affection.

One of the boys from their Columbia group joined them. 'We're going to be covered!' he told them. 'I saw them on my way here!'

'Great!' William said.

'What are you talking about?' Sherry asked.

'The press,' William told her. 'Photographers and reporters are here. We should get some coverage on TV and in the newspapers.'

Someone somewhere blew a shrill whistle. Then someone started beating a drum. And the crowd began to surge down the steps and on to the street. Like a tidal wave, the mass of humanity turned on to Wall Street and marched to the slow, steady rhythm of the drum.

And someone started a chant.

'Two, four, six, eight,

Wall Street has to integrate.'

Then everyone was chanting, repeating the words over and over. Sherry took William's hand – surely he wouldn't mind that small affectionate gesture nobody would notice.

He didn't mind. In fact, he gripped hers so tightly it almost hurt. And yet, at the same time, it felt so good.

Eventually the chanting stopped and singing began.

'We shall overcome, we shall overcome,

We shall overcome some day . . .'

Sherry sang lustily, until she became aware of two women staring at her. She smiled, but the women didn't smile back.

'What have *you* got to overcome?' one of them asked.

William heard her, and turned in their direction. That was when the two women saw that he was holding Sherry's hand. They both gave him a look of disgust.

Jealous, Sherry thought. But she knew their reaction meant something beyond that.

William looked away. But he loosened his grip on Sherry's hand, and then let it drop.

It was that moment when someone high up in the building they faced emptied a bucket of water out of a window. Sherry could see folks looking up in surprise. A second later, a few feet from her, something red flew through the air and hit a sign. Tomato juice ran down the word 'equality'.

And then all hell broke loose. More tomatoes, and eggs too. Sherry had no idea where they were coming from. The singing turned into shouting and yelling, and the crowd began moving in all directions. Sherry tripped on someone's dropped sign, but William grabbed her before she could hit the ground and get trampled. Wrapping a protective arm around her, he began to push through the crowd.

Suddenly it seemed as if photographers were everywhere, taking pictures of the chaos. A guy with a film camera that bore the name of a local TV station tried to balance himself on a fire hydrant to get a wider shot of the crowd.

With his arm still around her, William got them both behind a telephone booth. A man with a camera came towards them.

An image suddenly flashed in Sherry's mind. Mama and Daddy, opening the daily newspaper tomorrow morning and seeing a photo of their daughter in the arms of a Negro. She could actually see their shocked faces, plain as day.

The photographer spotted them and he lifted his camera. But before he could aim, Sherry slithered out from under William's arm and turned so her back was to the man.

'What's the matter?' William asked. Then he saw the photographer.

A voice from a bullhorn blared over the noise. 'This is the police! You are all required to leave the area immediately!'

'This way,' William said. He led her down a side street and then into an alley. There they stopped under a shop awning to catch their breaths.

Another boy and girl, a Negro couple, came running down the alley. They paused, and the boy's eyes darted between William and Sherry.

'What's wrong, brother? Can't find a sister?'

William studied the pavement.

The boy sneered at them and moved on with the girl.

William leaned against the wall. 'What a mess,' he muttered. 'You OK?'

'I'm fine. William . . .'

'What?'

'Why didn't you say anything to that guy just now?'

He was looking straight ahead, not at her. 'What would you want me to say?'

'I don't know. But you looked like you were ashamed of me.'

He met her gaze. 'Why did you hide when that photographer tried to take our picture?'

Sherry shifted her weight from one leg to the other and shrugged.

'Didn't want your picture taken with a Negro?' he asked.

They didn't speak for several moments.

Sherry broke the silence. 'Gloria said it was dangerous. You and me.'

He nodded. 'Yeah, that sounds like something she would say.'

'Is she right?'

He attempted a smile, but it wasn't much of an effort. 'Well, we're not going to win any popularity contests as a couple.'

'I told Gloria we could deal with the problems,' Sherry said. 'Now I'm not so sure. I don't know if we're strong enough. Either of us. What do you think?'

He didn't respond. He didn't need to. She could see the answer on his face. Or she thought she could. He'd become very blurry.

Was that a tear coming down his face too? Or maybe it was the rain.

It had just started, a light, soft, summer rain, like the one they walked into after being locked in the building. But this time it felt different. And there would be no kiss under the rain this time.

She turned and started walking towards the subway. He didn't follow her.

Chapter
Twenty-Two

Pamela stood before the full-length mirror in her bedroom and scrutinized her reflection with more care than she'd ever taken before in her life.

The day before she'd splurged on a visit to a renowned beauty parlour, one frequented by beauty editors of all the major fashion magazines. Her hair was now freshly blonde, without a trace of roots, and teased up into a frothy cloud of pale golden spun sugar. She'd worked for ages on getting the perfect wing on her eyeliner, nothing too flashy, just a touch of Cleopatra. Her cheeks were lightly rouged, and her mouth was a rich pink.

The ice-blue cocktail dress was heavenly. It offered a hint of cleavage, and the crisp taffeta skirt billowed out and made her waist look positively tiny. Of course, a cocktail dress wasn't normal apparel for eight o'clock in the morning, but in this particular situation it was perfect. It had cost her an entire week's wages, but it was well worth it, she thought. She considered it an investment. If she'd been able to afford a long ball gown, she would have bought one.

She moved in closer to the mirror to examine her

complexion, checking to make sure that the pancake make-up had erased any trace of shadows under her eyes. She wished she had one of those magnifying Hollywood mirrors with the lights all around it. She was dressing up for a role, and she had to be ready for her close-up.

She could hear Allison pottering around in the kitchen, and she tottered off on her stiletto heels. In the kitchen, she found her roommate with her back to the entrance, putting the kettle on to boil.

'How do I look?' she asked.

Allison glanced over her shoulder. 'Fine.'

'Allison! You didn't even look at me!'

She actually turned this time. Then her eyebrows shot up. 'That's what you're wearing to the office?'

'I'm not going to an office today. Don't you remember? This is the day of my audition.'

'Oh, right. Sorry, I forgot.'

'How could you forget? It's only the most important day of my life! Now, watch this. The host says something like, "and today, you could win this deluxe frost-free refrigerator." And I do this.'

She flung out a graceful arm in the direction of their refrigerator.

'Fantastic.'

It was the right word, but Allison hadn't said it the right way. In fact, Pamela thought she detected a note of sarcasm.

'OK, Miss Radcliffe College, this might not seem like much of a job to you, but I'm not getting a fancy university education. I'm never going to be a doctor or a lawyer or a professor. This is a big deal for me!'

'You're right, I'm sorry. You want a cup of coffee?'

'No, I'm too nervous as it is.'

Allison sat down with her cup. 'I know I haven't been very supportive lately. I guess I'm feeling a little down.'

Pamela couldn't sit – she was afraid of wrinkling the taffeta. But she did put her hands on a chair and lean sympathetically in her friend's direction.

'Thinking about Bobby?'

'I guess. I just feel so . . . I don't know. Alone.'

Pamela nodded with feeling. 'Believe me, I know how that feels. Remember how I was last summer when Alex threw me out?'

'But you've got Larry now,' Allison said wistfully. 'And he's crazy about you, it's so obvious. You're very lucky to have found someone like that. I hope you appreciate that.'

Pamela was checking her reflection in the metal of the toaster. 'Mm,' she murmured, adjusting the pin curl by her ear.

'Do you think it will last?'

'Will what last?'

'You and Larry!'

Pamela shrugged. 'Who knows? I mean, if I get this

job, everything's going to change for me. I'll be making real money, I can get my own apartment and—'

Allison interrupted. 'What does that have to do with your relationship?'

'I haven't finished. Larry's a great guy, but I'm being realistic. Think of the kind of men I'll be meeting! Did you know that three soap operas are filmed in that building? Including *The World Keeps Spinning.* I could meet Buck Fontaine!'

'I don't even know who that is,' Allison said.

Pamela ignored that. 'And you know, not all the contestants on *What's That They Say?* are librarians from Chicago. Sometimes they have special celebrity editions.'

Allison smiled. 'That will be nice for you.'

'Forget about Bobby, Allison. If this works out for me, I'll be introducing you to big stars – rich, famous, gorgeous men.'

'No, thanks,' Allison said. 'I've had about enough of men in show business.'

'Well, have it your own way,' Pamela said brightly. 'But if I get this job, I want to be available!'

Images of Steve McQueen and Sean Connery danced in her head as she sailed out the door. True, neither of them were on soap operas, and she doubted the game-show celebrity editions would include stars of that rank, but even so, once she became a television star – who knew what doors could open? And Sean

Connery just might be behind one of them.

She'd been stunned, utterly amazed, when she got the call from the producer's secretary, inviting her to come in for an audition to replace Tippy Turner. She wondered if that old lecher Bret Styles had recommended her, and if so, would she have to fool around with him? And how far would she go to get this job?

Arriving at the network building on West 67th Street, she presented herself to the receptionist in the lobby. The woman dialled some numbers on her phone, spoke to someone and within minutes a young man in an usher's uniform appeared.

'Miss Mackle? This way, please.'

She was led back to the studio where *What's That They Say?* was recorded. This time it was practically deserted, with the exception of one bored-looking man standing behind a camera. Then she saw three men sitting in the front row seats. One was the producer she had met with Larry at the taping they'd attended. Another was someone she'd never seen before. The third was Bret Styles.

The producer rose and came towards her. 'Ah, Miss Mackle. I'm Herbert Johnson, producer of *What's That They Say?* Thank you for coming.'

'Thank you for inviting me, Mr Johnson,' she replied sweetly.

'As you may know, we are seeking a new prize

hostess for the show, and you have been strongly recommended.'

She couldn't help glancing in the direction of Bret Styles, but the man was slumped in his chair with his eyes half closed. He didn't even seem interested in what was going on.

The producer gestured towards the two seated men. 'These gentlemen are Stan Foster, the casting consultant, and Bret Styles, the director.'

Did Mr Johnson not remember that she was already too well acquainted with the director? Apparently not. Styles himself only gave her a vague salute, like he'd never seen her before. Maybe this was just showbiz, where everyone made passes at everyone else and then forgot about it. Well, she could play along with that.

'Pleased to meet you,' she said.

'Now,' Mr Johnson continued, 'we would like you to go up on to the stage, and I will call out directions. We want to see how you would look on the screen, so the cameraman will be filming, and we'll be watching you on a monitor.'

She went to the stairs at the side and walked up them to the game-show set. The curtains were already opened to show the day's prizes – a dining table and chairs, a hi-fi system and some jewellery.

'OK, show us the hi-fi,' the producer called out.

She glided over to the waist-high object. They probably expected her just to point at it, but she'd watched enough game shows to know how it should be done. With her left hand, she lifted the lid, and with her right, she gestured towards the turntable. Then she turned and smiled brightly towards the camera.

The men were watching the monitor. 'Nice,' the casting man said.

'Now the necklace,' the producer instructed her.

Pamela glided gracefully over to the next table on which rested a velvet-lined box. With both hands she lifted the pearl necklace and held it to her own neckline, knowing full well it would accentuate her cleavage.

Her intuition paid off.

'*Very* nice,' Mr Herbert said. 'Let's see how she looks with Dominick.'

Someone fetched the game-show host, who looked very grumpy as he strode on to the set.

'How many times do I have to do this?' he barked.

'She's the last one,' the producer assured him.

Pamela's spirits rose. Surely the last girl seen would leave the strongest impression. Despite the fact that Dominick Dupont didn't even speak to her, she smiled brightly at him.

'Good morning, Mr Dupont,' she said cheerily.

He grunted in response and took his place behind the podium.

Bret Styles dragged himself out of his chair. 'OK, action.'

The game-show host's expression changed dramatically. 'And now, say hello to . . .' he stopped. 'What's her name?'

'Pamela Mackle,' Mr Johnson said. 'Wait . . . Dear, do you mind if we call you Pammy. And maybe we could change your last name to Packle. Pammy Packle. Yes, I like that!'

As far as Pamela was concerned, they could call her Puppy Pickle. 'That's fine, Mr Johnson.'

Once again, the director called, 'Action'.

'And now, say hello to Pammy Packle!'

Pamela walked to the podium and turned up the wattage on her smile. 'Hi, Dominick!' Then she turned to the camera. 'Hello, everyone!'

'How are you today, Pammy?' the host asked.

'Just fine, Dominick. And all set to show off some wonderful prizes.'

'Thank you,' Mr Johnson called out.

Without even saying goodbye, Dominick Dupont hurried off. Below her, the three men huddled and mumbled. Then the producer approached the stage.

'Congratulations, Miss Mackle. Or maybe I should say Miss Packle. You are America's new game-show sweetheart!'

The words seemed to wash over her. And for a moment she wondered if this was all just a vivid manifestation of her usual fantasies.

'Did you hear me? You've got the job!'

For the first time ever in her entire life, Pamela was speechless. Fortunately it didn't last long.

'Thank you! Thank you so much, Mr Johnson!'

Her head was spinning, the room was spinning, and as she shook hands and accepted kisses on her cheeks, she even half-expected to hear the sound of an alarm clock waking her up from this dream.

But it was happening. It was really happening.

'Now we'll have to get down to business and talk about your contract,' the producer said. 'I don't suppose you have an agent—'

'Oh yes, she does!'

The owner of that familiar voice came down the aisle of the room.

'Larry!'

He waved at her, then handed the producer a card. 'Call this fellow at TV Talent. He'll be representing Miss Mackle.'

'Packle,' Mr Johnson murmured, and looked at the card with distaste. 'Fine, fine. We'll be talking to your agent, Pammy.'

Bewildered, Pamela stepped down from the stage and joined Larry.

'But . . . how did . . . what . . . ?' she wasn't even sure what to ask first.

Larry put an arm lightly around her shoulder. 'Shall we go?'

Somehow she managed to stammer out another

round of thank-yous to the men, received more congratulations and allowed Larry to escort her back up the aisle, through the lobby and out on to the street.

Larry looked at his watch. 'Too early for champagne,' he said. 'We'll have to settle for a celebration breakfast.'

Still in a state of shock, she walked with him across the street to a coffee shop. It wasn't until they were settled in a booth that she was able to put enough words together to form an actual sentence – a question actually.

'Larry, did you set that up?'

He grinned. 'I told Johnson that if he wanted my client to sponsor the show, he had to give you an audition.'

'And that business about an agent –'

'An old school friend who works for a talent agency. I asked him if he'd represent you.'

'But how did you know I'd get the job?'

He shrugged. 'Because you're perfect for it! They'd have to be crazy not to hire you.'

She didn't know what to say.

Suddenly he became serious. 'And listen, Pammy – all I did was open the door. You got yourself the job. You don't owe me anything for this.'

'What do you mean?'

'I didn't do this so I could hold on to you. Like I said, I opened a door, but now a lot of doors are going to open for you. You'll be living in a whole new world, you'll meet lots of new people. And I know . . .' He stopped.

'You know what?'

'I know I could lose you.'

Pamela understood what he meant, but now she was completely bewildered.

'Then why did you do it? Why did you set up this audition and get me the chance?'

'Because you deserve it,' he said simply. 'You're beautiful, you've got a good heart, you're warm and you're kind and you're generous and you should be doing something other than typing all day.'

She agreed – she'd always believed that. She just never thought anyone else did.

A waitress appeared at their booth. 'What can I get you folks?'

They hadn't even looked at menus, but Larry spoke decisively.

'How's your cheesecake? Is it fresh?'

The waitress shrugged. 'It was fresh yesterday.'

'No good,' Larry declared. 'What about your pie?'

The waitress brightened up. 'We've got a cherry pie that just came out of the oven. It hasn't even been cut into yet.'

'OK, we'll take that. And what about your coffee? How long has it been sitting?'

'We're brewing up a fresh pot right now. You might have to wait a couple of minutes.'

'We'll wait,' Larry said.

The waitress jotted down the order. 'You're a fussy one, huh?'

'Not for myself,' Larry said. 'But I only want the best for my girl here.'

The waitress grinned at Pamela. 'Lucky you. I'd say you've got a keeper here.'

Pamela considered that.

'Yes. I'd say you're right.'

Early Friday afternoon, Tom Markham handed Allison her last cheque.

'There's a little something extra there,' he told her. 'You've done a wonderful job this summer.'

'Thank you,' Allison replied. 'It's been a great experience for me.' Gazing across the room at Karen, curled up reading in an armchair, and Tommy on the floor building a Lego tower, she had to admit they were her main source of pleasure over the past couple of weeks.

She crouched down next to the little boy. 'I'm leaving now, Tommy.'

His eyes were glued to his tower. 'See you tomorrow.'

'No, you won't see me tomorrow. Remember how we packed your suitcase this morning? You're going on vacation, to the beach. This is my last day with you.'

'Oh. OK. Bye.'

At least Karen showed a little more emotion at their parting. Allison actually got a hug from her.

'Joan is going to be our new mommy,' she whispered in Allison's ear.

'I know,' Allison whispered back. 'How do you feel about that?'

'I think it's a good thing.'

Allison smiled. 'So do I.'

She meant that too. She wasn't ready to be a mother, and all her fantasies about getting together with their father had sprung from something that had nothing to do with him, or them. She'd miss them all, but it wasn't that hard to say goodbye.

Back at Fifth Avenue, her summer apartment seemed unusually empty and quiet. She'd become accustomed to being alone there – Pamela had been out so much with Larry – but now Pamela was really, truly gone. She'd received an advance on her first month's salary as the new game-show hostess, and she'd immediately gone out in search of an apartment. She'd found something on the Upper West Side, very near where Larry lived. This was surely a good thing, since it appeared to Allison that they were just one ring short of becoming engaged. Pamela too had forsaken her fantasies. But *she'd* given them up for true love.

Allison became aware of her eyes burning, and she knew she was dangerously close to tears. Snap out of it, she ordered herself. Tomorrow morning she'd be boarding a train to take her to Boston. She hadn't even started packing, and tonight she was expected for dinner at Sherry and Donna's place. Sherry's parents were visiting from Georgia, and they wanted to meet their daughter's closest chums. It would be the last time the four former interns would be together for a while, and she had a feeling it would be a late night, so she'd better pack now.

But first she had to do something about the silence. She went to the hi-fi, and shuffled through the few albums she'd brought with her. Bob Dylan, Joan Baez, Pete Seeger . . . *The Greatest Hits of Bobby Dale* – definitely not that one. She settled on Bob Dylan and headed to the closet to drag out her suitcase.

Packing didn't take as long as she thought it would. She finished in half an hour. It was only four o'clock, too early to start getting ready for the evening. She decided to do a real search of the apartment, to make sure she wasn't leaving anything behind.

It was while she was feeling around under the sofa cushions that she found the watch.

She remembered when Bobby told her he'd lost it – it was just before their break-up. He was afraid he might have left it at one of the places where the film had been shooting, and he was upset about it. The watch had been handed down to him by his grandfather. Now she realized that he must have taken it off one night when they were fooling around on the sofa . . .

She had to get it back to him. But how? Mailing it would be a hassle – she'd have to pack it properly and have it insured. She could leave it with his grandmother – but then she'd have to explain to her why she hadn't been around for a while.

You're being silly, she told herself firmly. You know what you have to do.

She found Bobby's shooting schedule crumpled in a ball in the bedroom wastebasket. They were at a studio in Queens today. She probably wouldn't even have to see Bobby – she could leave the watch with someone on the crew.

When Allison got off the subway, she found herself in an industrial area she didn't know at all and it took her a while to find the building. She wasn't even sure it was the right place until she made her way through the parking lot and spotted the trailers where the actors changed their clothes.

And then she saw something else which assured her she was in the right place. Some*one*, actually. Beverly Gray, hurrying towards one of the trailers. And she wasn't alone. Lance Hunter, the star of *Tangled Hearts* was with her. And when they reached the trailer, they went into a major clinch.

Allison ducked behind a truck so they couldn't see her. Their kiss went on forever. Then they both ran up the steps and entered the trailer. Presumably to continue where they'd left off.

Allison became aware of conflicting emotions. So now Bobby would know how *she'd* felt when he betrayed her. She supposed there was some satisfaction in that. But at the same time, she couldn't help feeling a little sorry for him.

She went into the studio building. There was one of the usual guards inside, who approached her with a stern expression, but he relaxed when he recognized her.

'Oh yeah, I remember you. Sorry, haven't seen you around for a while. You're Bobby's girl.'

She didn't bother to correct him.

'They're watching the rushes from this morning,' the guard said.

Allison had no idea what that meant, but the guard showed her to a darkened room where a screen had been set up. She entered silently, and no one saw her.

Bobby wasn't in there. The director and some others were watching a scene that must have been shot that day – Beverly was dressed in the same clothes Allison had just seen her wearing.

It was yet another romantic scene between 'John' and 'Marcia'. From their words, Allison could assume they'd had some sort of disagreement, and now they were making up – and making out. She watched Bobby tenderly stroke Beverly's hair, and then they went into a kiss that looked every bit as passionate as the one she'd observed outside. She recognized the expression on Bobby's face – it was the way he looked when they used to embrace.

Allison slipped back out of the room and wondered if she should give the watch to the guard. She started back towards the entrance, but paused at a door that was slightly ajar. It seemed to have been set up as some kind of lounge, with a coffee machine and a sofa.

Bobby was sprawled on the sofa, and for a moment she thought he was asleep. But then she saw that his eyes were open, and he was staring at the ceiling with an expression that was new to her. He looked depressed. Maybe he'd just learned about Beverly's new affair.

She went in, and his head turned in her direction. Then he sat up. 'Hi!'

'Hello. How are you?'

'Not great.'

She reached in her bag and brought out his watch. 'Maybe this will cheer you up,' she said.

He took it from her. 'Where did you find it?'

'Under a sofa cushion.'

'Thanks.' He strapped the watch on to his wrist.

'You still look depressed,' she said.

'I am,' he replied.

'I can understand that,' she said pointedly.

Was that too harsh? The sadness in his face was almost unbearable to see.

'You do?' he asked.

GL♥SS

'Of course I do. Now you know how I felt.'

There was absolutely no comprehension in his eyes. 'What do you mean?'

'I saw Beverly with Lance Hunter.' She tried to look sympathetic. 'I'm sorry it didn't work out for you.'

To her surprise, he leaped up, clenched his fists and looked as if he was about to scream. Alarmed she took a step backwards.

'There was nothing to work out!' he yelled.

She turned worriedly towards the open door. 'Shh!'

He took a deep breath. 'You want to know why I'm depressed? Because you broke up with me! And for no good reason!'

'I had reason,' she said stiffly. 'Are you telling me now that you're sorry?'

He raised his eyes, as if seeking guidance from above. 'No, I'm not sorry. I can't apologize to get you back because I never did anything to apologize for!'

He came closer. 'Can you get this through your red hair and into your thick skull? There was never anything between me and Beverly. I love you. I've loved you from the first moment we met!'

'Wait a minute. I've heard that before. Aren't those the lines you said to Beverly?'

'For your information, I happen to have turned into a damned good actor.'

'Are you acting now?' she asked.

'You tell me,' he replied. With no warning, he lunged,

wrapped her in his arms and planted a kiss on her that lasted even longer than the one she'd seen Beverly and Lance Hunter share. She could have pushed him away, or kicked him, or done something to resist.

But she didn't. Because she didn't want it to end.

Finally he released her. 'Well?' he asked.

She considered the possibilities. Either he was the greatest actor in the whole wide world, or he really truly loved her.

She searched his face, his eyes, she tried to read his mind.

And then she kissed him again.

In the studio at *Gloss*, where Donna had spent the afternoon putting together a set to look like a classroom, her boss was getting impatient.

'Where *is* she?' David growled.

'Hair and make-up,' Donna told him.

'She's been in there for forty-five minutes!' he complained.

It was another five minutes before Bonnie Bailey sailed into the room. 'Sorry, David darling. Donna! It's been ages!'

Actually it had been only two weeks since they'd last gotten together. On the very day that Bonnie signed the exclusive contract with *Gloss*, she'd met the brand new man-of-her-dreams, and it was still going strong. Donna was off the hook.

GL♥SS

David directed her into a pose.

'How do I look?' Bonnie asked.

'Fabulous, beautiful,' David responded automatically in a monotone. 'Radiant.'

'That's because I'm in love! Madly, wildly in love!'

'That's nice,' David murmured. 'Can you tilt your head to the right?'

That put her facing Donna, and Bonnie winked. 'Men, they just don't understand. But I know you do.'

Donna smiled thinly. 'Sure.'

'I mean, you and Jack . . . you're still going hot and heavy, right?'

Donna tried to sound casual. 'Well, it's kind of cooled off.'

'I doubt that,' Bonnie said. 'Not on his part.'

'What do you mean?'

She cocked her head towards the door. 'Well, he's only been out there waiting for at least forty-five minutes!'

Donna stared at her. 'What?'

'Shut up!' David said. 'I'm trying to shoot!'

But Bonnie took no notice. 'He was sitting out by the desk when I arrived, and when I came out of make-up he was still there.'

Donna froze. She'd managed to avoid him for two weeks, ever since the meeting with his mother. When he called her at work, she had the receptionist tell him she wasn't in. At home she made Sherry answer the phone and say she wasn't there either. If Sherry wasn't home when the phone rang, she just didn't pick up.

Surely he'd get tired of waiting out in the hallway. She'd stay in here and work late, until the custodian came to lock up and made her leave.

'Damn!' David cried out. 'I need a new lens. Donna, go get me one.'

Donna was horrified. 'Now?'

'Yes, of course now!'

She could only hope Jack had given up and left. But he hadn't.

She had to pass him to get to the supplies closet. As soon as he spotted her he jumped up from his seat.

'Donna –'

She kept her eyes focused on the closet door and pretended to neither see nor hear him. Inside the closet, she found the appropriate lens and went back out.

But now Jack was standing just outside the studio door, blocking her from getting back in.

'We have to talk.'

'Not now, Jack. I'm working.'

The door opened, and a frazzled-looking David stood there. He took the lens from Donna and then he noticed Jack.

'You can take your coffee break now,' he said to Donna, and went back inside.

'So now you have time to talk,' Jack said.

He was dressed for business, in a suit and carrying a

briefcase. She focused on the knot in his tie so as not to look at his face. And she concentrated on keeping her face, her expression, as still as possible so he couldn't see how much pain she was in, being this close to him again.

'I only get ten minutes,' she murmured.

'That's all I need,' he said, his voice stern. He glanced at the receptionist behind the desk, who was watching them curiously. 'Is there someplace we can talk?'

David had left the door to his private office open so she led him in there. There was a small settee against the wall, so they had to sit uncomfortably close. At least, she was uncomfortable. He just looked grim.

'I'll get right to the point,' Jack said. 'Tell me the truth. There's no old boyfriend who suddenly turned up, is there?'

She swallowed. 'Yes, there is.'

He shook his head. 'You're not a very good liar.' He paused. 'At least, not *this* time.'

She drew in her breath and forced herself to look at him. 'I don't know what you mean,' she whispered, but she knew she sounded unconvincing.

He set the briefcase on his lap and opened it. 'I found this.' He handed her a folder.

She didn't have to open it to know what it contained. There was a label on the front – Carruthers and Clark, Private Investigations. It was the file his mother had put together on her background.

'So now you know,' she said dully.

He nodded. 'And that's why you made up the story about the boyfriend. So my mother wouldn't give me this.'

There was no point in denying it. 'Yes,' she said.

'Why? Why did you make up that background – Boston, Beacon Hill, private school?'

'Because I didn't think you'd be interested in a girl like me.'

'A girl like you,' he repeated. 'A beautiful, intelligent, kind, thoughtful girl like you.'

She shook her head. 'A girl from a trailer park, who didn't even finish high school. A girl who was married and pregnant at seventeen. A girl who ran away from her husband.'

He cocked his head quizzically and asked an unexpected question. 'Were you ever really in love with me? The truth!'

'Yes! Oh yes.'

'I don't understand how. Not if you thought I was the kind of person who wouldn't love you if you weren't from my kind of background.'

'I . . . I just thought–'

She was glad he interrupted her, because she had no idea what she was going to say.

'Donna, I was furious when I found out what my mother had done. And I was pretty angry with you too. For thinking I couldn't love you whoever

GL♥SS

you are, wherever you came from.'

She bowed her head. He touched her chin and raised her face to meet his.

'Donna . . . my mother is a snob. A materialistic, superficial, condescending, patronizing and pretentious snob.' He paused, and then he added, 'But I'm not.'

'I know,' she said. 'But by the time I figured that out, I'd dug a hole too deep to climb out of it. So I just kept right on lying. It was too late to do anything else.'

'It's never too late,' he said.

Then she was in his arms. It was going to be all right, better than all right. And in the back of her mind she had a feeling she'd be taking a longer-than-usual coffee break today.

Chapter Twenty-Three

Sherry looked around the living room worriedly. The bowls that had been filled with olives, nuts and pretzels were now empty, and she had nothing more to put in them. She'd done something unheard-of for a properly brought-up girl of the South – she'd run out of appetizers. It wasn't her fault. She'd only planned for six people – her parents, herself, Donna, Allison and Pamela.

But when Pamela turned up with Larry, what could she say? And when Donna came home with Jack in tow, good manners required her to invite him to stay for dinner.

Thank goodness there was a huge lasagne in the oven that would be ready any minute now. She wished Allison would show up so she could get the meal set out before people got too hungry.

Sherry was relieved to hear the buzz of the house phone.

'Send her up,' she ordered the doorman before he could even speak.

'It's so lovely to meet Sherry Ann's friends,' her mother was saying to Donna and Pamela. 'And you girls have certainly found yourselves some nice young men! I just wish our little girl could meet someone special.'

Sherry silently groaned, and hurried to respond to the knock on the door. At least now her mother would see that she wasn't the only unattached girl in New York City.

But she almost groaned out loud when she saw Allison with Bobby. Her reaction must have been evident.

'Gee, I thought you'd be happy to see us back together,' Allison said.

'I am, I am,' Sherry said hastily. 'Surprised, that's all. Come on in and meet my folks.'

She made the introductions, then went into the kitchen to pull things together. There weren't enough chairs at the dining-room table for them all to eat there, so they were going to do a buffet-style meal. She set a stack of paper plates on the table, some plastic forks and spoons and paper napkins. Mama would be horrified when she saw all the disposable stuff, but that was just too bad.

Back in the kitchen, she looked at the clock and frowned. The lasagne had been in the oven for what seemed like ages. She should have heard the ding of the timer by now.

Taking advantage of a few minutes alone, she sat down on the step stool and took a deep breath. She was feeling tense, but she knew she had no real reason to. Her parents' visit was coming along nicely. They were staying in a pleasant midtown hotel and had spent their days sightseeing. They'd taken her out to a fancy restaurant one night and to a Broadway show on another. They'd talked about family and people back home, and her mother dropped her usual broad hints about how Sherry's hometown sweetheart was still unattached.

The only really awkward moment was when her father mentioned an argument that had been going on in the local city council.

'Now this new law says public schools have to be integrated, and that's fine. But we have neighbourhood schools, and Negroes and white people don't live in the same neighbourhoods. So now they're talking about bussing Negro children to the white school and white children to the Negro school.'

'Which is just plain silly,' her mother added. 'When they can walk to their local schools.'

'But maybe it's for the best in the long run,' Sherry pointed out. 'If Negro and white children go to school together, they'll socialize, they'll become friends, and by the time they're adults, they'll be comfortable living next door to each other. There won't be separate neighbourhoods any more.'

Her mother didn't agree. 'But, Sherry Ann, how much socializing can they really do? I mean, it's not like they can date each other.'

'Why not?' Sherry asked.

GL♥SS

Her father chuckled. 'Sugar, since when did you become such a radical thinker?'

Since I fell in love with a Negro, she wanted to say. But she couldn't. And what would be the point anyway? It was all over.

But she hadn't stopped thinking about William. When pictures from the Wall Street demonstration appeared in the newspapers, she searched hungrily, now wishing that photographer *had* gotten a shot of her and William together. Just so she'd have a memory she could hold.

She'd hoped she'd pick up news about him from Gloria at work. But just days after their break-up, Gloria had turned in her notice at *Gloss*. She'd finished her accounting training, and she'd already been offered a job.

None of this mattered, not really. She didn't need a photo, she didn't need to see his sister. William's face was etched into her memory in indelible ink.

Her mother poked her head in the kitchen. 'Sugar, we're all getting a little hungry out here.' Then her expression changed. 'Sherry Ann, are you all right? You look like you've been crying!'

'I was just cutting up onions for the salad, Mama,' she lied. She went over to the oven. 'I don't know why that timer hasn't gone off. The lasagne must be ready by now.' She put on oven mitts, opened the oven door and reached in.

It smelt terrible and it looked even worse. What was supposed to be lasagne was a blackened mess.

'Oh dear,' her mother said. And Sherry burst into tears.

The guests must have heard her, because suddenly they were all at the door.

'What happened?' Donna asked.

Sherry's mother explained the calamity.

'It's not the end of the world,' Donna said briskly. 'We've got a wonderful pizza parlour down the road that delivers. I'll go call them right now.'

Everyone settled back in the living room, and Sherry went to the bathroom to wash her face and reapply some make-up. She'd just come back out when the house phone buzzed.

'My goodness,' her mother said. 'They *are* fast.'

'It can't be the pizzas already,' Sherry said, picking up the phone. 'Hello?'

She heard the familiar lazy voice of the doorman. 'Pizza delivery guy's here.'

And then, in the background, she heard another familiar voice.

'I am *not* the pizza delivery guy!'

'Well, who the hell are you?' the doorman barked.

'I'm coming down!' Sherry yelled into the phone.

She hurried past the startled faces in the living room. 'I'll be right back,' she called out as she left.

She'd never run downstairs so fast in her life. She

was out of breath when she burst into the little lobby area.

Thank goodness he hadn't stormed out. William was still standing there with a pizza box in his hands.

'What's the big deal?' the doorman growled. 'I thought he was the delivery guy, so what?'

'Well, he's not,' Sherry said. 'He's my friend.'

However offended he'd been by the doorman's assumption, William looked calmer now. But he spoke stiffly.

'I've been thinking about you. And . . . I thought I'd bring along a peace offering.' He looked down at the box.

Aware of the doorman's curious face, she smiled brightly. 'That's totally unnecessary, but appreciated nonetheless. However, I don't think it will serve ten.'

'Ten?'

'I've got friends here. And my parents. Fortunately the real pizza delivery man is on his way.'

William nodded. 'Then I guess I'll take this home and eat it myself.'

'Are you crazy? Absolutely not. You're coming upstairs.'

He raised his eyebrows. 'Are you sure?'

'Yes.' She glanced at the doorman. 'When the delivery guy comes, please send him right up.'

They climbed the stairs together silently. Words, if they were even necessary, could come later.

'How's this for a funny coincidence?' she called out gaily when they entered the apartment. 'My friend William decided to stop by and surprise me with a pizza! So we can all nibble on this as an appetizer while we wait for the main course.'

She placed the pizza box on the table and then escorted William around the room to make introductions. She didn't miss the widened eyes on the faces of her guests. Was it because none of them knew about William? Or because of William's race? With her friends, she was certain it was the first reason. With her parents, she couldn't be so sure.

'And do you work with Sherry Ann?' her mother asked when she met him.

'No, we're just friends.' He looked at Sherry and they exchanged a silent message. That was all the parents had to know for now.

'William's a student at Columbia University,' Sherry told them.

Her father was impressed. 'Columbia! That's an Ivy League school, isn't it?'

For a moment Sherry tensed up. Would William think he was surprised that a Negro could attend such an important university? Would he come back with one of his chip-on-the-shoulder comments?

But no, William smiled. 'Yes sir, it is. I'm studying political science, in the pre-law programme.'

Now Sherry's father looked astounded. Sherry

jumped in. 'Actually, Daddy, I'm thinking about applying to Columbia myself. They have a very good journalism department.'

Her mother was looking more than a little dazed. 'Well . . . and how did you two meet?'

'At a civil-rights meeting,' Sherry told her.

'Oh?'

She was going to have to say more. 'And we've been spending some time together.'

Her mother's smile was wearing thin. 'Talking about civil rights?'

'And other things,' Sherry said.

Her parents looked at each other, and Sherry thought she could read a million emotions in their expressions. Curiosity, bewilderment . . . fear?

The room had fallen silent. A sudden knock on the door made everyone jump.

'That must be the pizzas,' Donna declared with unmistakable relief.

The arrival of the food got people moving, picking up plates and serving themselves. Conversations were humming, and everyone seemed to relax.

Except for her parents, who sat down stiffly and looked as if they were in a state of shock.

'He's cute!' Allison told Sherry softly.

Pamela looked even more enthused. 'And he's going to be a lawyer! They make big money.'

Sherry just smiled. She got herself some pizza, and

then she and William sat on some pillows she'd laid on the floor. Side by side. But not too close. She'd already given her parents enough to worry about.

The others made a real effort to distract her mother, and her mother responded, but the strained expression never left her face. Her father was talking in his usual hearty way, but to Sherry it seemed forced. At least this had put the plastic forks and paper plates in perspective.

It was going to take time, Sherry thought. A long time. And she didn't know if they'd ever come around to feeling good about this. But they were good people. So hopefully they would try.

But it wouldn't be easy.

She looked at William. He smiled. Then he glanced towards her parents.

'Rocky road ahead,' he murmured, and he wasn't talking about ice cream.

'I know,' she said.

But at least they would be travelling it together.

Marilyn Kaye

A long hot summer in the city that never sleeps.

New York, 1963. Fashion, music and attitudes are changing, and there's nowhere in the world more exciting.

GL♥SS

Sherry, Donna, Allison and Pamela have each landed a dream internship at *Gloss* – America's number-one fashion magazine. Each girl is trying to make her mark on New York and each finds herself thrown head first into the buzzing world of celebrity, high-end fashion and gossip. But everything isn't as glamorous as it seems – secrets from the past threaten to shatter their dreams.

They're finding out that romance in New York is as unpredictable and thrilling as the city itself.

Stella

HELEN EVE

Seventeen-year-old Stella Hamilton is the star blazing at the heart of Temperley High School. Leader of a maliciously exclusive elite, she is surrounded by adulation – envied and lusted after in equal measure. And she is in the final stage of a five-year campaign to achieve her destiny: love with her equally popular male equivalent, and triumph as Head Girl on election night.

By contrast, new girl Caitlin Clarke has until now lived a quietly conformist life in New York. With the collapse of her parents' marriage, she has been sent across the Atlantic for an English boarding school education, only to discover that at Temperley the only important rules are the unwritten ones. It's a world of the beautiful and the dangerous, and acceptance means staying on the right side of Stella Hamilton, the most beautiful and dangerous of them all.

Not everyone is happy to be under the Hamilton rule. But fighting the system means treading the same dark path as Stella – and if Caitlin puts a foot wrong, it's a long way to fall.

FANGIRL

Cath and Wren are identical twins and until recently they did absolutely everything together. Now they're off to university and Wren's decided she doesn't want to be one half of a pair any more – she wants to dance, meet boys, go to parties and let loose. It's not so easy for Cath. She would rather bury herself in the fanfiction she writes where there's romance far more intense than anything she's experienced in real life.

Now Cath has to decide whether she's ready to open her heart to new people and new experiences, and she's realizing that there's more to learn about love than she ever thought possible . . .

A tale of fanfiction, family and first love

RAINBOW ROWELL